SO WE LOOK TO THE SKY

SO WE LOOK TO THE SKY

A NOVEL

MISUMI KUBO

TRANSLATED FROM THE JAPANESE BY POLLY BARTON

Arcade Publishing • New York

First English-language Edition

This is a work of fiction. Names, places, characters, and incidents are either
the products of the author's imagination or are used fictitiously.

Originally published in Japanese under the title ふがいない僕は空を見た
(Fugainai Boku Wa Sora Wo Mita) by SHINCHOSHA Publishing Co., Ltd.

English translation rights arranged with SHINCHOSHA Publishing Co.,
Ltd. through the ASIA LITERARY AGENCY and Japan UNI Agency, Inc.

Visit our website at www.arcadepub.com.

10 9 8 7 6 5 4 3 2 1

Library of Congress Cataloging-in-Publication Data is available on file.
Library of Congress Control Number: 2021933411

Cover design by Erin Seaward-Hiatt
Cover illustration: © George Peters/Getty Images

ISBN: 978-1-951627-71-3
Ebook ISBN: 978-1-951627-93-5

Printed in the United States of America

Contents

SO WE LOOK
TO THE SKY

1

Mikumari

LET'S SAY FOR THE sake of argument that a typical, healthy sex life for the dopey kids who live around these parts is the kind that my classmates have: stopping off on the way home from school at someone else's house, or a cheap motel, or finding a deserted spot outside and doing it two, or three, or as many times as the mood takes you, then making your way back home, crotch still tingling, and putting on your best butter-wouldn't-melt face as you eat dinner with your family, eyes pinned to the TV news—well, if that's the case, I guess at some point I strayed pretty wildly from the typical, healthy path.

With the end-of-term ceremony over with and my report card in my bag, I walked straight past my house and crossed the bridge. On the road running along the other side of the river I turned in to an apartment building and took the elevator to the top floor, checking that the coast was clear before making my way toward the apartment at the very end of the hall. The door was unlocked. I opened it just a crack and slipped through, entering the small room closest to the entrance.

Inside the room the blackout shades were drawn, and it took some time for my eyes to adjust to the darkness, but my ears were alive to every sound. My hearing was pretty good in general, and I was always the one to hear my friends' phones when they vibrated and stuff. Laid out on the double bed was Anzu, dressed up as a character from some anime. "Anzu" was the name she'd taken for herself, and I had no idea what her real one was. The outfit, modeled loosely around the sailor uniform most high-school girls wore, had an incredibly short skirt. The thighs jutting out from underneath made me think of tree trunks, and the blond wig with attached cat ears was also seriously unflattering.

I approached the bed and Anzu opened her eyes a little, pointing wordlessly to the costume that was waiting for me on its hanger in the corner of the room. As directed, I unbuttoned my school uniform, letting it drop to the floor, and put on in its place the silky lab-coat type thing that would transform me into another character from the same anime. I capped it off with the long blue wig and pair of small spectacles also laid out for me, then went and stood beside the bed. I could hear a whirring noise like an electric toothbrush. Flipping up Anzu's skirt, I saw a pink electrical cord trailing out of her skimpy panties. I pulled the panties down until they hung around her right ankle, and I propped up her knees.

Anzu made a gulping sound, as if she was swallowing a whole mouthful of saliva. When I tugged slowly on the cord trailing out of her body, a load of liquid came spilling out of her, leaving a big wet patch on the sheets.

"I see you've been waiting for me like a good little girl."

I was now fully in the role of this character, whoever the hell he was, which meant I was obliged to come out with gross lines like that. That was part of the agreement I had with Anzu. As I spoke, I saw her body jerk, her back arching so it lifted off the sheet.

Before we had sex, Anzu would write a script. I would act according to the script, come out with the lines she'd written for me, and then we'd do it. That was the deal.

I put Anzu's index and middle fingers in my mouth now and sucked on them in the perviest way I could muster, with lots of slurping sounds. That, too, was part of the script.

Anzu groaned, a perfectly unsexy groan as if she'd just been kicked in the stomach. I moved the vibrator onto her clitoris, and began sliding Anzu's fingers around in my mouth. Instantly she began wailing at a pitch that was strangely grating, "Oh, Lord Muramasa, I'm coming!"

"Not yet," I said in a stern voice, as the script had demanded.

I opened Anzu's legs up into an *M*-shape and moved my face right up to its center. I stuck my middle finger into the place where all that slimy, glistening liquid was coming from. Then I took it out, smeared the liquid I'd scooped up across her clitoris, and began to move the vibrator around and around on top.

"Aaaaaaah! Lord Muramasa, it's too much! I'm cooooooooommmmming!!!" Anzu said, arching her body back like a bow and shaking so violently that all the flab on her lower half shook, then falling totally still. I could only assume

Lord Muramasa was the guy I was cosplaying as. Truth be told, I didn't know a single thing about this anime series that Anzu was so obsessed with.

"What a naughty little girl you are," I said, patting her head.

When she'd got her breath back, Anzu sat up and unzipped my jeans. My cock had been starting to get hard from more or less the moment I walked in the room. Now she took it in her mouth, coating it in her saliva, then quickly changed posture and straddled me. By this point, the room was so warm that the little spectacles had steamed up. I lay there faceup on the bed as Anzu rocked back and forth on top of me, reaching out my hands from time to time to fondle her nipples through the fabric of her uniform. She moaned rhythmically, *mm, mm, mm,* and with every movement, more of her warm juices caught in my pubic hair. Glimpsing the rolls of fat on her belly, her wig that was now askew, I felt myself starting to lose it. I shut my eyes tight and concentrated on the feeling of being inside her.

"I'm gonna come," I blurted out, and Anzu leaned over and whispered in my ear in the tiniest of voices, "Come as much as you want."

It wasn't the voice of some cosplay character, either—it was her real voice. The moment I heard it there was no holding back anymore, and I shot hard inside her.

It was at the beginning of my first year of high school when Anzu—well, hit on me, basically. A friend had dragged me along to Comiket, a huge comic market in Tokyo, and I was hanging around there kind of bored when Anzu came up and told me that I looked exactly like so-and-so from this anime, took a photo of me, and then all but forced my email address out of me. We started texting, and I was pretty surprised to discover that she lived in the exact same part of town outside of Tokyo that I did, in an apartment building directly across the river—that was some coincidence. That surprise, though, was nothing to when I discovered that she wasn't the same age as me, as I'd assumed, but twelve years older, and married. In other words, when I actually thought about it, what I was doing was *having an affair with someone's wife.*

I don't watch anime or TV at all, so a good part of what Anzu said went straight over my head. I just knew that, so long as I was in this room, I wasn't allowed to be my normal self. I had to wear the cosplay outfits she prepared for me, make my face up white, and sometimes put in color contacts, too. When she saw me all done up, she'd go all dewy-eyed and take a ton of photos.

The first time Anzu invited me over to her apartment, I sort of forced her back on the bed, not really thinking for one second that she'd be up for it, but it turned out she was. The one condition was that the sex had to be in cosplay. From that day on, I'd been coming around once or twice a week after school and we'd been going at it like crazy, barely an unscripted word passing between us.

Anzu was my first, and she taught me all kinds of stuff about sex I had no idea of—that there were lots of different positions you could do, and equipment you could use. Not always, but often when we were through, Anzu would apologize to me and slip me a ten-thousand-yen note. At first, I didn't really grasp the significance of that neatly folded note, so I didn't really feel that bad about it. I thought of it like the "little something" an aunt or someone would give you when you went around to visit. But even a brain as stupid as mine couldn't resist the truth of the matter forever, and one day it finally filtered through to me: Anzu was paying me to fuck her.

I was lying back on her bed afterward, smoking a cigarette, listening to some kid running down the hallway outside. *What the hell am I doing?* I wondered to myself, as all the while my non-smoking hand fondled Anzu's crotch. I felt the smooth skin growing sticky beneath my fingers. Anzu began making little noises, then her hand reached out for my cock. I hadn't once worn a condom with Anzu, not from the very first time—which was my very first time, ever.

"It's fine," Anzu would always say, "I can't get pregnant," and I'd always had the sense that I shouldn't ask any more, but today, for some reason, I did.

"Are you not going to have kids?"

I felt the heat instantly drain from Anzu's body, and she got up from the bed.

"It's none of your business," she said, in her regular voice, and left the room. I waited a while but she didn't come back, so I got up, picked off a sliver of tissue that was stuck to the head of my cock and threw it in the trash, then changed out of the lab coat and back into my uniform. I remembered what my mom had said to me a bunch of times: *You can't just go blurting out whatever damn thing comes into your head.* And today, of all days, when I'd had something to talk to Anzu about. Oh well, I thought vaguely as I put on my shoes at the entrance. It'd just have to wait till next time.

I came out of Anzu's building and walked across the bridge in the direction of home. Letting all the strength drain from my body and dragging my feet, I watched the enormous evening sun as it sank down behind the mountains. Looking down off the bridge, I saw a man in a yellow T-shirt and track pants emerge from his makeshift home of vinyl sheeting and wooden boards and take a piss.

I opened the door to my house, and a loud moaning greeted me. My mother was a midwife, and she ran a maternity clinic out of our house, which meant, more often than not, there were women giving birth in my home. It was just a regular sort of house, with no soundproofing or anything like that, so wherever you were in the building, you could hear the sounds of women in agony. I found it so weird to think that people made the same sounds when they were having sex as they did when they were in labor. Honestly, if you weren't told that these sounds were the sounds of someone giving birth, you would definitely assume it was just porn with the volume turned up really loud. Growing up in this house, that had been the soundtrack to my childhood.

As I was picking at the bowl of simmered daikon left out on the kitchen table, my mom came rushing into the kitchen.

"Got a minute?" she said, and without waiting for an answer, led me through to the tatami-floored birthing room at the back of the house. The woman's husband, who was supposed to be her birth partner, had been held up at work, and my mom wanted me to step in and rub the woman's back in his place.

"It's the sacrum you want to focus on, okay?" my mom instructed me.

"Yeah, yeah, I know. I know *everything*," I said, placing the palm of my hand so it adhered exactly to the flat plane above the tailbone and rubbing gently.

"I do apologize," said my mom to the woman giving birth. "The other nurses are on summer holiday, and this delinquent son of mine is the only one around."

The young woman's face, all crumpled up in agony, suddenly relaxed.

"No, no! He really knows what he's doing," she said, and smiled at me. It was such a pretty smile, I felt a pang go shooting through my chest.

"See?" I said, and my mom grinned as if she was genuinely pleased.

Sometimes, when the other midwives were off or there was nobody to accompany the women in labor, I was called in to help with the deliveries—only when the women gave their permission, of course. I guess I must have taken after my mom after all, because whenever I saw women giving birth in real pain, I would be overcome by an urge to do something to help them, to make their pain less bad. Today, thanks to my expert sacral massage technique, the delivery was over in no time at all, and a new person entered the world.

* * *

I'd gotten a summer job as a lifeguard at the local pool, together with Ryota from my class at school. I was crouching down outside the door to my house, eating a freeze pop, when Ryota turned up to pick me up on his bike. Mine was broken, so he gave me a ride to the pool on the back of his.

"I've got some good news for you," Ryota yelled without turning around, standing up as he pedaled. "Nana's got a job at the pool reception desk."

Ryota was my best friend at school, but even him I hadn't told about Anzu. Nana was a girl in my year, and I'd had a crush on her since I'd first got into the school. The more wrapped up I got in my sex life with Anzu, the more I'd put my thoughts of Nana on hold. But then, just after the end-of-term tests, she came up and asked me out.

"Give me some time, okay?" I said right away, thinking, of course, of Anzu. I kind of surprised myself, to be honest, not going down the two-timing route. Apparently, I had a little pocket of decency left in me after all.

As I was waiting for Ryota to lock up his bike in the racks, someone grabbed my arm from behind. I turned around to see Nana, a good ways shorter than me. She gave me a big smile, then let go of my arm and went tottering off toward the pool entrance, just like a little kid. Her front teeth were on the long side, and when she smiled, she reminded me of a squirrel happily clutching an acorn.

I got home that evening to discover three boxes of condoms waiting for me on my desk. I went tearing down the stairs and slid open the door to the tatami room where my mom was kneeling at the low table before a stack of papers.

"What the hell are these?" I said, holding up one of the boxes.

"Use them!" she replied, without lifting her head.

"Who gets given condoms by his own mother?" I shouted.

She looked up, grinned at me in the way she did when she was on to a secret of mine, and held out a hand. "If you don't want them, give them back." As I was standing there at a loss for words, she added, "It's not just about pregnancy, you know. You can end up with a penis like a cauliflower if you're not careful!"

Hearing my mom say the word "penis" always sapped the strength from me, immediately. It had been the same ever since I was young. In any case, I knew it was useless to try saying anything to her when she was being like this, so I closed the screen door without a word, my condoms still in my hand.

"I'm not ready to be a grandma yet, okay?" my mom bellowed from the other side.

That evening, I had a message from Nana, so I ate dinner early and set out for the riverbank. Outside my front door, I stopped and turned around, ran back up to my room, and stuffed two of the condoms into my back pocket. The sun had gone down some time ago. I ran all the way to the place we'd arranged to meet, overtaking the leisurely old couples walking their dogs and the young kids scurrying home from summer school.

Nana was standing by the bike path, a lone figure silhouetted by the light of the vending machine. Something about the sight of her standing there so small and alone made me want to cry. We walked along the path talking, Nana pushing the bike she'd come on. For some reason, the whole scene felt deeply satisfying to me: walking along above the riverbank with Nana, pushing a bike, the summer break only just begun. I had this feeling like this was a stage I had to pass through in order to move on. No sooner had the thought formulated itself than I asked myself, *On to where?* I didn't have a clue.

"You're going out with someone, right?" Nana said, looking up at me. I knew instinctively that it was best not to give any details, so I simply nodded, and then, after a pause, added,

"I want to make a clean break with her before you and me start anything."

Now it was Nana's turn to nod silently.

The following day, on the way home from work, I stopped in at Anzu's apartment. Just as before, Anzu was lying on the bed, all dressed up in her cosplay outfit, love egg in, eyes closed. Ignoring the costume she'd laid out for me, I went up beside the bed and looked down at her. I am pretty shortsighted, and from afar like that, with her face painted so white that it was impossible to see the skin underneath and her fake eyelashes on, Anzu could have been someone from my school. When I crouched down close beside the bed, though, I could make out a couple of wrinkles at the corner of her eye. I took a deep breath and then moved my mouth close beside Anzu's ear.

"I'm not going to come here anymore," I said, surprising myself by how cold my voice sounded.

Anzu opened her eyes slowly. After a while, in such a quiet voice I struggled to hear, she said, "You have to."

"I'm not going to," I said.

"You can't stop," Anzu said, this time springing up from the bed and flinging her arms around me. I could hear the whirring of the love egg.

"You're married, aren't you?" I just about got the words out when Anzu's hand came clamping down across my mouth. Her other hand grabbed one of mine and guided it to her crotch. As ever, her panties were soaked through, and I could feel with my fingers the whirring of the love egg.

Now her hand came reaching out toward my crotch. I brushed it away.

"I'm underage. What you're doing is a crime," I said, in the most expressionless voice I could muster. I instantly felt disgust at myself for coming out with a line like that. If it was a crime, then we were in on it together.

Suddenly, Anzu grabbed my arm and bit down on it with all her might. The pain was so intense I almost cried out, but I managed to hold it back. My right arm was now branded with two sets of Anzu's tooth marks, beads of blood rising to the surface.

"I'm not going to see you anymore," I said once more and made to leave the room.

"I'll curse you for this," Anzu shouted, as a pillow came flying in my direction. It struck my back and fell to the floor. I could barely even feel it.

"You'll be back here. I know it!" screeched a voice at my back as I closed the front door to the apartment.

* * *

I'd never split up with anyone before, so I didn't know if that counted as the official breakup or if there was more to come. Knowing Anzu, I figured she'd probably start texting me and calling me endlessly, stalking me, posting photos of me in cosplay and other sketchy stuff around the neighborhood and who knows what else, but in fact there was none of that. The messages she'd been sending me every day stopped abruptly.

I saw Nana at the pool every day, and every day she looked cuter.

While I felt kind of bad ditching Ryota, I started going to and from the pool with Nana, with me pedaling and her perched behind. Her hair, her skin, her ears, her lips—they all seemed somehow bursting with moisture, like she was glistening from the inside out. Her skin tissue, even her cells seemed young. At first, when I wrapped my arms around her, I could see Anzu's teeth-marks there on my right bicep, but they soon started to fade until in no time they were barely visible.

There was always someone at home in both Nana's house and mine, so we would ride in the opposite direction to our preferred spot at the foot of the bridge. There we'd lie, concealed by the grass that grew taller than Nana's head, and I'd feel her up like crazy.

Nana gave off a sweet, cheap smell, like American shampoo or something. I was lying there, staring down at the whorl on the top of her head, which came up to my chest, and thinking of the strange time I'd spent with Anzu in that room, when Nana suddenly piped up,

"Your mom's a midwife, right? I want to be a midwife, too."

"There's nothing good about being a midwife," I said. "You don't get to sleep or take holidays, and there's no money in it."

Nana looked up at me and said with her squirrelly grin, "But I just love babies so much!"

There was something about this that seemed like a reflection of something shallow in Nana. It put me in mind of something I'd heard my mom say a bunch of times when I was growing up: *It's not a job to do because you like babies.* Goodness knows who she was trying to convince. After my dad had left home for another woman, my mom had raised me all by herself. I'd grown up listening to the screams and wails and cries of the women as they brought all those new people into the world.

I'd had my eyes opened to the world of sex by the medical textbooks in my mom's study, full of countless gynecological photographs. Not long after I got into middle school, I read a passage in one of those book that explained: *From the time of their birth, women's ovaries are filled with several million primordial follicles, which can later develop into egg cells.* That sentence shook me to the core. Reading it, I felt the same sense of disgust I got when I swatted a cockroach and saw the eggs come spilling out of its abdomen. Until that point, salmon roe marinated in sticky soy sauce had been one of my favorite dishes, but from that day on, I went right off it. Sometimes in class, I would start imagining the belly of the girl next to me jam-packed with all those tiny eggs, and I'd feel the bile rising to the back of my throat. For a good six months, I lost all trace of the interest in sex I'd previously been feeling.

Somewhere along the line, I'd managed to forget about my aversion entirely, but now, out of the blue, I started thinking about all that tiny roe hidden away inside Nana's body and let out a deep sigh. Whenever I got to thinking about these *things* that we men and women got stuck with and had to go carrying around with us until the day we died as they caused us endless kinds of trouble, I felt so exhausted that my head would grow numb. To try and dispel the feeling, I kissed Nana hard. As usual, when I stuck my tongue inside her mouth and began fishing around in there, Nana instantly pulled away.

"It's scary when you do that," she said with a smile.

As all that was happening, I could hear a dry rustling, and then a homeless man suddenly popped his face above the dense grass, grinning at us. I grabbed Nana's hand and began to run, up onto the mound of the riverbank. When we finally came to a standstill back where Nana's bike was parked, I felt a stinging in my calf. I looked down to see a cut running straight across it, the blood dribbling down.

"Oh, no! You've cut yourself really badly! Are you okay?" Nana said, pulling out a pack of pocket tissues from her bag and wiping away the blood. *Anzu's curse*, I thought to myself immediately.

Sometimes, when you're thinking about a person all the time, you end up bumping into them in the most unexpected of places. It always really shocks me when that happens, as if the contents of my head had gotten out and materialized right in front of my eyes.

That particular day, I'd gone to the shopping center in the next town over to buy onesies for my mom. It was the middle of summer, but that hadn't stopped it from raining solidly for a week. Unable to do any laundry, my mom was about to run out of spares, or so she said. Shopping for onesies or diapers or sanitary pads or whatever didn't bother me in the slightest, as it would have some people. I'd made a note of what was needed on the back of my hand in marker pen—*4 l-sleeve muslin, 4 s-sleeve muslin*—and was making my way through the baby section, glancing down at my hand from time to time, when I noticed someone in one of the aisles. It was Anzu. Right in the middle of the baby section, deserted of people despite its being the summer break, was Anzu. She was staring down at a pair of baby socks, so small that they fit in the palm of her hand. She was taking her time, comparing the patterns and sizes the way a mother would do. Concealing myself behind one of the shelves, I stood there and watched, like a stalker.

Needless to say, Anzu wasn't in cosplay. She was dressed like a student, in jeans, a T-shirt, and a gray zip-up hoodie. Suddenly, a thought occurred to me, and I felt a dull pain shoot through my stomach, a chill coming over me. Surely, I said to myself, surely it couldn't be. I moved closer. Noticing me beside her, Anzu looked up in surprise.

"Are you pregnant?"

My mouth went dry the moment I opened it, and I could hear how thin and papery my voice sounded. Anzu shook her head and attempted to smile, but the expression she managed was more like a child being told off. We stood there, our eyes locked on one another's for a while, and then Anzu put the baby socks back on the rack they came from and moved off quickly in the direction of the escalator.

From that day on, the only thing I could think about was Anzu.

Maybe, I thought, maybe I've fallen in love for the first time ever.

I kept replaying the image of Anzu with the baby socks in her palm, in slow motion, frame by frame. At work I was a total mess. I got a telling-off from my boss for failing to notice a child who was on the verge of drowning. Some lifeguard I was. Nana got so upset with me for responding like a zombie that she was now totally ignoring me.

At home, the births weren't letting up. "It's because it's a full moon," said my mother resignedly. She had barely slept for days. When I was younger, I used to think my mother was some kind of witch because she came out with stuff like that.

The deliveries went on throughout the night, and even when I shut my eyes, I could still hear the moaning. Unable to sleep, I jumped up, put on a pair of sandals, and ran down to the river.

I walked across the stretch of grass until I could hear the sound of the water. I picked up a few pebbles and, flicking my wrist, skipped them over the pitch-black surface, listening to the sound they made as they moved across the surface of the water. Disappointed by how dull it was skipping stones in the dark, I picked up another stone at my feet, this time the size of a baby's head, and hurled it out toward the river, like I was throwing a shot put. It plummeted into the water closest to my feet with a dull plunking sound. With the palm of my hand I wiped away the lukewarm spray that had landed on my cheek, and then I walked back in the direction of the bank. Crouching down in the grass, I lit a cigarette, sucking the smoke deep into my lungs.

The full moon peeked its head from beyond the clouds, lighting up the river.

I looked toward Anzu's building on the other side. I could feel the tears streaming down my cheeks like water out of a tap. I didn't bother to wipe them away, just let them run down my face, dripping from my chin onto the grass at my feet. The day my dad had left, I'd come here and cried, staring out at the river like this. I'd stood on the bank and wailed out loud, and then I'd gone back home and seen the patch of greenish, unfaded tatami where my dad's chest of drawers had used to be and cried all over again. I hadn't seen my dad since that day. Back then I'd been a child, powerless to stop myself from being hurt. To be hurt so spectacularly like that was one of the special privileges of childhood. But I wasn't going to be that wounded child forever. It was me, after all, who'd severed the tenuous thread tying Anzu and me together. Suddenly, I felt utterly pathetic, sitting here on the bank lamenting over Anzu, and I screamed out as loud as I could.

"AAAAAAAAARRRGGGGGHHHHH!"

Clasping my head in my two hands, I went rolling down the sloped riverbank. Blades of grass snuck inside my T-shirt, and the chirping of the crickets rang deep inside my ears.

* * *

The following day, I skipped work without telling anyone and went to Anzu's instead.

A slim man in a suit I passed in the hallway shot me a suspicious look, so I made sure he'd gotten in the elevator before I rang the door to Anzu's apartment. After a little while, I heard Anzu's voice over the intercom.

"Hello?"

"It's me," I said. The intercom cut out, and then, after another pause, Anzu opened the door a crack and stuck her head out. Her face looked dozy, like she'd just woken up. The summer sun coming through the door lit up her face, the freckles spreading like galaxies across her cheeks. I forced the door open and stepped inside. Anzu, dressed in a black tank top and a wraparound skirt with flowers on, looked up at me with a fearful expression on her face. Still standing there by the door, I seized her by the arms and kissed her. Her mouth tasted like salty bacon.

I had no intention of holding back the thing that was rising up in me thick as magma, and I couldn't have, even if I'd wanted to. Anzu didn't resist. With our mouths still locked together, I kicked off my shoes and pushed Anzu up against the wall of her hallway, which was for some reason stacked with cardboard boxes. I thrust my hands inside her skirt, using one hand to pull down her panties and the other to squeeze her butt. There was already spit all around our mouths. I undid my belt and, with my trousers and my boxers only half off, entered her. She wasn't totally wet, but she felt incredibly hot. The noise she was making was louder than any she had made before—AAAAAAHHHHHH!—and it turned me on even more. In that unstable position up against the wall, I began to move my hips. It only took a few thrusts before Anzu was coming, and then so was I.

Still panting, Anzu took me by the hand and led me, for the first time, down the hall into the living room. There was a dining table laid with two people's dirty plates and cups from breakfast.

We closed the curtains, then Anzu took off her clothes and then mine, kissing all the while. It was like some kind of game-show challenge, where you weren't allowed to lose contact with the other person's lips. Finally, we fell back onto Anzu's sofa. In the dim light of the curtained room, I saw Anzu's naked body for the first time. Her largish breasts, which had lost some of their firmness, hung down at an angle across her chest. I took one of her small, pale nipples into my mouth, and with my tongue moved it around my mouth like a boiled sweet. I tried sucking hard, then flicking it gently with the tip of my tongue. Anzu sat there with her eyes wide open, watching me as if she was trying to imprint the sight into her memory.

The warm juices that came flooding out of Anzu's insides left wet spots on the sofa. I lifted one of her knees up on the sofa, and stuck my tongue right into the source of all those juices, pulling it out and sticking it in again. My jaw started to feel tired almost right away, but I kept at it. I hadn't eaten anything for breakfast, and soon my stomach began to rumble. I wanted to fill myself up on these juices of Anzu's, coming out of the place from which no babies could come. As I sucked away, Anzu's moans grew louder and louder. With her hand she pushed my head closer into her body, until I felt like I couldn't breathe.

"Point your tongue."

Her voice was quiet, but it was unmistakably an order. I curled my tongue into a U-shape, to make it as pointed as I could, and flicked at her hardened clitoris. She lay there moaning for a while, then suddenly looked at me straight in the eyes and said, "I want you inside me."

Just those words were enough to almost push me over the edge, but I managed to control it and entered her.

Taking hold behind her knees and pushing them up toward her head, I began moving my hips. Before, Anzu had always done her best to wriggle out of the missionary position as soon as we got into it, but today she stayed there, making noises, her eyes locked firmly on my face. Her pelvis was moving in time with mine. She reached her index finger inside my mouth and moved it around. Then I felt the tip of my penis brush up against something hard inside her, and Anzu let out a wail like a baby, and I knew couldn't hold it any longer. I saw a thin ray of light go streaming through my head, and my nose tingled with pleasure. The next moment, I exhaled and released what felt like endless amounts of semen inside her.

When I detached myself from Anzu's body, white cloudy liquid dripped down from inside her. Anzu reached out a finger, scooped some up, and licked it.

"It doesn't taste very good." She looked me right in the eye and smiled. I took one look at her smile and moved straight back inside her.

* * *

After we'd had sex more times than I could count and taken a shower together, we sat down at the kitchen table to eat slices of watermelon Anzu cut for us, and that's where we were when Anzu announced, "I'm going to America for a while."

". . . America?"

"Yep."

"Whereabouts?"

She pronounced a place-name, a cluster of harsh consonants. I'd heard of it, but I had no idea where it was.

"I'm going to meet someone who'll give birth to our baby."

"Whose baby?"

"Mine and yours."

I choked on my watermelon.

"Just kidding," Anzu said, straight-faced, and took a bite of her watermelon. "I'm going to meet someone who might be having a baby for me and my husband."

Outside the window, I could hear the cry of the cicadas. A picture floated into my head of Anzu, all dressed up as her favorite anime character, cradling a newborn baby.

I sat there, staring at the watermelon on Anzu's plate, not moving a muscle. The slice bore a clean U-shaped set of tooth marks, the exact same shape that she'd left on my right arm. Instinctively, I looked down at my arm now, but there was no longer a trace of any teeth.

"Thank you for everything," said Anzu quietly, her face deliberately free of any emotion, and bowed her head.

"Don't go," I said, without a moment's hesitation. "You can't, I don't want you to. Don't leave me here."

In that moment, I truly believed that if I behaved like a total brat, if I threw a tantrum in the most immature way possible, then maybe Anzu wouldn't have to go anywhere. I was still a child. Anzu looked at me for a moment with a look like she was about to cry, and then said, in an even quieter voice than before, "I think it's time for you to be getting home."

The sinking sun had stained the sky the color of honey. I stood in the middle of the bridge, staring out at it, wondering if a fall off the side would be enough to kill me. I guessed not. I imagined myself hobbling my way into the start-of-term assembly on a pair of crutches.

Over to the west, the sun was sinking behind the mountain. I'd climbed that mountain with my dad once when I was young. I remembered him telling me how the water coming out from a crack deep in the rocks turned into this river that we lived beside. At that time, it seemed unbelievable to me that water so clear could be connected with the filthy river flowing near our house. When I looked down now under the bridge, the paltry stream had parted into two sections, exposing a section of dried white riverbed underneath, before rejoining farther on to form a single, narrow stream.

Come to think of it, both my mom and my dad had taken me to the mountains after they'd had a fight. I'd been with my mom, and I'd been with my dad, but I had no memory of the three of us going together. The moment my dad got into the mountains, his pace would quicken, and I'd have to run along behind him so as not to lose sight of his sturdy shoulders, his rucksack. When I went with my mom, she'd pick up a twig and beat down the grasses and foliage growing on either side of the mountain path. She, too, would plow steadily ahead without ever looking back at me.

Once, just after my father left, before my mom started her own maternity clinic, she took me along to a shrine hidden away in the mountains. I remember staring up, mouth agape, at the huge stone column, with the four Chinese characters engraved on it. I'd only just learned to read them, and they looked to me like they meant *moisture shrine*.

"It doesn't mean 'moisture' here," my mom said. "The shrine is named after the gods who give us water, and that's just how you write their name. It's pronounced 'mikumari.' It's the Mikumari Shrine."

Then she started up the flight of steps up to the shrine building, her feet ringing out against the stone. I chased after her and found her standing there with her eyes shut and her hands clasped together in prayer. I imitated her at first, but she was there for so long that after a while I gave up and squatted down at her feet, showering sand on top of a line of ants. Eventually I got bored even of that and tugged at my mother's arm.

"Mom, what are you praying for?"

"For children," my mom said, her eyes still shut.

"For me?"

"Of course you're included. I'm praying for all children. For all the children that are going to be born, and all of them who couldn't be. Children who are alive, children who are dead. All children."

A slap on my backside shocked me out of my reminiscing. I turned around to see Nana there behind me, straddling her bike. She looked at me and mouthed the syllables, "Ass—hole," and then went pedaling away.

I stumbled dizzily back to the house. The moment I opened the door, my mom came pattering down the hall.

"Come on, foolish boy! Quick! Wash your hands and come with me!"

With that, she dashed back into the birthing room at the end of the hall.

I did as I was told, washing my hands and face in the sink, then followed after her.

"Wipe away her sweat and give her some water," my mom barked. Lying on a futon laid out in the middle of the room was a woman with her legs opened into an *M*-shape, looking exhausted and letting out short, sharp pants.

I sat down behind her, supporting her from the back so she didn't topple over, and gave her a plastic bottle with a straw stuck in the top to drink from. The baby's head was already peeking out from between her wide-open legs, and my mother's gloved hands cupped it gently.

"NYYYYAAAAAGGGGHHHHHHHH!"

Without warning, the woman let out an animal roar, almost too giant to have come from her tiny frame, then reached her hands over her head and gripped my arm with such force I thought it might snap. There was a splashing sound, as the amniotic fluid poured out from between her legs.

My mom had barely finished saying the words, "It's coming," when the woman let out a piercing scream, and the baby's body slid out, covered in white vernix. The baby stretched out two little fists as if grasping at the sky, opened a toothless mouth, and started to cry. When my mom lifted the baby, still attached by its umbilical cord, and placed it onto the woman's chest, I caught a glimpse of his dick. It looked enormous in comparison to that tiny body. *That thing's gonna cause you a whole lot of trouble, man*, I told him silently.

My mom opened the window, letting a lukewarm breeze into the room. I sat there to one side, watching my mom as she cut the cord and took care of the afterbirth, and the screaming baby, lying there on the pale chest of the woman who'd just become his mother. I wanted to join in with his wailing. I wanted to scream and cry, too, because Anzu had sucked my tongue and my cock, and they were stinging like hell.

2

The Enormous Spiderweb
Covering the World

THE ELEVATOR JIGGLED ABOUT a bit on its way down, before coming to a stop at the fourth floor. The doors opened, and in stepped Mrs. Kimura and her daughter. The two of them wore their huge masses of hair wound into buns at the top of their heads and had on matching dresses in identical gingham fabric, the floaty kind that tastefully obscured the shapes of their bodies. They had the whole mother-and-child look down to a tee, I thought. Releasing a hiss of pent-up air, the elevator doors swept shut and we began our descent again.

"I'm a huge fan of your blog! I'm always checking it."

I'd barely got the words out of my mouth before I noticed Mrs. Kimura tense up. Taking hold of her daughter by the shoulders and drawing her closer, she looked around at me and said, very quietly, "Thank you."

The honest-to-goodness truth was I had stumbled across her site by total accident one day while browsing the internet for dinner ideas. It seemed to be very famous and was always somewhere in the ranking of the top ten cooking blogs. Mrs. Kimura made sure to blur out her daughter's face in the

27

photos she uploaded, but I'd instantly recognized the view from the balcony where she kept her solid wooden table and chairs, and the arrangement of the beams on the living room ceiling. Even the placemats that often appeared in her tabletop shots were from the same hundred-yen shop I went to. That was how I figured out that the woman with the username "mrs mi" was one and the same as the Mrs. Kimura I had met a bunch of times in the residents' weeding sessions.

But! It seemed like once again, I'd gone and put my foot in it. Just because I knew who Mrs. Kimura was didn't neces-sarily mean she remembered me. The only reason I had said anything was because I just couldn't bear that awful, awkward silence inside that cramped little space. Still, I guess that even if you do live in the same building as someone writing a famous blog, it doesn't do to bring up the subject. It doesn't do to tell them you read it. I get it. Or rather, I get that it's exactly because I don't get these kinds of things that I'm such a useless excuse for a human.

I find it all kinds of weird, though. Why would someone make that kind of face when you tell her you've read her blog, as if you've put her on the spot? All feedback should be expressed only via the comment box provided, is that it? Or is it more like, in her heart of hearts, she doesn't want people to read it? But, the information on the internet is put out to the entire world. If you don't lock your front door, then you're basically inviting all kinds of strangers to come marching into your apartment, right? That's the deal. That's how the world's set up. So, surely it's hardly surprising someone you don't know would be looking at your blog? But then again, I suppose it's because I go around overthinking this sort of stuff that people don't like me very much.

Keiichiro once told me that the "www" in website addresses stands for "World Wide Web" in English, which basically means an enormous spiderweb that covers the entire world. Keiichiro always explains the stuff I don't understand in such a way that even someone as stupid as I am can get it. When he was telling me about the internet, he told me lots of other stuff about how it actually works, but those parts were a little too difficult for me. But the idea that the entire earth is covered in all this soft, transparent thread that glistens whenever information passes through it? It seemed to me kind of beautiful. So, while Keiichiro explained the technical stuff, I sat there thinking about how there must be a huge spider or two sitting up by the North Pole, churning out all that thread. After a while, Keiichiro smiled at me and said, "You tuned out again, right? I can always tell."

The elevator reached the first floor. It must have been pickup time for the nursery bus, because there was a swarm of mothers with little kids in tow standing outside the entrance. Mrs. Kimura and her daughter immediately dissolved into the swarm and soon began smiling and chatting away with the others. As I went hurrying past them, lowering my head in a sort of bowing-greeting thing, I thought I sensed Mrs. Kimura shooting a look in my direction. She was probably going speak about me to the other mothers. Yeah, no doubt.

"See that woman over there?" she'd say. "She was in the elevator with me just now, and she was really creepy."

"No way!" the other mothers would say, and listen with fascination to the rest of Mrs. Kimura's story.

If I had the kind of friends I could speak to about minor incidents like this, probably my life would be more enjoyable. But I went to an all-girls' school from the age of twelve and was bullied the entire time I was there, so I still find groups of women pretty difficult to handle. Even just catching sight of a crowd of them from a distance, like those mothers, is enough to raise my pulse rate, or that's how it feels anyway. It's been nearly a decade since I left school for good, but when I think back to that time of my life I still get a squirming in my stomach, and I end up feeling a little panicky.

I got on the little bus that runs in a big loop around the area, headed for the women's clinic in the next town along. The bus wound its way through the pear orchards, coming out at the foot of the small mountain where the clinic is located. Consultation hours hadn't started yet, but the parking lot was already full. Opening the door and seeing all the women sitting there on the pink fake leather sofas, I let out a sigh. Looked like I was in for a long wait, again.

I gave my name at reception, then settled down in a chair in the corner, pulled out my iPod, and put on some anime songs. I wasn't sure why, but I didn't find the women who came to this clinic very intimidating. Even on the days when I took anime magazines or fanzines out of my bag, the people around me didn't bat an eyelid, and none of them looked like the sort to start spreading rumors about me being a geek or an *otaku* or whatever. I guess they must all have been way too caught up in their own problems. Funnily enough, I didn't at all mind being among self-absorbed people like that, though I did wonder about what would happen if these women did manage to get pregnant and have babies of their own. Probably it wouldn't take very long before they'd start finding me gross and creepy, like Mrs. Kimura did.

The clinic had a really good reputation in the fertility-treatment world, and patients traveled from far and wide to be seen there. Its doctors, nurses, and reception staff were never anything but smiley and polite, and the décor of the place was very heavy on pink, which is apparently supposed to encourage female hormone secretion. There was a permanent smell of lavender wafting from who knows where, and healing-style music with lots of running water sounds playing in the background. I sat there in that space, its every last feature designed to bring reassurance and comfort to women desperately wanting children, and waited for my number to come up. Out of respect for people's privacy, names were not used in the clinic. Patients had to watch for their numbers to pop up on the LED display above the reception desk.

It's not that I don't like children, exactly. It's just that whenever I think about the children Keiichiro and I would have, it doesn't really feel real to me. Keiichiro says it's the same for him. I suppose that if I did manage to get pregnant, I wouldn't mind having the baby. I'm pretty sure I must be the only patient at this clinic who feels this degree of uncertainty about the whole "having kids" thing. If you're wondering how someone like that ended up coming to a place like this, it's because the idea was suggested to me, kind of forcefully in fact, by Keiichiro's mother, Machiko.

"If there's still no patter of tiny footsteps after five years of marriage," she said, "something must be up." That was her view on the matter. She not only discovered the clinic but even made the appointment for me and dragged me along to it.

When I first started coming here, they carried out all kinds of tests on me. I bit my lip and bore them as best I could, the painful ones and the frightening ones alike. The tests revealed that both Keiichiro's body and mine had issues that effectively meant we'd be hard put to get pregnant just by having lots of sex. Thanks to an STD I'd contracted in college and let go untreated, my fallopian tubes had narrowed so much that any eggs would have a tough time making their way through, and I was told there was also some kind of disorder with the little parts that were supposed to catch the eggs when they came out of my ovaries. They also found a problem with Keiichiro's sperm. His count was less than that of other men his age, and the sperm he did have weren't very active. Lastly, they told us they had discovered an antibody in my vaginal discharge that identified Keiichiro's sperm as a foreign body and attacked it. That kind of floored me. There I am doing my best to love Keiichiro while, unknown to me, my discharge is attacking his semen. How am I supposed to get my head around that one? What does it mean? Does my discharge not love Keiichiro? Just thinking about it all made me feel weird and bad.

Still, when we heard all the reasons why we couldn't get pregnant, both Keiichiro and I felt pretty relieved. It seemed like a message from the gods: *It's okay, you guys don't need to have them!* But Machiko wasn't so easily satisfied. She wanted to know everything they'd said, and started asking lots of probing questions. I fobbed her off by saying I hadn't really understood all the complicated stuff the doctors had come out with, but I'd been told that I'd been born with very narrow fallo-pian tubes which would make it difficult to conceive naturally. Telling Machiko that there was some kind of problem with her beloved son's body would have taken a level of courage I didn't possess. When I finished speaking, Machiko looked right at me for a few seconds, and then said with a big, broad smile, "In that case, you really must try artificial fertilization. I'll cover all the costs."

In that particular moment I found her very frightening. The sad truth of the matter is that neither Keiichiro nor I have the power to go against what she says. So the two of us agreed between us to go along with Machiko's proposal for a year or two, until she started to lose interest.

Finally, one hour after my appointment time, my number was called and I went into the consultation room.

"Unfortunately, the treatment was not successful this time."

With a detached air, the doctor revealed the failure of the latest artificial-fertilization attempt. Even before hearing the official verdict, I had somehow sensed from the way my body felt that I wasn't pregnant. I felt awful about making the doctors go to such efforts, tiring them out, causing the other patients to wait even longer, when I didn't really want a baby at all. How many times in the course of today would this doctor, whose hair was almost entirely gray, have to sit in front of a woman and tell her that she hadn't managed to get pregnant? I wondered about such things.

The appointment was over in less than five minutes, and I went back into the reception area to pay the bill. It was still full of women patiently waiting their turn. The room was quiet, yet I could sense that the air was saturated with a kind of determination—a single-minded zeal to imprint their and their husbands' DNA on the world. That was exactly the kind of thing that Keiichiro and I so lacked, and I always found it a little stifling when I encountered it. Whenever I left that clinic, I'd discover myself walking at a slightly faster pace than usual.

I listened to anime songs on my iPod again that evening while I prepared dinner. I soaked the salted wakame in water to rehydrate it, and lightly dusted some cucumbers with salt. The sauce and the mashed potato, which would go with the hamburgers I was making, seemed to have turned out pretty well this time. I sang along to the music as I formed the ground beef in the bowl into patties. All of a sudden, I found myself being squeezed from behind.

"I could hear your singing from all the way down the hall." Keiichiro removed one earbud so he could speak into my ear. "It's burger night tonight, eh?"

He went to the bathroom to wash his hands.

Keiichiro is about the same height as me, but when he comes home from work he always seems much shorter than he did in the morning, as if his body has shrunk over the course of the day. Keiichiro works in a pharmaceutical firm as something called a medical representative. I wondered if maybe the doctors had been mean to him again. Since he'd been put in charge of the private clinicians a while back, it was rare for him to get home this early. Apparently, there was one really tricky guy who Keiichiro was responsible for and who was always making Keiichiro accompany him on day-long golf sessions on his days off or sort out tickets for the boy band concerts his daughter wanted to go to, or else forcing him to stay out for the late-night karaoke sessions that Keiichiro hated more than anything. It was a very different story from when he'd been working with the university hospitals.

Despite saying my hamburger "wasn't at all bad," Keiichiro didn't seem to be making much progress with it. As I watched him not eating, I remembered something Machiko had said about how much weight Keiichiro had lost since we'd got married, and started to feel slightly upset. Until getting married, I'd basically never cooked in my life, so there was little to no hope that the food I rustled up would ever match up to that of veteran homemaker Machiko, who made housewifery look like an art form.

"I was at the clinic today."

At this, Keiichiro put down his chopsticks and looked at me.

"It didn't work."

Keiichiro blew on the steaming liquid in his teacup, then nodded silently and returned the cup to the table.

"Sorry, is it too hot? Shall I add some water?"

Keiichiro has a low tolerance for hot things. One time, just after we were married, he lost it with me for serving him steaming rice straight from the rice cooker. Feeling very nervous, I got an ice cube out of the freezer and transferred it into Keiichiro's teacup with a spoon. In my haste, a little of the tea splashed over onto the tabletop. When I went to wipe it away with a cloth, Keiichiro stood up from the table, saying, "I'll leave it to you to tell Mom."

Then he went to his room, leaving more than half his burger on the plate, and I told myself I was going to have to make more of an effort with my cooking.

"There's just no way that a kid who'd inherited genes from two bully-magnets like us could ever make it in this world." That was Keiichiro's opinion on the matter. I agreed with him, though I sometimes wondered if he really had been bullied at school like he said he had. I wanted to ask him about it, but I wasn't brave enough.

The ice cube in Keiichiro's teacup had melted, so the surface of the liquid swelled up over the rim of the cup. It looked as if it might overflow at any time. What was this called again? Was it "surface tension," or was that something else? I felt like asking Keiichiro right away, but going by the way he'd been acting at dinner, I guessed it was better to wait until the following day. Just one more drop of water in this cup, and the tea would spill over. I could hear the sound of a TV blaring and a kid shrieking with laughter, likely coming from the apartment next door. The cherry blossoms were out already, meaning it was officially spring, but the nights were still pretty chilly, and I shut the door to the balcony that I'd left open. I hadn't yet started on my hamburger, so I wrapped it in cling wrap and put it in the fridge. That would do for lunch tomorrow, I thought, and as I worked my way through the remains of Keiichiro's burger, I listened to the sound of water from the tap dripping into a mug I'd left in the sink.

I know this is probably a totally clichéd thing to even think, but back at school I'd often pictured a cup sitting there inside my chest, like the one in the sink. Every time I was bullied or teased, it was like another drop of liquid falling into the cup, building up slowly inside me.

I still don't know exactly what it was that prompted the bullying. What I do know for a fact is that I was fat, ugly, stupid, bad at sports, and just generally slow, and I probably came out with a lot of dumb stuff—the kind of stuff you weren't supposed to say, like I had today with Mrs. Kimura. Back then my eyelids were so swollen that my eyes became these little slits, and when I looked at someone—even if just in a regular way—they'd act like I had been glaring at them and call out: "Whoa, Satomi gave me the eye again!"

The school wasn't particularly academic, but it was Catholic, and there were strict rules about how we should behave, so maybe the kids were looking for someone to take their stress out on. But actually, there probably weren't any clear-cut reasons why it began, especially. They just wanted to pick on someone and there I was, an easy target. When I messed up tons of times in our softball game for the school tournament, a group of kids locked me in the recording studio and started in on me, saying how it was my fault our class hadn't won, swearing at me and insulting me and that kind of stuff. Thinking about it now, that recording studio was the perfect spot for bullying people. So long as that soundproofed door was closed, nobody outside could hear so much as a whisper from within.

I spent break and lunchtimes sketching my favorite anime characters. One time I came back from the bathroom to find the notebook I'd left on my desk with its pages all ripped up. On the cover someone had written in black marker GROSS OTAKU SCUM. The thing was, I didn't have any friends I could talk to, and I'd got into the habit of talking to myself inside my head, so when I saw what was written, the thought that went through my head immediately was, *Oh, I'm scarcely worthy of being called an otaku!* This seemed pretty funny to me at the time, so I sort of tittered to myself, but I guess I was being watched because I heard someone say: "Whoa, she's so creepy!"

Of course, it got me down when that kind of stuff happened, but my dad had been so delighted when I'd got into this middle school that I resolved never to miss a day. My mom had died of breast cancer when I was still a baby, and my dad, who ran a Korean barbecue restaurant and a love hotel, brought me up all by himself, never remarrying. When my first period came, soon after I'd started middle school, it was my dad who sorted me out, rushing out to the pharmacy to buy me supplies. What he bought, as it turned out, wasn't tampons but those little squares of cotton that people use for removing makeup. Since it was my first time I didn't know any better, either, so although I always found it kind of weird wedging those small, creaky squares of cotton between my thighs, I just kept on doing it until eventually my aunt—my father's elder sister— got wind of it. When she saw what I was using, she let out a great roar of laughter that soon morphed into a sob. Then she rushed out and bought me some regular pads.

"How's school, Satomi? Are you enjoying it?" Dad would ask me every day, and every day I would respond with a big smile. But by that point, the cup lodged inside my chest was full to the brim. It had reached the stage where it felt like just one more drip could make it spill over. The bullying got worse each day, until finally everyone around me began to act as if I literally didn't exist. Nobody in my class spoke to me, or looked at me, and my time at school was spent simply sitting silently at my desk, willing the minutes to pass. When I got home, I was so weary I could barely move, and each evening I'd grow a little feverish. I'd lay in bed with the lights turned out; watching hours upon hours of anime on the tiny DVD player Dad had bought me. Then it would be morning, and I'd try to keep the nausea down as I put on my uniform and made my way to school. I didn't want to think that being bullied was better than being ignored, but in truth, it was. It was a tough time. And it went on and on, right until school finally ended.

The first time I had sex was in college. It was a fourth-rate place, the kind that even someone with grades as poor as mine had no problem getting into. No sooner had class begun than I realized that I was pretty popular with the guys. As a reward for getting into high school, Dad had paid for me to have cosmetic surgery to form a crease in my eyelids, and it was possible that had something to do with it. I don't know, but in any case, lots of guys spoke to me, and I had sex with all of them. I was so just happy that they were talking to me and, also, I had no idea how to say no. I'd rather have sex with a person, whoever they were, than see them pull a face when I turned them down. As ever, I didn't have any female friends, but I had a bunch of guy friends who I could talk to about my favorite anime and manga series, and that made me really happy. I pretended not to see the notes I sometimes found stuffed inside in my bag saying things like PIG-FACED SLUT and the emails asking if I shouldn't be praying for the souls of all the children I'd aborted.

During my four years of college I had sex with lots of my guy friends, but I never really found it pleasurable. Once, looking up at myself reflected in the mirror of the love hotel, pinned to the bed by a man's large expanse of back, I had the thought that having sex wasn't all that different from being bullied. I watched how his butt muscles rose up every time he moved his pelvis and wondered to myself why sex had to involve such a ridiculous set of movements. I wondered, too, if other people burst out laughing in the middle of the act.

But even though the sex didn't feel particularly good, I noticed that when I was doing it lots of warm liquid would spill out of my body. Looking at the man thrusting away so strenuously that he was drenched in sweat, I felt kind of guilty. If I made little moans and dug my nails into his back, he'd grunt into my ear: "You can come if you want." And when I screamed out in a piercing voice, "I'm coming!" just like I'd seen people do in the erotic anime I'd watched (of course, I wasn't actually coming), his thrusting would double in speed, and he'd come right away.

They did their best, those guys, they really did. They twiddled my clitoris with amazing persistence, rubbed away at the inside walls of my vagina with their assorted middle fingers, and changed positions on a minute-by-minute basis. I felt terrible about it, but the truth was the only time I would come was when I touched myself looking at boy-on-boy manga.

After I graduated from college, a business associate of Dad's helped find me a job in a small company that manufactured vending machines. I had never been any good in an academic environment, but I was even worse in the office. There was something about me that meant whenever I touched a photocopier or a fax machine or a computer, something was bound to go wrong with it. My boss was constantly hurling abuse at me for the fact that the phone messages I took from our clients had an accuracy rate of 30 percent.

Six months in, my dad died from a sudden brain hemorrhage. I'd been under the impression that he had plenty in savings, but it turned out that most of the money went toward paying off his debts, and just when I was starting to worry I'd have to live out the rest of my life in this company being yelled at, I met Keiichiro.

Keiichiro said he'd spotted me a few times in a restaurant where I often went for lunch, but I have no memory of ever having seen him there. But then, one day, I left my phone in the restaurant and went home without realizing it. Late that night, my landline rang, and I picked up to hear a man's voice on the other end.

"Look out at the streetlight beneath your window," said an unfamiliar monotone.

Since Dad had died, I'd been living in a studio apartment by myself, so this gave me the heebie-jeebies. When I peered down through the gap between the curtains, I saw a guy I didn't recognize standing under a dim streetlight, holding up my cell phone in one hand and smiling.

"I'll bring it up right now," he said, and hung up.

Sure enough, my doorbell rang. It kept ringing, over and over. I was debating whether or not to answer when my next-door neighbor kicked at my wall with a great thump. I quickly turned on the light in the hall, opened the door a crack, and saw a man about the same height as me, kind of pudgy, and wearing small silver glasses and dressed in a suit.

"I wanted to bring it sooner, but I had to work overtime," he said, reaching his hand through the crack in the door, which still had the chain on, and handing me my pink cell phone.

"Thanks. So much," I said, but still he showed no signs of leaving. He lingered, staring at me as I stood there in my thin pajamas with just a cardigan on top. Thinking he might be angry because I'd not been thankful enough, I tried again.

"Really, thank you so, so much, I really appreciate it," I said.

At this, he tried to pass a box containing a tiny cake to me. In a fluster, I undid the chain and opened the door. He cast his eyes around my room, then took his business card out of the pocket of his suit jacket and handed it to me. At great speed, he rattled off: "My name's Keiichiro Okamoto, I've liked you for some time, please will you go out with me?"

I had no idea what to say. As I was looking down at the business card, he thrust the box with the cake inside toward my chest. Then he said, "OK. I'm going," and stepped quickly back out through the door.

Wondering to myself what on earth all of that had been about, I put the cake in the fridge and went to bed. I'd stood so long by the open door in my bare feet that my legs were frozen right down to the tips of my toes, and I found it hard to get to sleep.

The following day, when I got back from the office, Keiichiro was standing in front of the door to my apartment, holding a box from the same cake shop.

Though I felt kind of alarmed, I bowed my head and said, "Thank you so much for returning my phone yesterday."

"How would you feel about some dinner?"

Keiichiro persuaded me to go with him to a restaurant in front of the train station. He gulped down beer from a huge tankard and went on and on about how terrible his job was. It wasn't exactly a thrilling conversation, so I just repeated the same three phrases over and over again as seemed most fitting: "Really," "Gosh, that sounds bad!" and "Yes, I'm sure you're right."

After a while, Keiichiro looked up at me and said, "I can tell you're a kind person." And then, looking as if he were about to cry, he reached out across the table and squeezed my hand.

Keiichiro is round-faced and short. He's the kind of guy who really isn't made for wearing a suit. In other words, he is, and was, basically the polar opposite of the kind of man I was usually attracted to, physically speaking. The honest truth was I felt neither any particular affection toward him nor any strong dislike. He proposed on our third date, and when he said I wouldn't have to work if I didn't want to, I agreed immediately. I guessed that a big pharmaceutical company like

Keiichiro's must pay well, and that there was no real chance of it going bankrupt. I was so worn down from being insulted at work every day, and I'd been so lonely since my dad died, so I was glad to have Keiichiro in my life, even when he turned up at my apartment unannounced several nights in a row or messaged me ten times a day. "Don't worry, Satomi. I'll take good care of you," he'd sometimes say to me, just like Dad had. When I heard that, I felt sure I'd make it through okay somehow.

Not too long after telling my boss that I'd be getting married and leaving the company, I was passing by the staff kitchen when I overheard someone saying: "Can you believe she's marrying that stalker?"

"Well, at least that's one less criminal on the loose."

I could see cigarette smoke leaking out of the room, along with their voices.

"He really should have been reported to the police, you know. You know Miss Shimizu from accounts basically had a nervous breakdown after he started turning up at her house every night?"

As I was standing there, I remembered I wanted to collect my favorite coffee mug to take home with me, so I went in. The moment they noticed me, everyone stopped talking and looked straight at me. As I was rooting around in the cupboard above the sink, one of them said in a very fake sort of voice:

"Oh, Satomi! Congratulations on getting married! We'll have to sort out a farewell party for you!"

"It's so great you've found such a good guy, from such a good company, so you can stay at home!" said another.

"Yeah, I'm so envious! What I wouldn't give not to have to commute."

"Those packed trains are *such* a nightmare!"

"Tell me about it! I'm so jealous!"

My mug wasn't in its usual place. I glanced around and, sure enough, I found it staring out at me from inside a clear plastic garbage bag in the corner of the room. I untied the bag and removed the mug, only to see there was a big crack in its handle. I dropped the cracked mug inside my purse, and retied up the bag. My colleagues watched me in silence.

"Thanks very much for everything. Don't worry about doing a farewell party or anything like that," I said, and bowed my head. My colleagues' faces took on slightly piteous expressions. Then, suddenly, one of them cried out. "Oww!" She stood up and flung her cigarette butt into the sink. "I think I burned my finger!"

"Gosh, are you okay?"

"Run it under cold water!"

My coworkers' interest quickly shifted to the colleague with the burned finger. I turned my back on the sound of their animated voices and left the kitchen.

We started our life as newlyweds in an apartment near the house Keiichiro had grown up in. Keiichiro often said to me things like, "I like that you don't boss me around like other people do, and you're not all quick and efficient," and, "I love touching your tummy, it's so soft and squishy. . . . It really calms me down," and, "It makes me feel happy to see you lazing around on the sofa reading manga." I knew some might find those kinds of comments pretty offensive, but I felt content. I was no good at cooking or doing laundry or cleaning but, as long as I managed to do the bare minimum, Keiichiro didn't complain. Yes, sometimes he'd fly off the handle about tiny things, like how the rice was too hot or his favorite shirt hadn't come back from the dry cleaners, but compared to being bullied at school or abused at work, that was nothing. All I had to do was bear those parts and then, when Keiichiro went to work, I could get lost in the world of manga and anime. Keiichiro seemed to have no interest whatsoever in geeky stuff like that but he never ridiculed me or showed any sign of finding my interests gross or weird. For Christmas, he even bought me the DVD I'd been trying to track down for ages and went shopping with me to buy fanzines. He was altogether very kind.

As I was clearing the table, the phone rang.

"Oh, Satomi, hi. How did your appointment go?"

It was Machiko. I knew Machiko noted my appointments at the fertility clinic in her planner.

"It was unsuccessful," I said, trying to inject a little sadness into my voice.

"Oh, dear. I'm so sorry, what a shame! Still, it's no good giving up after just two tries. I know a woman whose daughter got pregnant on her sixth go! And, Satomi, please don't fret about the money. I've got that all covered. Oh, yes, and I was thinking, I know you don't like exercise, but it's so lovely out this time of the year! Why don't we have a walk by the river one of these days? Did you know they say acupuncture can really help women with fertility problems? There's a really good acupuncturist in the next town, so I'll take you along, how about that? We can shop while we're there for some lovely new silk lingerie—I read that's also supposed to be effective for infertility. It'll be my treat. And remember, it's about to start getting warmer, but you mustn't go gulping down lots of chilled barley tea or anything like that, okay? Hot tea only, it's always got to be warm. Although green tea is actually supposed to cool the body, so it's not recommended for people with fertility problems. *Hoji-cha*, you're best sticking to hot *hoji-cha*."

Machiko talked so fast there wasn't space for me to say anything other than "yes" and "okay." Her voice was pretty loud, too, so I had to hold the receiver away from my ear. Every time she used the phrase "women with fertility problems" I'd have to think for a minute before I realized, oh, she's talking about me. When people used words like "fat," or "ugly," or "slow," I knew immediately who they were referring to, but somehow "fertility problems" took me longer. Still, I knew this had now been added to my list of attributes. I was now not only fat, ugly, and slow, but I had fertility problems, too.

With Machiko going to such efforts, I felt a little bad about the fact that neither Keiichiro nor I really wanted a baby. As I went on listening to her and inserting the right responses into the right spaces, I eyed the clock. The program I wanted to watch on the anime channel was about to start, but I was too frightened to interrupt Machiko's everlasting monologue and break off the conversation.

Eventually, after about an hour, Machiko said, "I think of you as my daughter, you know, Satomi. So I want you to think of me as your real mother! If there's anything you ever want or need, don't even hesitate to ask!"

Then she hung up.

Machiko often came out with that kind of stuff. The truth was, though, I had no memory of asking my real mother for anything, so I didn't really know how to do it. If we really were mother and daughter, for example, would it be okay to say, "There's an anime program I really want to watch, so do you mind if I go now"? I wasn't sure if that was allowed.

After I put the receiver down, I breathed a long sigh. Machiko was very kind and treated me well, but speaking to her for extended periods of time left me totally exhausted.

I opened the door to Keiichiro's room as quietly as I could and peeked inside. He was lying on top of his duvet snoring, his bedside lamp still on. Keiichiro was naturally baby-faced, but those gray circles under his eyes gave him the look of a middle-aged man, exhausted with life. I guessed his job must really be tough. With that wide, domed forehead and those thin lips, Keiichiro was the spitting image of Machiko. I had the feeling that if I ever got pregnant, my baby would come out looking exactly like that. As I stood there watching, Keiichiro turned his face away from the light. On the left side of his neck was a diagonal scar about ten centimeters long, stretching from his earlobe down toward his collarbone. I'd once asked him what had happened, if he'd been involved in some kind of accident, but he'd just replied, "I was bullied at school, too."

He didn't elaborate. Whenever I spoke about my experiences with bullying, Keiichiro would pat my head and say, "I just put a curse on your bullies to bring them bad luck, so it'll all be okay now."

I was grateful to him for saying it, but seeing him come home every day looking so ground down, I couldn't help suspecting that he didn't have the strength to curse anyone.

Keiichiro said he finds it hard to sleep well when he's sharing a bed with another person, so from the very first we'd slept in separate rooms. On weekends, Keiichiro comes to my room in the evenings to have sex. He gives me a few peck-like kisses, squeezes my boobs, and fiddles with my clitoris some, and then, still lying down, enters me from behind, and comes after a few thrusts. I don't make any noise or feel any pleasure. The doctor at the clinic said Keiichiro has a low sperm count and that his sperm aren't very energetic, and I can't help but wonder if that's related in some way to how lifeless our sex is. I kind of suspect the important task of passing on your genes to the next generation might be just too much for a person like Keiichiro. I've no complaints about our sex life, but sometimes I can't help thinking back fondly to the wild times I used to have with my various guy friends in college, where I felt as though they might devour me right then and there.

On Saturday, as I was putting together a late lunch, the doorbell rang. On the intercom monitor I saw Machiko standing there in a matching fuchsia jacket and skirt.

"Guess where I've just been!" she said. "The morning farmers' market in the square in front of the town hall. Just look how fresh these vegetables are! Let's get them down you right away!"

Machiko set down a heavy-looking paper bag and some of the soil sticking to the daikon leaves fell onto the floor.

"Have you not eaten yet? It's late to be having lunch, isn't it?"

"We both slept in today."

"These sandwiches look nice," she said as she peeled back the bread with her finger to look inside. "But not half enough vegetables. Hold on a minute. You just put your feet up and watch TV for a while now." And as she said this, she pulled an apron from her purse and began washing the mud-caked vegetables in the sink.

Thinking the sandwiches would dry out, I hurriedly wrapped them in cling wrap. Machiko hummed to herself as she stood there, busying herself in my kitchen. I found myself rooted to the spot, unable to speak, just staring at the broad back of this woman who had come bursting in on us and our day. Still, I realized there was nothing to be done. I took a seat on the sofa and stared at the TV, though it was totally impossible to relax.

"Lunch is ready!" Machiko eventually called out in a sing-song voice.

Keiichiro came traipsing into the room, face still swollen with sleep.

"I thought I recognized that smell," he said, as he put his hand up inside the hem of his faded sweatshirt and scratched his belly.

"What time do you call this, young man? Go on! Off you go and wash your face," said Machiko, with obvious delight. The table was laid with bowls of steaming vegetable soup and daikon salad.

Keiichiro always claimed that the only thing he could stomach when he'd just woken up was coffee, but now he practically threw Machiko's soup down his throat, commenting on how good it was. Neither Machiko nor Keiichiro touched the sandwiches I'd made. But I couldn't deny that Machiko's soup and salad were far better, so it made perfect sense.

"Oh, yes! I've brought something for you," she said, pulling a small box out of her purse. "This, my dear, is egg vinegar. They make it by pickling the eggs of silkie hens. So healthy. A friend of mine told me her daughter drank this and got pregnant almost instantly! I thought it might be the thing for you." She opened up the bottle and poured out some of the liquid, the color of milky coffee, into a small plastic measuring cup.

"You only need a little. Here, give it a try."

It didn't seem as if I could refuse, so I drained it in one go. It wasn't as sour as I'd expected it to be, but it had a very strange taste that spread out right across my tongue. I hurriedly took a sip of tea.

"So, you just drink that every day from now on. It's ever so good for you."

Next, Machiko brought out of her bag several Tupperware containers containing various nutritious salads like simmered hijiki with soybeans, and sautéed lotus and burdock roots.

"If only your mom had been alive, of course, you'd have been able to eat all these healthy foods when you were going through puberty, when your body really needed them."

At this, I felt a prickly, stinging feeling in my chest. Machiko seemed more formidable than ever today. What was she trying to imply about my body? Was the idea that if I'd eaten more seaweed and root vegetables when I was younger, then I'd have been pregnant by now? Her uninterrupted stream of conversation leapt from one thing to another. One moment it seemed the topic was her friend's daughter who had a shotgun wedding at the age of twenty after getting pregnant unexpectedly, but then before I knew it Machiko was speaking about which nursery schools had the best teachers, and then to how tough elementary schools were these days. Finally, she landed upon what seemed to be the heart of the matter: how her friend had been terribly shocked by suddenly finding herself with a grandchild. I listened and made appropriate noises as best I could, but somewhere along the line I must have zoned out because I heard Machiko say, "I really do," and then stop speaking entirely. She reached out and grasped my hand, and I looked up in surprise. Noting the expression on my face, Machiko repeated herself.

"I was *saying*, I think it's worth trying IVF, Satomi, I really do. I know that money is a concern for you, but I've got the savings that Keiichiro's father left, and I'm sure that up there in heaven, he wouldn't be against my using it to give him grandchildren. Let's give it a try, eh? As many goes as it takes. People with excellent genes like you two are the ones who need to be passing them on, not all these hopeless parents with the DNA of stray dogs. Trust me, it's better to give birth before you turn thirty. Children prefer a young and beautiful mother."

Keiichiro had disappeared off to the sofa, where he was stretched out reading the paper. I was sure he could hear what Machiko was saying, but he didn't make any comment on any of it. My heart was thumping in my chest, and I started to say, "Actually, we're not entirely sure if—"

Machiko gripped my hand and started to speak even more loudly.

"You know, in the past, men were told that if their wives didn't give them children within three years they had to leave them. I hate to say this, but we really should have had you checked at the hospital before you two got married. If we had, then we wouldn't have found ourselves in this—this—"

I could feel her great booming voice vibrating inside my ears. Hearing Machiko begin to snivel, Keiichiro looked up in surprise from behind his newspaper. I really hoped he would say something at that point, but, after a moment, he returned his gaze to the print. Machiko removed her tinted glasses, sank her large body down onto the table, and began to cry in earnest.

A voice inside me was saying, *I really can't be bothered with this*, but I did all I could to push it down to the bottom of my chest. I'm not very good at dealing with these kinds of situations, and my impulse was just to run out of the apartment, but I knew the minute I left I would lose my right to ever return. It concerned me that the people next door would hear Machiko's wailing. It went on and on, and though I didn't really feel sorry, I figured that if I didn't apologize she'd be there wailing forever, so I rubbed her back and said, "I'm sorry, Machiko."

She lifted her face, her makeup ruined with tears, and said with a smile, "So you'll give IVF a try, then?"

I heard a drop of water fall from the tap into the sink.

No sooner had I begun preparations for IVF than I understood how much of a step up it was from artificial insemination. They may both have been classified as infertility treatments, but IVF was in a different league from anything I'd tried before. I had to have daily intramuscular injections to ensure my ovaries were producing healthy eggs. The injections themselves were painful enough, but worse was the dull pain in my stomach and the nausea that came on afterward. I would lie in bed, and Machiko would bring meals around for me. Once, seeing me lying there green-faced, Machiko said: "If you're suffering this much, it's guaranteed to work!"

When several of the follicles that contained the ova had reached the right stage of development, a needle would be inserted into the ovary to suck them out, the doctor explained. Just hearing the phrase "insert a needle" was enough to make me feel faint. Yet everything that had to be done was done quietly, and without incident. One of my eggs that had been artificially matured was successfully fertilized inside a culture vessel with Keiichiro's sperm, which he'd had to masturbate in the clinic to produce. After this, the cleavage stage began. Two days later, when the fertilized egg would be returned to my womb, Machiko showed up unannounced at the clinic. Right before I entered the treatment room, she handed me a talisman of brocaded silk, saying, "You've nothing at all to fear!"

The talisman had come from a shrine just outside town, where people went to pray to the god of children. I had never been.

Even after the fertilized egg was inserted into my womb, I had to continue taking hormones. It was two weeks before they would tell me officially whether I was pregnant or not, but Machiko was behaving as if her grandchild bun was already in the oven, buying cute baby clothes and bringing them around to our apartment along with her homemade meals.

The first IVF attempt failed, as did the second. The third time, the fertilization was successful, but then the cells suddenly stopped dividing. My guess was that the zygotes made up of mine and Keiichiro's DNA were somehow too weak to make it. It really seemed as though the gods had determined that our children were not supposed to be born into this world.

The late summer day I found out at the clinic that the third attempt had also been unsuccessful, there was a huge typhoon, and the water level of the river rose dangerously high. Even after dark, I could hear sirens racing all around town, and it made me feel very on edge.

Machiko had told me to let her know as soon as the results were in. I picked up the phone a few times to call her, but I found I didn't have it in me to tell her when I was alone, so I decided to wait for Keiichiro to come home. The truth was, I was kind of hoping he would make the call, but it was clear the moment he came in the door late that night that he was in a terrible mood. I guessed he must have had a bad day at work again, and I couldn't bring myself to ask him.

"It was unsuccessful again," I began to say into the receiver, and then the line went dead. Not long after, Machiko turned up at our apartment, soaked to the skin. There must have been some wind out there, because the flower-print umbrella she was holding was turned completely inside out, its wires all bent. Not stopping to take off her olive-colored raincoat, Machiko came flying through the door at me, forcing me backward down the hall.

"Why do you find it so difficult?" she yelled, as the raindrops leapt from her coat in all directions. "I never wanted him to marry you in the first place, but he insisted! He insisted, so I turned a blind eye to your situation!"

Machiko wasn't crying, but in her excitement her eyes had turned bright red.

"S-Situation?"

"A little money can get you anything, you know! Pay someone to do some research, and it all comes out of the woodwork! You can find out anything! Anything you like! Oh, yes, I know all about your student days, all those immoral sexual relations you had!"

I'd been called a slut plenty of times before, but this was the first time anybody had ever accused me of having "immoral sexual relations."

"But Keiichiro was determined to marry you, and I thought to myself, well, as long as you'll give him children, then, it doesn't really matter what kind of girl you are. I just want grandchildren. That's it! It's very simple! So tell me! Why isn't it happening?"

With these last words, Machiko was yelling, and the yell tuned into a scream that sounded as if it were being wrung from the back of her throat, and then she put her handkerchief to her eyes and began to cry.

"It's not just my fault we can't get pregnant," I said. It was the first time I'd ever spoken back to Machiko. It took all the energy I had to say those words, ever so quietly. I could hear my own voice shaking like crazy.

Machiko glared at me.

"What are you trying to say?"

"They found problems with Keiichiro, too," I said, but I couldn't get the words out to tell her about Keiichiro's low sperm count or his general lack of interest in sex.

"Don't talk nonsense! Just look at how Keiichiro is working himself to the bone just to keep you fed! If you'd only put some effort into the food you make him, there'd be no problems with his body whatsoever! From the day he was born until the day he married you, I poured every ounce of love I had into bringing him up properly. He was my treasure. But you! Just look at you! You hang around the house not doing a thing, and you can't even cook! And now it turns out, you can't even get pregnant! Do you know there are women in this world who work full-time, do all the housework by themselves, and still manage to raise three or four kids? I don't know how you managed to trick him into this! He really drew the short straw with you!"

With every new line Machiko came out with in that booming voice of hers, I felt like I was being sucked farther and farther inside some cheesy soap on TV, and it drained all the strength away from my body. Machiko had her own storyline all figured out. In it, she was the poor woman who had brought up her son with such loving care, only for him to be stolen away by a stupid bitch incapable of doing any housework, who couldn't even conceive. In her story, Machiko had the starring role and I was the villain; while for me, Machiko was like the last boss who showed up at the end of a game, the hardest enemy to defeat. If I did manage to finish her off, I wondered vaguely to myself, would my marriage and my life come to an end, like they did in computer games? Keiichiro was still sitting on the sofa, staring at the floor, not moving so much as a finger. Was he my enemy, too? If he was, I felt like he was one of the minor ones. Even I could take him down in an instant.

"It's because you don't try hard enough," Machiko was saying. Apparently, she still wasn't done with abusing me.

Since elementary school, I'd always struggled with things. Whether it was kickovers on the bar in gymnastics or sewing on buttons in home economics, it took me at least twice as long as other people to master new tasks. Even when I was trying my best, my fingers and my body just wouldn't move in the same way as other people's. I remembered all those tough times I spent after school in the classroom or the playground trying to complete some activity, and how the teachers and my classmates who were watching me would call out, "Come on, try harder!" as if by just *trying harder* I would miraculously become able to do the thing. It was the same now. I wasn't about to go and get pregnant just because someone told me to make the effort.

It seemed as though the storm outside had begun to rage even harder, and from time to time a gust of wind sent the rain whipping loudly against the balcony door. Leaving Machiko shouting and raving and Keiichiro still sitting silently in the living room, I ran into my bedroom and locked the door. Machiko came stomping after me with that great big body of hers, twisting the doorknob frenziedly and pounding on the door.

"Open up right now!"

I covered my ears with my hands to shut out her screams. Then I heard the muffled sound of someone's body—I didn't know whether it was Machiko's or Keiichiro's—slamming against the door.

I looked toward the door and said, "I'm sorry. I just need to rest a bit."

After a while, Machiko changed tack.

"Now listen, Satomi," she began. "Don't go getting any funny ideas in there, okay?"

First, I was thoroughly abused for being the way I was, and then I was told not to think anything "funny." What on earth did Machiko want me to do?

Eventually, I must have passed out. I slept very deeply, curled right up in the duvet, and when I woke, both the bed and I were drenched in sweat. I got up to change the sheets, and when I opened the closet I found my MAGICAL GIRL☆LILLICA cosplay outfit there on its hanger. Lillica is one of my favorite anime characters, and I'd bought her costume, along with the cat-eared wig and magic wand, just to have rather than to actually wear. Now though, on a whim, I took off my sweat-soaked clothes and tried the costume on. The outfit, which was modeled around a sailor-style school uniform, had an incredibly short skirt, and I could feel the air skimming my thighs. It was supposedly "one size fits all," but the waist was very tight, and though I just about managed to do up the buttons, it seemed as though it would pop off at any minute. I put on the wig with the attached cat ears, and then stood in front of the full-length mirror. No, I thought. It wouldn't do for Lillica to have a face like this, like a regular downtrodden housewife. I spread out every item of makeup that I owned across the floor and began to do myself up. I never usually wore foundation, but now I daubed it on carefully and evenly, adding mascara to lengthen and thicken my eyelashes, making my lips shiny with gloss, and finally applying a light dusting of blusher to my cheeks. Then I stood in front of the full-length mirror again. The person standing there wasn't Satomi, the fat, ugly, stupid, infertile housewife. Anybody looking from a distance would have taken her for a slightly plump Lillica.

Though it was still the middle of the night, I heard sirens sounding in the distance again. I wondered if the water level of the river had risen even higher. I picked up Lillica's wand, and shouted in as hushed a voice as I could, "Parallel Princess Version Up!" That was what Lillica said when she wanted to transform from a regular schoolgirl into MAGICAL GIRL☆LILLICA. When she spoke those magic words, every wish of hers came true.

I wished that Machiko and Keiichiro would always be nice to me. I wished I didn't have to go through any more painful fertility treatments. I wished I didn't have to go out into a world filled with bullies. I wished I could do the bare minimum amount of housework and then spend the rest of my time doing whatever I wanted.

Each time I repeated Lillica's magic words, I could feel the power building up in the base of my stomach. A siren started up again from outside like the wail of some dying beast. How good it would be, I thought, if the river would overflow and flood the town, washing away all the people who'd ever bullied me in a muddy torrent. It could wash away Machiko while it was at it, and Keiichiro, too.

Standing there in my Lillica costume, I kept striking poses in front of the mirror until it started to grow light outside the window.

I don't know what was said between Keiichiro and Machiko that night, but from then on, Machiko stopped coming over so frequently. Occasionally, she would call the house, but she only ever spoke about normal, day-to-day stuff and I no longer heard the words "pregnancy" or "children" from her lips. Life for me and Keiichiro went on just as it had before. Keiichiro's work got even busier, and he often came home way past midnight. I didn't feel great about the fact that he had made no attempt to save me from his mother, but I was still grateful for him for not kicking me out. Maybe Lillica's magic spell had worked. I returned to a life where, so long as I carried out all the basic domestic tasks, I could immerse myself in the world of anime and manga to my heart's desire.

It was around this time that I started making my own cosplay outfits for my favorite characters. I got into it initially because the costumes that were on sale were too small for me. I was so clumsy that learning how to use a sewing machine was a mighty undertaking, but friends of mine I'd met on online forums would help me out and, besides, I knew I could take as much time as I liked without having to worry about being told off by teachers or bosses or whomever. Even if the costumes weren't exactly prize-winning quality, I still had a great time making them.

After I'd finished the costumes for the three magical girls in MAGICAL GIRL☆LILLICA, a friend of mine named Kurumi, who I'd met at last year's Comiket, asked me to make her a costume for another Lillica character named Lord Muramasa, a physics teacher who was also a sorcerer. Kurumi was tall and skinny like a boy, so I figured she'd be perfect as Lord Muramasa. I bought some shiny purple satin and set about cutting and sewing. I got so carried away that I was still at it when Keiichiro came home from work. He knew I was making cosplay costumes, but, as with everything, he'd never said anything to me about it.

Seeing me struggling with the buttonholes, Keiichiro came up to me.

"Let me try," he said.

In a flash, he was sitting in front of the machine, slitting the fabric with a U-shaped tool called a seam ripper and creating four perfect buttonholes.

"That's amazing! How come you can do that?"

"I was a member of drama club for a while, in college. We made all our own costumes, so I had to learn how to use a machine and to sew by hand as well," Keiichiro said, somewhat proudly. That was maybe the first time I felt pure respect for him. It was also the first I'd ever heard about drama club. I thought the reason I knew so little about Keiichiro was because he didn't like to talk about stuff, but I guess it was also my fault for not asking more. I was so happy to have discovered this totally new side to my husband that, without thinking, I said, "Hey, why don't you try it on!"

"No way! Why?"

But I kept on at him, saying, "Please, please, go on! Just this time!" and eventually he took off his suit and stepped into the newly completed Lord Muramasa costume. I looked at him, standing there in the purple gown. Chubby, short, hunched, pale-faced, with dark bags under his eyes, Keiichiro didn't suit the costume at all. I mean, it made total sense. Keiichiro was working himself to the bone, putting up with a job he hated in order to feed me, and that's why he looked the way he did. I knew that, and I knew it was bad to even think those kinds of things about him, let alone say them. But still, seeing how old and haggard Keiichiro looked in the bright lights of the room, I became a little frightened. I didn't feel at all sure that I could keep this marriage thing up, watching as this person right in front of me went on aging with every day that went by. And of course, I'd get older, too. I'd be following right after him. Thinking that, I felt a tiny hole open in my chest and a gust of cold wind go blasting through it.

I guess Keiichiro must somehow have sensed my disappointment. In a second, he was tearing the costume off, saying,

"Why did you make me do that? You knew it wasn't going to look any good on me."

He went into his room and shut the door.

"Anzu, look! Over there!"

On that fateful day at Comiket, Kurumi was the first to see him. I looked in the direction she was pointing, and there I saw Takumi standing in a white T-shirt, jeans, and green Converse. He really looked like someone who'd found himself in the wrong place by accident. He was tall and gangly, and though he wasn't desperately good-looking or anything, he had the kind of face that you could tell would look really ace when it was made up.

"I'd love to see him in this," Kurumi said, fingering the collar of her Lord Muramasa costume. Before that day, I'd never once gone up and spoken to a boy, but I was there with Kurumi and I'd already had my photo taken as Lillica by a bunch of people, so I guess I was feeling braver than usual. Takumi seemed kind of taken aback to be approached by two girls in cosplay and even more so when I asked him for his email address, but he gave it to me nonetheless.

After exchanging a few emails, we found out that we lived in the same part of town, and when I invited him over, saying that I just wanted to take some photos of him in cosplay, Takumi immediately agreed to come. I felt a lot like one of those pervy old men who trick schoolgirls into letting them take nude photos. Although actually, what I was doing was a lot worse than that. Admittedly, it was Takumi who pushed me down onto the bed, but I was the one who had enticed him into doing it.

The first time we had sex was Takumi's first time ever, and he was trembling like crazy. Still, I showed no mercy. I told him I wanted him to fuck me as per the scripts I would write for him. He wore the costumes I'd made without complaint, and learned the scripts I wrote by heart. I was having exactly the sort of sex I wanted to be having, so needless to say it felt amazing, but afterward I was always ridden with guilt and would often slip some money into Takumi's palm.

Strange as it sounds, Takumi's body always had a milky smell to it, like a baby's. I wondered whether that was because he was still young and, compared to me at least, fresh from the womb. But even though Takumi was just a kid and still didn't know what to do in bed, he never treated me roughly like my boyfriends in college had. If the art of touching people tenderly was something that came naturally to some people, then maybe Takumi was a kind of natural-born genius in that way. I remember once, when we were having sex and I was on top, Takumi reached out to rest his hands on my hips and suddenly said, "You're chilly here."

I was so taken aback that I stopped moving.

"It's important for women to keep this part of their bodies warm."

It was the sort of thing that Machiko was always saying to me.

"How do you know that?"

"My mom . . ." he began, and then I watched as his face turned crimson. I can see how it might have felt pretty embarrassing to mention his mom while he was inside me. I thought it was cute, though, and as I laughed I began moving my hips back and forward very fast.

"When you laugh, I can feel it," he said, and came inside me, panting. His neck was pure white, without a single spot or wrinkle. I bit into it, gently. Somehow I sensed that Takumi was even less intelligent than I was. He was probably so dumb he couldn't name all the Japanese prefectures—though actually, saying that, I'm not super confident I could, either. Yet I had this feeling that if the two of us were washed up on a desert island, we'd get by. Somehow or other, we'd pull through. Those are the kinds of things I'd started to think about as I was fixing dinner for Keiichiro in the evening.

Keiichiro's job had become so busy that the only time we really talked was at breakfast. His visits to my room for sex had fallen to just once a month. Perhaps because he was so exhausted, he'd recently started doing it with me regardless of whether I was awake or not. If I were fast asleep, he'd just pull down my panties and wedge his way inside me. Usually, I just put up with it. After all, otherwise he was looking after me, so it seemed only fair. But there was one particular day, I guess maybe he'd drunk a lot with his clients or something, because he had that ripe smell that boozed-up guys on the last train have. He was moving back and forward inside me over and over, apparently unable to come, and I was dry as anything. I never got sad when I was having sex or anything like that, but this time was so sore that I really thought I was going to cry with pain.

"Stop!" I thrust an elbow toward Keiichiro, who was clinging on to my back.

"What's with you?" He gave my hair a tug.

"It really hurts. Can you please give it a rest today?"

Keiichiro clicked his tongue in irritation. "That wet patch on your sheet was distracting me. It feels gross."

"Sorry. I spilled some water there before." Of course this was a lie.

"If you're in the house all day long, you could at least change the sheets," Keiichiro spat out, before clicking his tongue again, louder this time, and leaving the room.

Takumi started coming over more often.

Once, while we were having sex, the doorbell rang. Pretty bad timing, because I was just getting close to coming. I pulled myself away from Takumi, sighed, and turned over so I was lying on my back. Takumi looked at me, so I put a finger to my lips and mouthed *shhhhh*. From my bedroom window that faced onto the hallway outside, I heard Machiko's voice.

"Satomi! Are you there?"

She began knocking at the window with her fingers and rattling the grate, saying in an affected voice, "Well, how strange!"

I lay there straining my ears, and after a while I heard her moving away from the window and returning to the door, ringing several times and turning the doorknob noisily, before giving up and going home.

Not long after, I got in the elevator again with Mrs. Kimura, the cooking blogger.

"Is it your brother who comes around to see you?" she asked me with a smile. When I said nothing, she said, "My daughter goes to the same nursery school as Mrs. Fujimura's little ones—you know, Mrs. Fujimura, who lives next door to you? She was telling me you've got a younger brother in high school who comes over a lot. She's always saying how handsome he is!"

Before Mrs. Kimura had finished speaking, the elevator reached the first floor. As the doors opened, I sensed the gazes of all the young mothers waiting for the nursery school bus fall on me. As ever, Mrs. Kimura melded in naturally with the others, and I walked on past quickly. I could feel their whispers following me down the street, lapping at my back.

I had the feeling that things couldn't go on like this for much longer, but even I was surprised by how quickly the dreaded day came around. Even knowing that I had to stop, that what I was doing was an outrageous crime, I still felt very upset when Takumi broke up with me. When he told me out of the blue that he wouldn't be coming to see me anymore and then left, I lay stunned on my bed for a while. Then I decided to go after him.

I pressed the button to call the elevator up from the first floor. When it reached the landing, the doors opened, and Mrs. Fujimura and her daughter stepped out. Mrs. Fujimura looked at me, her eyes perfect circles of surprise. Her daughter pointed a finger at me and said loudly, "Look Mommy, it's Lillica!"

The little girl wouldn't take her eyes off me, and Mrs. Fujimura had to drag her down the hall by the arm to their apartment. I watched as the doors to the elevator closed in front of me, and the elevator started out again for the first floor.

Looking down at my feet, I noticed I wasn't wearing any shoes. The toes of my white knee-high socks were gray with dirt.

One evening, about two weeks after Takumi stopped coming over, I came back from buying food for dinner to see Keiichiro and Machiko's shoes arranged neatly side by side in the entranceway. It was getting dark, but there were no lights on in either the entranceway or the hall. Opening the door to the living room, I found Keiichiro with his head on the table, sobbing, and Machiko stroking his back. Keiichiro's laptop was open on the table. The glow from its screen was the only source of light in the room, but the picture itself was dim, and at first I couldn't tell what it was they were watching. Keiichiro's sobbing drowned out the noise from the computer, but after a little while I clearly heard my own voice say, "Lord Muramasaaaaaaa!"

As my eyes began to adjust to the darkness I saw that there, on the computer screen, was a video of me and Takumi in cosplay. The shopping bag fell from my right hand, and an onion went rolling across the floor.

"It's because you don't have children," Machiko explained quietly. Her face was lit up by the glow of the screen. "This kind of thing wouldn't happen if you had children. When women have too much time on their hands, they always get up to no good. Keiichiro's been suspecting something was up for a while. There's been a hidden camera in there for some time. Did you really not notice?"

I shook my head.

"I've talked it all over with Keiichiro. Even in the light of all of this, he says he doesn't want to split up with you. So the question is how can we go about ensuring you have kids. If artificial fertilization and IVF won't work, we need to think of another way. If only I could give birth for you!"

The image of Machiko with a great swollen belly passed through my mind. I instantly felt the skin across my body begin to crawl, and nausea rise up from the pit of my stomach. So long as they're happening within the confines of anime and manga, I can forgive weird procreation plotlines, however ridiculous they might be—Human Instrumentality Projects, or transmutation, or humanoid interfaces, or what have you. But the idea of Machiko giving birth to Keiichiro's and my child was definitely, 100 percent out of the question. I may have been a perverted housewife who had made a schoolboy dress up in cosplay to have sex with her, but there were some things even I couldn't agree to.

"I'm very sorry, Mother," I said, kneeling down on the floor and bowing until my head touched the ground. "Please let me divorce your son."

I'd seen people adopting that position on TV and stuff a lot, but it was the first time I'd ever done it myself and I didn't know if it was really appropriate for the occasion. It was the first time I'd ever called Machiko "Mother," too.

"There's an excellent hospital in America that finds surrogate mothers for couples wanting babies," Machiko began. "They have a Japanese coordinator who'll arrange everything. It doesn't matter if you can't speak a word of English. I think we should go, the three of us, to take their test. To America. Of course, I'll pay for everything."

Entirely ignoring the way I had prostrated myself on the floor, Machiko spoke in as cheery a tone as if she was suggesting a family outing to a spa resort.

"This way you won't even have to go through the pain of childbirth. It doesn't get any easier than that! And there'll be nothing to worry about afterward, either. I'll be there to take care of the baby. You can lie around and read manga all you like, or do whatever. Aside from these kinds of antics, of course."

"I'm comingggg!" bleated my voice from the screen, as if on cue. Machiko shot a glance at the laptop. A deep frown formed on her face, and she sighed, loudly. Face still buried in the table, Keiichiro let out a sob. Machiko gently rubbed his back the way people did to lull children to sleep.

"He's such a kindhearted boy, my Keiichiro. I'm sure you must think so. I was always determined to have a nice, kind child, and I did my best to make sure he turned out that way. But then, of course, when he got into school, he was so badly bullied. The truth is, in this world of ours, it's not enough just to be kind. You know this scar? Wait, have you not heard about it? Oh, heavens, he doesn't tell you anything, does he? Well, it's time you heard. When Keiichiro was in middle school, he tried to take his own life. Slashed his neck open with a knife, right here. That was a shock, I can tell you! When I went to wake him in the morning, his bed was drenched in blood. My husband wouldn't let me hear the last of it, saying that if we lost our only child, it'd be all my fault. He's very kind, and he's got a good head on him, but he's so very weak, that's the thing. I started to regret the way I'd brought him up. To think I'd made some kind of mistake. But everything's going to be okay. With yours and Keiichiro's child, I'll make sure that everything turns out fine. Everything goes better the second time."

I pressed my forehead to the floor once again and said, "I'm begging you. Just let us get divorced. I'll leave."

At that, Keiichiro lifted his head abruptly from the table.

"I won't let you go. If you insist on divorcing me, I'll spread these videos and photos everywhere. I'll send them to his parents' house and his school. I'll spread them around the world."

The light of the screen picked out Keiichiro's face, a mess of tears and snot, from the darkness surrounding him. If it ever arrived, our child would probably be weak and ugly, just like Keiichiro and me. I didn't know if I had it in me to love a child like that. I heard my voice say, "Lord Muramasaaaaa, I'm coming!"

Keiichiro let out a long thin wail that worked its way deep inside my ears.

With Machiko in charge, the preparations for our America trip came together in no time. I took the bus to the shopping center one day to pick up a bunch of small items I needed for the vacation. In the department store, beside the lingerie section, I found myself in an area selling baby stuff—onesies and outer clothes, that sort of thing. A baby mannequin smiled out at me from its stroller. If the process of finding a surrogate mother went smoothly, I could be walking around with a baby of my own by next year. I had no home to go back to, and I couldn't work to make a living, so in a way, Machiko's plan wasn't so bad. Just like she said, I wouldn't have to go through the pain of childbirth, and I could leave all the childrearing to her. I'd be able to spend my time reading manga, watching anime, and making cosplay outfits, just as I had until now. I knew that was a lazy approach to take, but that was how I'd started to think about the whole thing.

I came to a halt in front of a rack of baby socks. I remembered something I'd heard someone on TV say: *Babies choose the parents they're born to.* Was there any baby in its right mind who would choose to come to me, knowing what I was like—or, for that matter, to Keiichiro the weed or Machiko the battle-ax? And all via the womb of some American woman we hadn't met yet? Maybe it would be pressured into it, forced by the others around it to come to me, against its will, in the same way that Keiichiro and I had been forced to do all kinds of horrible things during our school days. I picked up a pair of baby socks. They were so small they fit inside my palm. I might not be able to love the baby that came to me, I thought, but I still wanted to stroke the soles of feet small enough to fit into these kinds of socks, in the same tender way Takumi had touched me.

Sensing someone standing close by, I looked up to see Takumi standing right in front of me, looking very serious. It had been a while since I'd last seen him. He'd gotten some sun and looked like he'd grown even taller.

"Are you having a baby?" he asked. His voice was quavering. I shook my head. I didn't know what to do next. I put the socks back on the rack and walked away. On the escalator, the thought struck me that if I were having Takumi's baby, I'd probably be able to touch it with even more tenderness. Just thinking that, I felt a warm, glowing sensation around my hips, the place where Takumi had once laid his hands and told me to keep warm.

Keiichiro had hidden cameras inside the clock, the stuffed toys, on top of the cabinet we used for dishes, and inside the flower-pots where we kept our houseplants, and there they remained. Everywhere I went in the apartment, I knew they were there, filming me. They were filming me that day as I opened up a notebook and began calculating how much money Takumi and I would need if we were to start living together, Keiichiro's and my dirty breakfast plates still on the table. I could have two jobs, day and evening, I thought. I leafed through the want ads in the newspaper, but there weren't any jobs I qualified for. Yet the fantasy of living with Takumi now seemed much more appealing to me than the idea of reading manga, watching anime, and making cosplay costumes all day. There was nothing to stop us from going to some far-off place and starting a new life. I was busy devising plans to apply for scholarships to pay for Takumi's school fees, thinking about the cost of renting somewhere, and wondering what kind of fabric would be best for our curtains when the door rang. It rang once, then after a while, again. When I picked up the intercom phone, I heard Takumi's voice.

"It's me."

I opened the door. The light rushing in from the hallway behind him prevented me from seeing his face properly. He seemed to have grown even taller than the last time I'd seen him at the shopping center, if that was possible. When he kissed me right then and there in the hall, my heart started squeezing itself into a tight little ball. Over and over it squeezed, sending out blood so hot it seemed as if it would boil over at any moment to the farthest reaches of my body. The blood that gathered in my lower half seemed to flow straight into my clitoris, making it swell, and the hollow part of me was crying out for him. I felt that if he didn't fuck me quickly I would go mad. Our tongues intertwined, and there was a clink of metal as Takumi undid his belt. He pulled down his boxers and entered me. He only had to push his pelvis up a few times before I was letting out an enormous roar, the kind I'd never heard anyone make before, and before I could stop myself I was coming. I took his hand, and led him into the living room, which he'd never set foot in before. We fell back together on the sofa.

I hadn't been that wet to start off with, but my first orgasm sent warm liquid spilling out from inside me like a tide. Takumi sucked it up noisily. From time to time, we could hear the voices of children playing in the courtyard outside or the twittering of birds, but the only noise I was concentrating on was the one his tongue made moving fast and then slow. He continued licking me, flicking at my clitoris with his pointed tongue, and when he switched to sucking hard, I climaxed again, without knowing I was going to. Quickly, Takumi clambered on top of me, grabbing tight hold of my wrists, which were up by my head, and watched my face as I let out a long roar like a wild beast. Then he stuck his hot tongue inside my mouth and moved it around and around. They called it climaxing, I understood then for the first time, because you were at the very peak of happiness. Takumi was different from how he'd been during our cosplay sex, when he'd always seemed kind of timid. Now there was none of that. When he touched me with his tongue, or his fingers, every movement he made was full of power. Every time his hot tongue or his cold fingers brushed roughly against my nipples or my armpits or the insides of my thighs, I'd get a tingling sensation in my temples. Takumi was the only person I wanted to touch me, ever. When I wrapped my arms around him, I noticed his shoulders had grown wider. And yet. Even this body of his, which was currently shooting up like a sunflower under the blazing midsummer heat, would one day dry up. It suddenly struck me that human bodies started aging from the moment they came into this world, and the thought made me want to throw back my head to cry and howl like a baby.

Cradling my legs, Takumi spread them wide, and then in one fluid movement, he entered me. The tip of him reached right to the very deepest part of me. When I felt him rubbing against me there, I began moving my hips in time with his, wanting to feel him even harder. The pleasure went on and on, so that I was shaking right to the very core of my body.

I realized that right in that moment, there wasn't a thing in this world I was scared of. Imagine, I thought, imagine if a child was conceived from sex that felt as good as this. What a happy thing that would be. Except that couldn't happen to me, because my body would malfunction and refuse to get pregnant. And because if it did, I wouldn't be able to see Takumi ever again.

For what seemed like the umpteenth time, Takumi let out a girlish scream and came inside me. I reached a finger down, and tried to taste the semen spilling from my body.

"It doesn't taste very good," I said.

As Takumi looked at me, his dark eyes lit up and once again he moved slowly back inside me.

The cameras all over the apartment went on capturing our sex from a multitude of angles. I guessed that when Keiichiro watched this footage, he'd bawl his eyes out again. I opened my legs as wide as I could so he'd be able to see. When I came, over and over again, I made sure to make as much noise as I could, so the next-door neighbors would hear. As he whimpered and wailed, Keiichiro would spread the images and videos of mine and Takumi's sex all around the world. Well, that was fine. He could go ahead and spread them all he wanted. He could show the world what Takumi and I looked like when we were making love. If people wanted to call me a pervert, a weirdo, they could sit there, wherever they were, pointing their fingers at me and laughing.

Our planet, floating in darkness, was covered in a web made of silky, translucent spider's thread, and every time words or images or recordings came and went across those spindly fibers, they would glisten very beautifully. This moment of mine and Takumi's would go traveling across that great web, traversing space and time, forever.

I'm sorry, Takumi. I guess having met me is one of those things that might stick to you, like those strands of spiderweb that brush against your face and seem impossible to remove. I'm a stupid, fat, ugly, perverted housewife with fertility problems, but I want you to know that I'm so, so grateful to you for all the time we've spent together.

3

The Orgasm from 2035

I ALWAYS THOUGHT THAT once I got into high school I'd get a little taller and my boobs would get bigger, but as things turned out, I've grown just a piddling *three millimeters* since the third year of middle school, and I'm still only an A cup. I guess being short isn't such a bad thing (I get a lot of people saying how "short and cute" I am) but I'm desperate to do something about my chest, which is basically no different from a elementary-school kid's. I've tried all kinds of stuff that's supposed to be good for boosting your bust size—making myself eat loads and loads of cabbage and chicken as well as various massages and exercises and creams. My friend Akutsu is always telling me not to worry, that boobs get bigger naturally when a guy fondles them, but she's never gone out with a guy and she's an A cup like me, so she's not exactly the greatest authority on these things.

The first time Takumi felt me up, I felt really bad for him that my boobs were so small. I was convinced they were going to be a major letdown for him, so I kept checking his expression, but his eyes were closed and he had this super-serious look on his face, so I really couldn't tell at all what he was thinking. Being fondled by him didn't really feel good at all, just a little tickly, but I put up with it on the basis that this was bound to make them bigger.

According to my plan, I should have lost my virginity to Takumi around the end of the summer. I was sure that if I had actual sex, then there was no doubt my boobs would grow. But then my plan kind of ground to a halt. It's a week today that Takumi hasn't come into work. I've sent him a few messages, but he hasn't replied to any of them. Which means the summer vacation's nearly over and I'm still a virgin in an A cup.

Monday was my day off from my summer job at the pool. It was two o'clock in the afternoon and I was sitting on the riverbank in the sweltering heat. The grass, which had grown as tall as the average adult ever hopes to get, stretched off into the distance. Akutsu got up on the only bench for miles around whose wood has started to rot and shouted: "It's so fricking hot!"

She tucked up the hem of her skirt and waved the promotional fan she'd been handed outside the station back and forth between her legs. The fan was advertising a new pachinko complex that had just opened. I was wearing shorts, and I felt pretty sure that if I stayed too long sitting on that bench baked by the midday sun my legs would actually start to cook, so I sat down on the grass alongside it instead. When I turned to look up at Akutsu, her head was blotting out the exact spot where the sun was, its edges blazing with scorching light. I quickly shut my eyes, watching the yellow afterimage flicker and float on my eyelids. The sky was gray like a dirty old sheet. I figured the pain in my temples must be something to do with the photochemical smog everyone was talking about.

"I've got something to show you," Akutsu had said when she called me earlier.

We met up for lunch at one of those chain family restaurants by the main road.

"So what's this thing you want to show me?" I'd asked, once we'd been chatting a while.

"No way, I can't tell you here! Not with all these people around. Let's go to the riverbank," Akutsu said, widening her eyes deliberately. And so it was that we'd ended up here, where nobody else was stupid enough to be hanging out at this time of the year.

Akutsu had been moaning about how the air-conditioning in the family restaurant was turned up too high and was making her shiver, but the moment we got on our bikes and started pedaling she'd moaned, "You've gotta be kidding, this is just *way* too hot. Hang on a sec."

She went into a nearby convenience store and came out with an ice pop sticking out of her mouth.

I tried getting up on the bench beside Akutsu. She was about as short as I was. When I stood on tiptoes, I could just about see the river way off in the distance, beyond the stretch of grass and the rocks that the heat had dried to a whiteish color.

"Show me that thing you were going to show me."

Akutsu nodded, crouched down on the bench, and took a small notebook out of her bag. I crouched down beside her.

"So my older sister is like really into anime and stuff. I mean she does all the full-on freaky stuff, like making fan comics and going to Comiket, and all that. So she sometimes looks at these online forums for hard-core cosplayers, and she started telling me that there are these photos that are like *huge* in the community right now. . . . God, this is so fricking sticky!"

Akutsu tossed the stick of her ice pop onto the grass, and wiped her fingers on her skirt.

"At first, I figured I'd just message them to you, but I thought it might shock you or whatever. My sister had printed them out anyway, thinking it might be someone from our school. Our printer's so old and crappy it's kind of hard to see, but look at this. Don't you think this—" Akutsu stopped suddenly mid-flow and looked me right in the eyes. "Look, Nana. Are you really sure you wanna see this?"

The sound of an ambulance passing over the bridge, siren blaring, came carried on the wind. I didn't say the word "yes," but I nodded, and Akutsu handed me a few sheets of paper stapled together and folded in quarters. On each sheet was a bunch of small photos, showing a guy in a purple costume like a lab coat, a long blue wig, and small spectacles. Looking at the full body shots on the first page, I had no idea who it was, but then I turned the page to see a selection of close-ups. When I saw the guy's profile, shot from the right, my chest started to sting like someone was piercing it with a long needle. All the makeup he was wearing had made them less noticeable than usual, but the two small moles beneath his right eye were still definitely visible.

"Takumi." I whispered his name without meaning to.

"So it is, right!?" Akutsu sounded almost pleased. "I can't believe he's into this kind of stuff! It's such a shock! Do you know this anime?"

"No. No idea. I, like, never watch anime."

As I spoke, I noticed how dry my throat was. I took a sip of the now thoroughly warm bottle of mineral water my mom had forced me to take to prevent me from getting heatstroke.

"I think my sister said it was Magical Girl something-or-other. They show it on Saturday mornings, and there's, like, *tons* of fan sites for it. My sister says the pictures were sent to one of the fan sites, with his name and address on them."

"You mean he sent them in? In his own name?"

"Can you imagine? Who in their right mind would do a thing like that, right! Apparently there's more stuff that's way weirder…"

Akutsu inserted her straw into a carton of sugary milk tea she'd bought at the convenience store and sucked at it thirstily.

"What do you mean by 'weirder?'"

"Hmmmmmm . . . Apparently, the videos are way more out there than the photos, even. By out there I mean . . ."

Akutsu once again put her mouth to the straw and sucked hard, gulping down the liquid.

"You mean, like, porn?"

With the straw still stuck in her mouth, Akutsu rolled her eyes toward me and nodded demurely.

"My sister figures it's the girl he was going out with who sent them in, actually. In both the photos and the videos, you can't really see her face, so it seems kind of likely. But honestly, can you believe it? Him, of all people? He's got such a goody-two-shoes vibe, but then it turns out he's doing all this sketchy stuff in secret! Skipping work, too. Well, I think he's a moron for letting himself get into this kind of situation."

Noticing how quiet I'd gone, Akutsu added, "Sorry."

As I listened to her talking, I remembered the time I'd followed Takumi to the old apartment building across the river. He hadn't seen me sneaking into the lobby behind him, and I watched him taking the elevator up to the seventh floor. I used the stairs to follow him and emerged just in time to see him stepping into the apartment at the very end of the hall. There was no hesitation to his movements, which made me think he'd done this a bunch of times before. I went up to the door and put my ear to it but couldn't hear a thing. Just as I was thinking about going home, I heard a woman's voice coming from a room facing the hall, the curtains in its window drawn.

I strained my ears to hear. The woman was moaning. I gripped the bars on the windows so tightly my fingers began to hurt. On the other side, Takumi was *having sex with someone*. Just thinking that, my heart started beating so hard I could feel it moving there, underneath the wires of my bra. I wedged my head in between the bars of the grate so I could get my ear even closer to the windowpane.

I clearly heard him say, "You can't come yet," and then the door to the apartment next door opened, so I dashed away and shot as fast as I could down the fire escape stairs. Maybe the person Takumi had been going out with was the woman who lived in that apartment. Maybe she was the one who'd taken the photos.

"So what's going on with you and Takumi?"

I had no idea how to reply, so I just shook my head, and then began: "It seemed to be going all right . . . ," but as soon as I blinked, I felt a big tear go running straight down my cheek, surprising even me.

"Whoa whoa wahh wah wah wah!" As she let out a whole range of totally meaningless sounds, Akutsu took out her handkerchief from her bag and handed it to me.

"Thanks," I said, wiping my eyes.

"I promise I didn't mean to make you cry, that wasn't why I was showing you, I just wanted to, like, warn you, you know? Let you know about the pervy stuff he's doing so you could watch out. So like, I mean, like . . ."

Akutsu grew incoherent again, then reached into her bag and took out a Snickers bar and tore off the wrapper.

"Do you want some?" she said, and held it out to me. When I shook my head, she bit into the half-melted lump of brown chocolate.

"Sorry for losing it," I said to Akutsu, but still couldn't stop crying.

"Look, let's drop this, okay? I shouldn't have shown you. It's totally my fault. I'll throw them away, right now."

She went to rip up the papers, getting ready to put all her strength into it, but I took hold of her arm.

"Hey, give them here."

"You want them?"

"Yeah. And the address of that website, too."

"You want to see the videos?"

"Yes," I said, blowing my nose loudly. Akutsu stared at me for a while and then let out a huge burst of crazy laughter.

"Hahahahahahahahahah!"

With her mouth wide open like that, I could see the chocolate all stuck in her back teeth.

"I still really like him," I said, and then felt like I was going to start crying again.

The house where my family lives is just across the street from the riverbank. Dad told me that one time, ages ago, a big typhoon caused the river to overflow, and it washed away a few of the houses. Hundreds of years ago, he said, the water used to come up as far as the red torii gates to the shrine on the top of the mountain.

Apparently, Mom kicked up a fuss when Dad announced he wanted to build a house here. But Dad was convinced that because a disaster like that had already happened, it wouldn't happen again, and so he went ahead and built it anyway. Mom often said with a sigh how the house had been a real splurge for someone like Dad, when you thought of it in terms of his salary from his job at the clothing company where he worked. But Dad had grown up in a very poor family, and he'd really hated living in their cramped, shabby old housing project apartment. As soon as my parents had kids, buying a house of their own had become Dad's top priority, whatever it took.

"As long as you give kids a good, strong house to grow up in, they'll turn out upright," Dad would say when he was drunk.

When I said that he'd grown up poor and in a housing project but had still turned out upright, he'd say, "I'm not upright at all."

Then he'd cackle, his face all red from drinking, and tickle me under the arms. Dad didn't particularly have any hobbies of his own, but watching him on Sundays as he pottered around the house fixing things or gardening, I thought he seemed super content. Now, though, he's not around anymore. His company sent him up north to manage a factory in Tohoku. He's working such long hours that he can't even come back home for the national summer holidays.

Akutsu and I stayed on the riverbank chatting, and, before we knew it, the sun had set, and it was growing dark. Riding back along the asphalt road, still hot from the feverish heat of the day, I noticed my brother standing on the balcony to his second-story room. It looked as if he were pointing his binoculars in my direction, so I waved to him, but he didn't make any movement. In the light of the streetlamp outside our house, his white shirt looked like it was glowing. I pulled open our rusty gates that always made a terrible screechy scraping sound and parked my bike beside the back door. Mom and my brother were both in, but still the house was pitch black. We had a big garden which, with Dad away, had now basically become a jungle. I guessed the insects in there must have liked it that way, and they were making one heck of a racket to show it. The sky was dark, but the pink crepe myrtle tree in the corner of the garden seemed artificially bright, like some kind of tacky toy.

"Mo-om!"

I went inside, turning on the lights in the kitchen to find the table set with plates of food, covered in plastic wrap. In the living room Mom was lying on the sofa, snoring peacefully. The coffee table was strewn with Korean drama DVDs and crossword magazines.

I put a hand on Mom's shoulder and shook her lightly. Her snoring stopped, and she let out a strange *gurghh* sound from her throat as she opened her eyes.

"Ah . . . Ah, you're back." She sat up heavily. "Oh goodness, it's dark already! You must be hungry. Dinner's all ready."

"You just stay sleeping, Mom, it's fine. Listen, if you're not feeling good, you don't have to make dinner, honestly. I can always just pick something up on the way home."

"No, no, no takeout, it's not good for you," Mom said as she got up from the sofa and began walking unsteadily toward the kitchen.

"Honestly, Mom, sit down. I'll do it."

I pulled at her arm so she sank back on the sofa, then draped a light gauze blanket over her. Thinking the room seemed a little chilly, I looked at the air conditioner remote to see it was set to 64 degrees.

I don't really understand what *menopausal disorder* is, but it seems like a terrible thing to happen to a person. Mom can be just eating dinner in a normal way when she'll suddenly break out in such a sweat that her hair will get as soaked as if she'd just come out of the shower, or else she'll suddenly clutch at her chest as if she's going to be sick. I've never known Mom to be ill in bed before, not even when I was little, so at first it was a real shock. I thought she might be dying or something.

Since Mom became ill, our house has grown messier and messier. I try to help with the cleaning, but even when I copy exactly what Mom used to do, it just never gets as clean as when she does it. However bad Mom feels, though, she still makes dinner for us every day, saying that's her "last vestige of pride as a mother." She's had to give up her part-time job in the supermarket, though. She says it's because it's too physically tough now she's got this menopausal disorder, and I'm sure that's true, but my guess is that there's another reason, which is that she's worried about my brother.

The microwave beeped, and I removed the plate. Taking off the cling wrap, I saw it was meatloaf with egg inside. *Yay!* I thought. This was one of Mom's special dishes, my favorite. It used to be my brother's favorite, too, and there was a portion laid out on the table for him as well. But it would most likely stay there untouched. The only things my brother would eat now were brown rice and steamed vegetables. He got up earlier than any of us and prepared his food for the day, put it into Tupperware containers, and then took it to his room to eat alone. Even those things he only ate the tiniest amount of, so his once-pudgy body had become super thin.

It was now fully dark, but the laundry Mom had put out to dry this morning was still hanging on the line on the balcony, so I went to bring it in. My brother was still there with his binoculars glued to his eyes, looking in the direction of the riverbank.

"What are you looking at?" I asked, yanking the clothes free from the pegs, knowing full well that if Mom saw me doing it this way I'd be in trouble.

"I am regarding the sinful acts of foolish individuals."

My brother came out with these words at such speed and with such a monotone, it took me a while to convert what he'd said into something that actually had a meaning.

"What kind of sinful acts?"

"Money, sex, violence, et cetera."

This was the first time I'd ever heard my brother say the word "sex." The way he came out with it so casually, without any embarrassment, took me so much aback that I threw the clothes I was holding in my arms through the open door to my room all at once. Also, I knew violence was bad, but I figured money and sex were kind of important and necessary, because they helped us survive.

"As soon as the Antarctic ice sheet starts to melt, this river will overflow. This house, this entire town, will be swept away by the flood," my brother pronounced, seeming very pleased at the prospect.

"If this house gets swept away, Dad's gonna be really upset," I said, but my brother ignored me.

"The 2035 total solar eclipse will herald the next paradigm shift. We must be sure to mend our ways before then."

Sometimes the things my brother said made no sense to me, but that wasn't a recent development. He had been that way since we were small; basically, he was mega-smart from the moment he was born. Mom said he'd done everything much earlier than other kids—turning over in his sleep, growing teeth, walking, talking, writing and reading. At home we had a poster we'd got free from the bank with the names of all the Japanese administrative districts and the location of their capitals, as well as the names of countries around the world and their capital cities, and my brother had memorized all of it by the time he was three. When he got into elementary school, he read through his textbooks in the first week and memorized the entire contents of those, too. Both Mom and Dad are of average intelligence levels, or maybe even below average, so everyone was pretty surprised by my brother's genius-like leanings and wondered where on earth they could have come from.

He used to come home from school crying because the lessons were way too easy for him and he found them unspeakably boring, so from the third year of elementary school on, my parents started sending him to cram school. The cram school in question was attended by kids preparing to pass the entrance exam for elite private schools, and it cost loads of money. That was when Mom began working at the supermarket, taking on a part-time job there to help pay for his extra lessons. I was in my last year of nursery school, but even so, I remember it well. After regular nursery had finished, I would go into the after-nursery club, looking out at the garden as it grew slowly dark, waiting for Mom to collect me.

When we got home, I'd have a rushed dinner and bath, and then get into bed, only to be woken up again just after ten in the evening when I'd go with Mom to collect my brother from the station on his way back from cram school. Mom was too scared to leave me in the house alone, so she'd strap me half-asleep into the child seat of her bike, and we'd ride to the station together. I would be desperate to get back to sleep, and it was freezing cold. In fact, there was basically nothing about those trips to the station not to hate, but I went because Mom promised that on the way back she'd buy me a red-bean-paste bun, the kind that she never usually allowed me to have. At the station, there were always lots of mothers waiting for their kids to come back from cram school.

"Your son is such a bright little boy!" they'd say. "And what a cute little girl you've got as well. I'm sure she'll turn out to be very bright, too!"

Mom would always brush off their compliments, but she seemed over the moon when people said that kind of stuff. But hearing it made me feel angry. Even then, I knew full well that I wasn't ever going to be "very bright."

When my brother, who was always top of his class throughout cram school, was nearing the end of elementary school, he began preparing for entrance exams for all the top private schools. Staying up until the middle of the night studying every day, he found it hard to wake up in the morning, so Dad would prepare hot, wet towels to press against my brother's neck.

"There's a big artery here, see," he used to say. "If you send plenty of nice hot warm blood to your head, you'll feel nice and awake." I would watch them through the door of the room, brushing my teeth in silence.

Unsurprisingly, my brother got into the best school in the area, a combined middle and high school, with the top examination score in his year. It was around this time that he began talking to me and the rest of the family in a weirdly distant and formal way, and, apart from the times he was eating, he always had his head in a book.

He'd begin conversations with me and Mom about whatever it was that he was immersed in at that moment, like, "Something that occurred to me reading Dostoyevsky's *Notes from Underground* is . . ." or "Ludwig II of Bavaria, who commissioned Neuschwanstein Castle, was in fact . . ." or "The Meiji Revolution is often referred to as a 'revolution without bloodshed,' but that's actually a total falsehood because . . ."

Mom, Dad, and I couldn't engage with what he was saying in any proper way, so we'd just smile vacantly in response. Maybe he realized that there was nobody in this house who he could have a decent conversation with, because he gradually began to speak less and less.

He didn't have to wear a uniform but always wore exactly the same outfit: a white shirt and jeans. The only thing that changed was the length of his shirtsleeves, depending on the season. Even when he was in high school, he wore the clothes Mom bought for him without ever expressing an opinion about them. Though it was hard for me to get my head around it, it genuinely seemed as if my brother had literally no interest in what clothes he wore. Equally crazy to me was the fact that he went to an all-boys' school. However clever he was, the idea that he was content to spend six whole years surrounded only by boys was unfathomable to me.

Once, I went along with Mom to an arts festival held at my brother's school and found the whole place full of boys *just like my brother*. Looking at them all from a distance, it was as if the whole school was made up of clones of the same person.

Everyone wore glasses, had the same haircut, was shy and dweeby-looking, and spoke quietly at high speed. If someone had asked me to find a boy to have a crush on from among them, I'd have been at a complete loss.

After a lot of persuasion from Mom, my brother would occasionally help me study for my own high-school entrance exams. I really hated those sessions. My brother would just explain at machine-gun speed the way he'd got his head around the problem in question. It seemed he had no idea that people like me, who could have something explained to them three times very slowly and *still* not get it, even existed in this world.

At the same time that I got into the second-worst school in the area, my brother got into the country's top university to study medicine, which was apparently one of the hardest courses to get into. Dad wasn't really the type to show his emotions, but when my brother got into Tokyo University he seemed totally over the moon. He went around telling everyone in his company about how his son had got in on his first try—to the point that his boss had to call him in and give him a talking-to.

My brother had always been weird, but after entering college he became even weirder. For a start, he began leaving the food Mom made him, which he'd previously wolfed down with such obvious enjoyment. He refused to eat meat. He stopped using a cell phone and wouldn't go near the microwave, saying that electromagnetic waves were bad for your health. He would sit for extended periods of time in his room with his legs crossed and his eyes shut, and pictures of men with Indian-style beards appeared on the walls of his room. He started to do his own laundry separately from the rest of ours, using a box of soap flakes he'd picked up somewhere or other. Their strange smell would get on the clothes of anyone who used the washing machine after he had. When I complained about this to him, he said, "Do you realize, Nana, that if you continue to use synthetic laundry soap, toxic particles will build up in your body, causing your future children to become sick?"

It felt like he was trying to threaten me or something.

"Yusuke's being really weird recently," I said to Mom one day.

"Yes," she said with a smile. "He's gone and got himself all into environmental issues. You know what he's like! Once he gets something in his head, he can't think about anything else."

I'd once heard someone on TV say that all mothers spoil their sons rotten. Now I realized my own mother was absolutely no exception.

It was just before the May holidays that my brother didn't come home. For the first day or two, Mom was pretty relaxed about it, saying stuff like, "Oh well, what can you expect from students!," "Boys will be boys!," "Maybe he's found himself a girlfriend!," and those kinds of things, but when a whole week passed without a word from him, she began to get worried and called Dad, who put all his work on hold and rushed back home halfway across the country. My brother didn't have a cell phone, nor did he have any real friends to speak of—or none that we knew of anyway. The school had no idea where he had gone. So, at a total loss, Mom and Dad filed a missing-person report. A month later, though, we still had no leads at all.

One day, I went into my brother's room to borrow an English dictionary and found all these great stacks of books like anthills, covering so much of the floor space it was hard to find anywhere to step. I approached his desk, knocking over anthills left and right as I went, and found a single book sitting on top of it. On its cover was a picture of the guy with the piercing gaze that my brother had stuck photos of all over his wall. I picked it up and opened it. Its first page was blank except for the words:

ABANDON THE PAST. LIVE THE NOW.

I wondered if my brother had the kind of past that needed to be "abandoned." He'd spent his whole life happily chowing down the burgers and potato croquettes Mom made for him, being kept warm and cozy by Dad, and studying. That was it.

"Could this be Yusuke, do you think?"

In June, when the strong rains had just begun, a classmate of my brother's named Hinata showed up at our house totally out of the blue. Mom, Dad, and I all craned over to peer at the photo he held out across the table. When I saw it, I came so close to bursting out laughing that I had to quickly cover my mouth with my hand. The picture showed my brother in a white collarless shirt, a long beard covering the lower half of his face, sitting alongside a plain-looking woman wearing no makeup and dressed in similar outfit. I'd never seen him smiling like that before.

"Where is this?" Mom said, practically pouncing at Hinata on the other side of the table, while Dad tried to restrain her. "Where is he?"

"It's taken at the headquarters of a certain organization, in Nagano."

Saying this, Hinata took out a book from his green tote bag. Just like the book lying on my brother's desk, it had a photo of that same shady-looking bearded guy on the cover.

"It was originally the Japanese branch of a religious society based in India. Actually, I was there recently myself to look for someone. I just returned."

Saying this, Hinata put his thumb and forefinger to the corner of his black-framed glasses and pushed them back up his nose. He wasn't scruffy like my brother. His hair looked like it was cut regularly at a salon, and though his T-shirt and the nice pink oxford shirt he wore open over it didn't look desperately expensive, it seemed as if he'd at least gone to the effort of picking out things he liked, and which suited him.

"When you say 'religious group'. . . Do you mean like a cult? Like the one that let out that poison gas in the metro?" Dad's face was sharp and serious as he turned to Hinata, who was sitting next to him.

"I don't know all that much about them, but their way of life doesn't seem exacting enough for them to qualify as a proper religious organization. There are similarities, for sure, but I don't think they have any relationship with the cult that caused that catastrophe. They don't seem to have an active agenda to change the world or anything like that. The only slightly worrying thing is . . ."

Hinata took a sip of the cold barley tea in front of him, darted a look in my direction, and blushed.

"It's a little hard to talk about with Yusuke's younger sister in the room."

He drained the tea in his cup, and Mom topped him up.

"Nana, will you go upstairs, please," Dad said, looking very stern. Of course, there was no way I was going to go upstairs now but I nodded, stood up, bowed at Hinata, and then went out and shut the living room door. I took off my slippers so they wouldn't hear my footsteps, then moved as quietly as possible to the kitchen, slid the sliding door leading through to the living room open just a crack, and stood listening.

"I suppose the official description would be Tantrism or something similar. Which is to say, they believe in using orgasms experienced during the sexual act to expand one's consciousness. They aim to utilize orgasms experienced by multiple men and women to release the energy buried inside all of us. The belief is, that if each individual can progress beyond selfhood in that way, then we may be able to prevent the apocalypse predicted to occur in 2035. That's the kind of nonsense that they come out with."

Neither Mom, nor Dad, nor of course I, listening in from the kitchen, had any idea what Hinata was talking about. I couldn't see my parents' faces, but I'd have bet anything that they looked totally stunned. Still, Hinata did his best to break it all down for them so that they could understand. He chose his words carefully and spoke slowly, describing in great detail all the things he'd seen back in Nagano. It was like he felt that doing so was a kind of duty on his part, or a mission that he'd been given. He wasn't really even friends with my brother. I guessed he must just have been a really earnest kind of guy.

"It seems as though, when they're trying to lure people in, they start out with environmental issues and so on, the kinds of topics students today are interested in. So they do have some kind of theoretical trappings but, speaking frankly, what they actually do inside those headquarters is just lunacy. Since the former group leader was arrested for possession and cultivation of cannabis . . ."

I heard a gulp, which I guessed was probably Hinata taking another big sip of barley tea.

". . . there's been a policy of free sex within the facility."

Now I found myself swallowing desperately. Did "free sex" mean the same thing as an orgy? Like having as much sex as you wanted?

"There are many students who go to Nagano for that reason alone."

I heard Mom start to weep. I knew it was bad to be thinking this kind of stuff when Mom was clearly in serious shock, but when I imagined my brother, who was always so deathly serious about everything, jumping at the chance to go off and have a bunch of free sex, I couldn't help grinning. Did that mean Hinata had also been tempted by the same thing?

"When I showed the photos I'd taken in the facility to people back at school, I was told that the person in this photo was Yusuke, and that he'd been missing for a while and everyone was terribly worried. Most students who make the trip out there leave after the first seminar, you see. This person in this photo with him is the current group leader. I believe she's the wife of the previous group leader, or at least, they're married by common law. They say it was she who recruited Yusuke . . ."

As Hinata spoke, I pictured the woman in the photo. Her long hair was parted down the middle, she was bare-faced, and she was pretty boring-looking and ugly. It was impossible to tell what age she was.

"They say that if the students don't have any sexual experience, then she initiates them. Sexually."

What did that mean, I wondered, to *initiate someone sexually*? I heard the flick of a lighter, and then cigarette smoke came wafting into the kitchen so I covered my mouth and nose with my hand to make sure I didn't cough. I figured that if Dad was lighting up without even checking with the people around him if it was okay, he must have been in a real state.

"I don't really know any concrete details. I just know that her role is to rectify all the mistaken information about sex that men absorb through pornography and so on. She shows them how to touch women, things like that. It's forbidden within the facility for people to form couples, but I've heard that Yusuke and this woman are pretty close. Were pretty close, I should perhaps say, because she's no longer there. It seems like she just upped and vanished one day. There are rumors she's gone to either Thailand or India. With its central figure gone, I'm guessing it'll only be a matter of time before the group disintegrates. It seems like the students with no other place to go are still there, living communally. The neighbors are kicking up a fuss, though, and I think they'll have to vacate at some point. It seems Yusuke just missed his opportunity to get out and is hanging on. I don't know him well at all, so I've no right to say this, but um . . ."

I heard the scrape of a chair, and for a while there was silence.

"Would you be so good as to go and collect him? I think it's better just to go, with no advance warning or anything."

I stood up and peered into the living room through a crack in the door. Hinata was giving Mom and Dad a very low bow. As far as I could see, there really wasn't any need for him to be pleading with them like that, given the circumstances. Dad urged him to sit down again, while Mom looked again at the grinning photo of my brother and dissolved into sobs.

Around the time the rainy season was ending, Dad brought my brother back home. Dad said he'd got in the car with surprisingly little resistance and then, in a service station nearby, had wolfed down not just one but two big bowls of rice topped with sliced *katsu*. Before reaching home, Dad took him to a barber, so when he arrived his hair was as closely cropped as that of the kids in baseball club. The car pulled up into our driveway and the two got out, and then, right in front of me and Mom as we were waiting by the door to welcome my brother home, Dad punched him in the face. He fell to the floor.

"Don't ever make us worry like that again," Dad said. Then he got back in the car, and drove off back to his work in Tohoku. Without even bothering to wipe his leaking nose, my brother bowed his head in apology at Mom and me, then ran inside and upstairs to his room, trailing drips of blood.

When I turned on the computer in my room, Akutsu's email was waiting for me.

"You'd better prepare yourself before looking at these," she had written, and underneath, pasted a bunch of long URLs. I took a deep breath, then clicked on the first link. The site it took me to was a very ordinary kind of cosplay forum, with lots of photos of people striking poses, dressed up as what I guess must have been anime characters.

Of course, in that world, stuff like white face paint, colored contact lenses, and wigs are not just relatively normal but actually *the norm*. It took me a while to get used to that, and at first my head felt totally scrambled. I scrolled down, looking at the photos in the order they appeared until I found an image of someone who looked like Takumi in the same kind of purple lab coat as in the photos Akutsu had shown me earlier. When I clicked on it, an even bigger photo appeared. In his wig and his purple lab coat, Takumi was scowling at the camera. I clicked NEXT IMAGE and another photo of Takumi appeared, then another. In each one, he was striking a different pose. He definitely looked good in makeup—handsome and well-put-together, a different person from the mopey Takumi I knew. I kept on clicking through the photos, as if in a trance.

When I'd seen them all, I tried out the next link from Akutsu's list. The bright red title jumped straight out at me: "Watch the DEPRAVED Cosplay Sex of T***Mi S**to from K%£?*@!"

I had no idea who would have made it, but this next one seemed to be a website entirely dedicated to endless photos and videos of Takumi's cosplay antics. Aware that my brother was in the next room, I plugged my headphones into the computer and clicked on one of the videos. Right away, the sound of moaning flooded into my ears, and I quickly lowered the volume. On the screen appeared a video of Takumi in cosplay, lying on top of some girl and banging away at her like crazy. I could see the girl's white thighs and knee-high socks, and her skirt, which looked like it was a kind of school uniform. I wondered what high school she was at. Takumi was making little grunts as he moved. His eyes were shut, and he looked like he was enjoying himself. A lot.

Now and then he would reach out for the girl's boobs, and the girl would call out "Lord Muramasa!" and grasp his arm. Each time Takumi thrust his hips, the girl's boobs wobbled. I wondered if it was having all that sex with Takumi that had made them so big. Her voice grew louder and louder, and Takumi's movements faster and faster. At some point I realized I was gripping my own chest really hard with my right hand. In the video, the girl screamed out "I'm commminnnggg!" *Lucky cow*, I thought, getting to have sex with Takumi like that. My plan had been to just take a look at one of the videos and then call it a day, but I ended up staying up until the middle of the night, watching them all over and over again.

When I drew my curtains in the morning, I saw Yusuke sitting cross-legged on the balcony. Seeing how Mom had tiptoed around him when he'd first came back from the Nagano camp,

I'd also made an effort not to say anything that would set him off. Now, though, as I looked at him and thought of how he'd been back two whole months and had stayed in his room the entire time, I started to feel riled up.

"Are you just gonna drop out of college? After everything you did to get in?" I asked.

He didn't reply. Someone jogging along the bike path glanced up in our direction.

"What are you gonna do? Are you gonna work or what? Couldn't you at least get a part-time job?"

My brother stayed stock-still, his eyes closed. The sun had disappeared behind a thick wall of cloud, and there was a breeze that felt surprisingly chilly for midsummer.

"Were you in love with that woman in Nagano?"

My brother slowly opened his eyes and turned his head to face me.

"You haven't been going to the riverbank much lately, have you?"

I didn't understand what he was saying at first, and I just gawped at him. He went on.

"You know, Nana, even when you believe you are concealed, there is always such a thing as a blind side."

I felt my cheeks suddenly burning.

"You prick! You're a total prick!" I said. I picked up a sandal lying on the balcony and hurled it at him. "You're the biggest prick in the world!" The sandal left a dirty footprint on his white shirtsleeve.

Still livid, I snatched up the lunch box Mom had made for me and headed out to work. When I checked my phone during a break, I saw I had a message from Hinata. Since my brother had returned home, Hinata had started visiting my brother at Dad's request. When I took coffee and snacks up to my brother's room, Hinata would blush and avoid my eyes. Sure, Dad had asked him to come, but to actually make good on that—was he some kind of a saint or what? I started to feel more curious about him and asked for his email address. Since then, we'd exchanged messages from time to time.

This message had the subject line HOW'S WORK? and it was full of emojis. I read through it, sighed, and threw my phone back into my bag without bothering to reply. Akutsu came into the break room. When she saw the expression on my face, she looked like she wanted to say something, but then the team leader called her and she went off to the locker room. There weren't many people in the pool today, maybe because it was cool outside. After lunch it began to rain, and the decision was made to close the pool earlier than usual. Takumi hadn't come to work at all. Just as I was wondering whether to leave my bike where it was in the parking lot and walk home with an umbrella to avoid getting soaked, Takumi's friend, Ryota, came up to me.

"I'm gonna go around to Takumi's today. Wanna come?"

I thought for a little before I nodded yes.

Ryota set off in the rain, so I quickly got on my bike and followed his. The fine mist, which reminded me of a steam room, got my face and my clothes entirely wet.

I'd passed Takumi's house before, but I'd never been inside. If it wasn't for the sign hung up by the door saying SAITO MATERNITY CLINIC, nobody would ever guess this old two-story wooden house provided some kind of medical service. In the entranceway, shoes, sneakers, and kids' sandals were strewn across the concrete floor. Ryota kicked off his flip-flops and went inside, heading quickly down the long hallway, and I did the same. I could hear a noise that sounded like a woman screaming.

"Hello? Mrs. Saito?" Ryota called out at the sliding door, and a woman's voice shouted, "Hold on a minute!"

From beyond the screen I could hear panting and, in between, cries of pain. After a while, a woman who I guessed must have been Takumi's mom slid open the door. Through the gap, I caught a glimpse of a pregnant woman wearing just a T-shirt, her legs spread open wide like a frog's. Leaning back against the man behind her who was holding her up, she was heaving these great long breaths that made her shoulders rise and fall and moaning loudly. Her black pubic hair and the reddish-black part below glistened as if they'd had water poured over them. Without thinking I looked away, as if I'd seen something I shouldn't.

"You're soaked through!" Mrs. Saito said, looking at me as she closed the sliding screen behind her.

She was tall and thin, and her eyes were a little like Takumi's. I bowed to her.

"Are you Ryota's girlfriend?" she grinned, fine creases forming at the corner of her eyes.

"As if!" Ryota said. "This is Nana. She's in our class. We're gonna go see Takumi, okay?"

"He hasn't left the room all day. Again. What a foolish boy, eh? Who knows what he's playing at."

Saying that, she plucked a couple of towels from a lidded wicker basket in the hall and handed one each to me and Ryota. "You'll catch a chill if you stay soaked like that. Here, dry yourselves off."

The woman inside the room let out a loud scream: "AAAAGGGGHHHH!"

"I'm busy right now, so just make your own way up, okay? Help yourselves to ice cream or juice or whatever from the fridge," she said, then rushed back inside the room.

With a very familiar air, Ryota made his way inside the kitchen near the front door of the house, took out three cans of tangerine juice from the big fridge, and handed one to me.

What I'd seen back there in that room had been my first-ever glimpse of childbirth, and I was in shock. I stood there, holding the can of juice in one hand, staring at the floor. Realizing the state I was in, Ryota said, "If you're not prepared for it, it can really knock you for a loop, right?" Then he drained the juice in one go, his Adam's apple bobbing up and down.

I followed him up a narrow, steep flight of stairs. He knocked on the door of the room closest to the stairwell.

"Hey, I'm coming in." Ryota opened the door. I saw Takumi lying on his side on a bed beside the window. "I brought Nana with me."

Takumi didn't move an inch. He wore a slightly grubby-looking white T-shirt with black shorts, and his legs poking out of them looked very thin. His room was smallish, with a tatami floor, the single bed by the window taking up half of it. The rest of the floor space was strewn with manga and CDs, leaving no room to stand. I quickly glanced around to check there weren't any cosplay outfits or figurines of anime characters in view.

"It's boiling in here," Ryota said, jumping up onto Takumi's bed and opening the window.

I saw his foot trample Takumi's shin, and Takumi let out an "Ow!"

"Do you want some juice?" Ryota asked, holding the can against Takumi's neck.

"Shit!" Takumi said, sitting up. "That's cold."

Cackling to himself, Ryota sat down at the end of the bed, stretched out a foot to press the HIGH button on the fan with his toe, and opened the can of juice he'd held to Takumi's neck. Takumi and I watched in silence as Ryota drained the juice in what seemed like a second.

"Okay, I'm off," Ryota said, handing Takumi the empty can and making to leave. I looked up at him, not knowing what on earth was going on. "I've gotta make dinner for my gran. See ya round."

With that, he left the room. Gazing at the door after him, Takumi and I listened to the sound of his feet on the stairs, stunned.

"What the hell's with him?" Takumi said, lying back on his bed and closing his eyes.

A cool draft came in through the window, and I wondered if the rain had got even harder. I pushed the manga books aside to create space and sat down on the floor, hugging my knees to my chest. From Takumi's window, you could see the bike path by the river, just like you could from my house. A group of small kids went racing along in the rain, speaking to each other in loud voices.

"So I saw that stuff online yesterday. Your, um . . . stuff."

I'd never expected to come straight out with that, and I surprised myself. From downstairs I could hear the woman screaming, now mixed with the sound of Mrs. Saito's saying things like "You're nearly there!" and "Try to relax!" in a loud, clear voice.

"You know about that, right? How the photos of you are all online and stuff?"

Takumi gave a little nod, his eyes still shut.

"They get sent to my phone every day."

I squeezed the can of juice I was holding, and the condensation went raining down on the manga books. I took a handkerchief from my bag and wiped them off. The fan rotating its head left and right ruffled my hair, still wet with the rain.

"Ahhh!" Takumi gave a big sigh, and stretched out his arms so one of them fell down from the bed. I could see the blue veins under his skin. I went over to the bed and lay down beside him, curling myself up on my side beneath his armpit like a little mouse in its hole. Closing my eyes, I breathed in the smell of his armpits. Wow, had I missed that smell. I looked up to his face. Under his jawbone, I could see a sprinkling of stubble. I thought of Takumi's face in the video from yesterday, all made up. I wanted to spread my legs wide and have sex with Takumi like the girl in that video. The world was so unfair.

I moved so as to press my face close to Takumi's. My hair fell down onto his face. I leaned in and kissed him, just brushing my lips against his. I knew my face was going red. Takumi didn't move an inch. My heart had started beating way faster, and I could hear a kind of hushing sound in my ears, like blood flowing. I climbed on top of Takumi, poked out my tongue, and slowly licked his upper lip, right to left, left to right. Then I did the same with the lower one. I realized that the groans of pain from downstairs also sounded a lot like groans of pleasure. I thought of the voice of the woman Takumi had been having sex with in the videos, and felt my lower abdomen grow heavy, hazy, and hot.

I slipped my body down and went to unzip Takumi's shorts, but he pushed me away.

"No," he said, and sat up. "Sorry."

For the first time that day he actually looked at me. His eyelids were all swollen, and he had yellow crusty bits in his left eye. Was that what happened when you slept all day?

"Go home, will you?" He lay back down on the bed.

I stared at him for a while but he didn't budge. I got up, picked up my bag, then ran out and down the stairs, slamming the front door behind me as hard as I could. It was only when I looked down that I realized I was still clutching the towel his mom had given me.

When I'd failed to get into the private high school I'd wanted to attend because I liked the uniform and only got into the three state schools that people called "the idiot league," I'd felt super depressed. Mom and Dad had both been really nice about it, trying to cheer me up by saying stuff like "We know you tried really hard." The truth was, though, that when it came to schoolwork, I really had not tried very hard. But that was how it was. Whenever little Nana did something that suggested she was making an effort in any way, Mom and Dad would instantly be full of praise for how hard she'd tried, what a good kid she was.

Since I was small, Mom had always said my brother was the Studious One and I was the Cute One, and as long as I smiled at people then everything would turn out all right. If I'm being totally honest, I'd been aware since I was pretty young that when I smiled, boys in my class or the adults around me would look slightly embarrassed or else really happy. If I made some kind of mistake, people would tell me to sit down, and they'd look after me. When I tried smiling at the mirror, I could see I definitely was cute. I figured that if I just kept smiling like Mom said, then lots of good things were bound to happen to me.

When I got into middle school, lots of boys started asking me out, but there wasn't a single one I was interested in. They were all too boyish for my tastes, brimming over with this big, clumsy energy in a way that was kind of scary. I found the whole being asked out thing a real pain, and I'd look down at the floor with a troubled expression and mumble, "I'm sorry," and then the boy would apologize, too, saying, "No, no, I'm sorry for putting you in this position." Then I entered one of the idiot-league high schools, and all the boys just seemed like idiots. I felt pretty fed up with the whole situation. But then, one PE lesson, something changed. The teacher had divided the athletic field into halves, the boys in one and girls in the other. Over in my half, a girl fell over mid-hurdle and sprained something, and as she was lying there crying on the ground, I watched Takumi come running over, hoist her onto his back, then run at full speed to the nurse's office.

"I wish he'd give me a piggyback, too," I said to Akutsu, who was standing next to me, but she just laughed.

In May, after losing to my classmates in a rock-paper-scissors game, I was given the position of one of the members of the Sports' Day committee, together with Takumi. He was mild-mannered and quiet, but he always seemed to be surrounded by people. When the boys in the year above grabbed his head and mussed up his hair, yelling out "Hairwaaaash!" or the girls in his class jumped on his back yelling, "Hey, hey, Takumi, it's my turn for a piggyback" (actually I wanted to try that move, too), he'd always brush them away, telling them to stop, but to go by his big grin he didn't seem to mind too much. It looked to me as though everyone was always finding reasons to touch him.

One day, as I was struggling to reach a box on the top of the lockers, someone came up behind me, took hold of my armpits, and hoisted me right up in the air, as you would a baby or a toddler. Dangling there in midair, I looked around in astonishment to see that the hoister was Takumi.

"Quickly, grab it," he said, looking at me.

From the hall I heard a boy call out, "Takumi, come paint this section!"

Clutching the dust-covered cardboard box with both hands, I thanked him.

"You're so light," he said, and then walked off.

It wasn't just my cheeks that I could feel burning but also the place where he'd touched me under my arms. He was the first boy I'd ever had a crush on, and the first one I ever asked out. Since we were at the same school, I figured he couldn't be any less of an idiot than I was, and he wasn't desperately good-looking, either. To make things worse, he was always shuffling wearily down the hallways, treading down on the backs of his shoes. Still, I really, really liked him.

Even when he asked me to hang on a bit, I felt really happy at the thought that all I needed to do was wait a while, and then I'd be able to go out with him. Hearing that he'd got a job at the local pool, I went and interviewed for a job in the same place, although I'd not actually been planning to work over the summer. For some reason Akutsu started saying she was worried about me doing a job like that by myself, and got a job at the same place.

The times Takumi and I hung out by the riverbank, hugging and kissing and stuff, I felt totally sure I was going to have sex with him. I got this sense like this summer break was going to be one I'd remember for the rest of my life. But in fact, unbeknownst to me, my most beloved Takumi was off having all kinds of cosplay sex with some stranger. It was almost too sad to be true, I thought to myself as I pedaled home, despised by Takumi, soaked through to the skin by the rain.

For once, the lights were on at home, and Mom was in the kitchen with an apron on, cooking something that was giving off a very loud sizzling sound. With her left hand, Mom dropped little flour-covered balls of meat one after another into a wok and then, with the large silver-cooking chopsticks held in her right hand, picked out the balls that were already deep-fried to a crisp golden-brown, and transferred them into a square dish. I moved behind her and said "Hello," but there was no reply. Thinking she hadn't heard me, I stepped closer.

"Stay back or you'll get burned." Her voice sounded gruffer than normal.

Mom is usually nice to everybody, but on certain occasions, when my brother's grades slip a bit or when she's had a fight with Dad, then this voice comes out. She never shows this side of herself to my brother or Dad, but she shows it to me. At these times, she always makes a huge amount of food—more than anyone could ever hope to eat. I glanced under the table and saw sheets of newspaper with broken plates and bits of food on them.

"Did something happen with Yusuke?" I asked, going up behind Mom and addressing her back. A glob of boiling oil came flying and landed on my arm. "Owww!"

"See, I told you!" Mom shouted. Not knowing what to do, I went to the foot of the stairs and called up for my brother, though I figured it was probably useless. Sure enough, there was no response.

"Just leave him. There's no point. He only eats what he wants to, and he only eats it in his room. Come and sit down at the table before it gets cold."

She heaped a small mountain of rice into my bowl. When Mom had this expression on her face, I got so scared that I just started talking about whatever came into my head, often giving away things I really didn't mean to be giving away.

"So there's a guy named Takumi in my year who's working at the pool with me, and the house he lives in is also a maternity clinic. I went over with a friend on the way home from school."

"I always wonder if those maternity clinics can really be safe," said Mom. "I just can't see why anyone would go and choose to give birth in a place like that when there's plenty of good hospitals around."

Mom wasn't even touching the food. Instead, she watched me fixedly. I bit into the fried meat, only to find that it wasn't the chicken seasoned with garlic, ginger, and soy sauce that she usually made, but plain liver, which I loathed.

"Mom, is this—"

"Yes, it's liver. I know you don't like it, but young women like you lose blood every month, so you have to make sure to eat these kinds of iron-rich foods."

The aftertaste was super disgusting. I did my best to wash the rest of it down with barley tea. Watching me eating my rice and drinking from my miso soup bowl, failing to reach for any more of the liver, Mom started to get irritated.

"By the way, Nana, you can use up all my sanitary towels. I won't be needing them anymore. Come on, eat some more liver. I've made plenty."

I had no idea why Mom was feeling the need to be so horrible. Her face was swollen, she had black circles under her eyes, she was wearing no makeup, and she was glaring at me in a really menacing kind of way. I knew the food on the table was stuff that she'd made with love, but I couldn't help feeling like I'd rather have had a ready-meal, even if it contained no love whatsoever.

"Come on! Eat it!" Mom suddenly reared up over the table and slapped me across the head. This was something she'd done very occasionally since I was small, but it had never particularly hurt, and I'd always felt that if it helped her feel better, then it was fair game. Now I'd reached high school, though, I'd assumed it was over. In my surprise, I shouted out.

"Stop it!"

Then I went on. "I know I'm not clever like Yusuke is, I know I'm stupid and stuff, but my head isn't here for you to use as some kind of punching bag to take your stress out on! Why did you have to go and make so much food if you knew nobody was going to eat it? It's nuts. If you're that keen on making something, why don't you try something that won't just disappear when people put it into their mouths?"

I hadn't finished speaking when I heard a loud slap and my left cheek started to burn. For the first time in my life, Mom had hit me in the face. I reached out my arm and pushed the plate with the deep-fried liver off the edge of the table. It smashed on the floor with a dull sound. I had the feeling that my brother had done a similar thing not long before. Treading pieces of battered meat underfoot as I went, I ran up the stairs to my room and shut the door.

Idiots, I thought, they were all idiots. Takumi, my brother, Mom, all of them. And Mom was a stupid liar to boot. You could go around giving people cute smiles all you wanted, but nothing good came of it. Nothing at all.

Three days after Mom slapped me, I found myself, for reasons I couldn't really explain, in a love hotel with Hinata. Or rather, I could kind of explain. I'd sent him a message saying "This is the worst summer vacation ever," and so he'd offered to take me to the aquarium I'd been wanting to go to forever. We stood for so long staring at Hinata's favorite jellyfish, which twinkled like Christmas lights, that I started to feel dizzy and then got all faint. Even after sitting on one of the benches in the aquarium for a while, my head was still spinning like crazy, so we left, with Hinata propping me up. He helped me into a taxi with a super-serious look on his face, and told the taxi driver a place-name I'd never heard before. When we arrived, I saw it was some kind of hotel district.

"I think it's a good idea if you lie down for a while. I won't lay a finger on you, so you don't have to worry about that."

I didn't believe Hinata for a second, but I lay down on the bed in that small air-conditioned room, looking as exhausted as I could. In fact, I was feeling totally fine by that point, but I had this feeling of not really caring about anything anymore. I felt like even if I ended up losing my virginity to Hinata right here, that wouldn't be such a terrible thing.

"Are you okay?" Hinata placed a towel that he'd soaked in cold water and wrung out on top of my forehead. I grabbed hold of his arm and stared into his eyes on the other side of his black-framed glasses. Hinata stayed looking at me like that for a while, then brought his face closer to mine, and kissed me. He was trembling a little bit.

"You're in love with someone else, aren't you?" he said.

"That doesn't matter anymore," I said, then sat up and kissed him. The wet towel dropped down from my forehead onto my chest. I picked it up and wiped away the beads of sweat on Hinata's forehead.

"I think you're more feverish than I am."

Hinata's hands grabbed at my boobs through my chiffon dress. Underneath I was wearing a really cute polka-dot bra I'd bought especially for losing my virginity to Takumi. Hinata lifted my dress, moved my bra aside, and took one of my nipples in his mouth. Then, as if something was hurrying him on, his cold, skinny fingers slid inside my panties and began kneading my crotch. He took off my dress and undid my bra. For whatever reason, he didn't remove my panties completely, but left them hanging half off my left foot.

"You're so sexy," Hinata said in a high-pitched voice, grabbing both my ankles and pulling my legs wide apart into an *M*-shape. The same position that the girl having sex with Takumi was in, I was thinking to myself, when the cold tip of Hinata's nose brushed against the hottest part of my body, and his rough tongue started moving up and down between my legs. Being kissed and having my nipples sucked, I'd felt nothing at all, but now I felt my breathing growing heavier. The tip of his tongue kept going up and down the sticking-out place between my thighs. I felt so embarrassed I thought I was going to die, but it also felt really, really good. The two feelings swirled around whirlpool-like inside me, like milk stirred into coffee.

"Mhhmm . . ." My mouth was closed, and the sound came out funny.

How were you supposed to moan in a sexy way, like that woman in the video with Takumi had? I couldn't seem to make any good noises, only heavy breathing sounds. I shut my eyes and imagined it was Takumi who was going down on me. Not cosplay Takumi, but the normal, droopy-looking Takumi, wearing normal clothes. I felt myself getting wet between my legs right away.

"Is this where you like it?" Hinata said, climbing on top of me. As he kissed me, he touched the sticky-out part, moving it round as if he was drawing circles. I shut my eyes and carried on imagining it was Takumi doing this to me, Takumi who was giving me all this pleasure.

All of a sudden, I felt Hinata break away from me and heard him unzip his jeans. I opened my eyes just a crack and saw Hinata's thingy pointing straight up toward the ceiling. Was it really possible that something that big was about to make its way inside my body? Would it hurt like crazy? What hurt more, doing it for the first time or childbirth? With his T-shirt still on, Hinata opened my legs wide and draped himself on top of me. As he did so, I felt something splash fast and hot against my thigh. Hinata buried his head on top of my left shoulder and lay there for a while, his breathing heavy.

What were you supposed to say in these kinds of situations? I had no idea, so I kept quiet and patted the back of his head. He breathed a basically silent sort of sigh.

"Sorry," he said, as he stretched a hand toward the tissue box on the bedside table and hauled it closer toward him. He wiped the liquid off my thigh. Just a minute ago it had been so hot, but already it felt cold.

"You were thinking about the guy you like, right?"

I felt so uncomfortable that I found it impossible to look him in the eye. He placed his palm on top of my head.

"I'm not blaming you. I think . . . I think everyone does it."

He rolled up the tissues he'd used into a ball and tossed them into the wastebasket.

"To tell you the truth, I . . . I'm really into someone at the moment as well, and as I was touching you I was imagining it was her. Wishing you were her, I guess."

I knew that I'd been doing exactly the same thing, so it didn't make any sense to feel hurt by what he was saying, but I did.

"I've always been really good academically, you know. Like your brother. I really thought that if I just kept on studying, then the things I didn't know about the world would gradually diminish. But the truth is that the older I get, the less I understand. About love, about sex, girls, even myself . . ."

If there were things that even someone as clever as Hinata couldn't understand, I thought, then I didn't stand a chance. Although maybe that was exactly it. Unlike Hinata, I'd never thought, even for a second, that one day I'd understand it all.

Hinata turned his back to me and slowly put his boxers and jeans back on. Then he sat down on the bed, next to where I was still lying stretched out.

"You know that woman in the photo with my brother, from Nagano? Was he in love with her, do you think?"

"I think so. My guess is that she's the first person he ever really fell in love with. I mean, he hasn't had a girlfriend before, right?"

I laughed and shook my head, and Hinata smiled.

"For someone as untainted as that, I guess Nagano might have been a real wake-up call."

"The free sex part?" I snickered, but Hinata pulled a serious face and rested his palm on top of my head again.

"Imagining someone you're in love with having sex with someone else right close by is tough for anyone."

The white thighs of the woman Takumi had sex with flashed in front of my eyes.

"I don't feel I can laugh at your brother or mock him for what he did. Sometimes when sex is dangled in front of you like a carrot, all you can do is run straight for it, however ridiculous you know you might look to other people. I think that's especially true of men."

I pictured Takumi grabbing hold of the white thighs and starting to thrust like crazy.

"It's really difficult to draw lines, you know. Between love and lust, and that sort of thing, I mean. I think the best thing would be to get to the point where you feel like there isn't any need to make those kinds of distinctions."

Saying that, Hinata took out a bottle of mineral water from the fridge and handed it to me. I decided to ask him something I'd been wondering about for a while.

"Did she give you a sexual initiation, too? That Nagano woman?"

"No, I . . . I went to the camp to see a girl. The first girl I ever fell for. Someone in my year. But she wasn't at the camp anymore, and after that she dropped out of school. I've no idea where she is now."

Hinata unscrewed the cap of the water bottle and drank noisily.

"I know it's weird to be saying this, considering I brought you here and everything but . . . You're still a virgin, right? And I—I felt like I shouldn't be your first. I mean, really, you want to do it with him, right? The guy you like."

As I listened to what seemed to me like a roundabout sort of excuse come spilling out of Hinata's mouth, it occurred to me, on a deep kind of level, that Hinata really didn't have feelings for me after all. I didn't feel anything for him whatsoever, yet that idea made me feel pathetically sad, as if I'd been dumped for the first time. Watching Hinata's face in profile as he drained the rest of the water in the bottle, I thought about how much I wanted to have sex with Takumi.

Suddenly, the fact that I alone was lying there totally naked, showing my A-cup boobs to Hinata, felt unbelievably embarrassing, and I hurriedly pulled the sheet up to cover my chest. My panties were still strung around my ankle, and my privates were still warm from all Hinata's probing. Of course I wanted to have sex with Takumi. That was what I really wanted above anything, but, right now, in this instant, I also wanted Hinata to touch me more, like he had before. The more I felt like that, the more I hated Takumi. Underneath the sheet, I put on my bra and my dress that Hinata had taken off. What I didn't know was that, at that moment, a little egg of lust was already incubating inside me, and it would grow and grow, just like a Tamagotchi, until it became nothing but big fat trouble.

Hinata rode with me to the station where I had to get off and bought me a plastic umbrella from the convenience store there.

Looking up at the sky when I emerged from the ticket gates, I saw it was covered by a low blanket of ash-colored cloud, and occasionally a large drop of rain would come smacking down onto my umbrella.

I checked my phone to see a message from Akutsu.

"It turns out the woman in that Takumi video is a housewife way older than him! He's even more pervy than we thought."

Since that time by the river, I'd been getting messages from Akutsu about Takumi practically every day. I was starting to get kind of sick of them, actually. But if it was a housewife, then maybe it really was the person who lived in that apartment building by the river. But seriously? A housewife, getting dressed up in cosplay and then doing that stuff? I felt confused about absolutely everything.

As I started across the bridge, the rain and wind suddenly grew harder, and when I looked down at the river I saw the water was spewing past with a scary churning sound. It looked like coffee-flavored milk. I wondered if that housewife had sexually initiated Takumi. I was standing there, lost in thought, when there was a huge great rumble of thunder directly above me. It gave me such a fright that I let go of my umbrella.

I watched it, that umbrella Hinata had bought for me just minutes ago, as the wind caught it and sent it sailing down off the bridge as if in slow motion. I watched it as it hit the surface of the water and was instantly sucked up in the seething current, carried away in no time. There was another clap of thunder, and I found myself screaming. I was too scared to cross to the other side of the bridge, so, with my hands over my ears, I ran back the way I'd come, the opposite direction from my house.

With my clothes and my hair all soaked, I stood in front of Saito Maternity Clinic. I opened the door and called out, but nobody came. Not sure what to do, I deliberated for a while, but then I took off my shoes and went up the stairs.

I opened the door to Takumi's room to find him lying there on the bed just like the last time, in the same T-shirt and shorts.

Treading across the manga-littered floor, I went to the bed. When I climbed up and sat astride Takumi, he opened his eyes and looked at me in surprise. I was even more drenched with rain than I thought, and droplets from my hair and clothes fell down and left little wet patches on his T-shirt. I scrunched my hand into a fist and punched his chest. I wanted to hit him much harder, but I couldn't find the strength.

"Are you not going to go out with me anymore?"

Takumi was looking at me, but it was as if he wasn't. I was still warm and sticky between my legs. The sensation of Hinata's fingers and tongue moving still lingered there.

"I really like you, you know."

I punched him again in the chest. A peal of thunder like a drumroll sounded somewhere in the distance. I took hold of the neck of Takumi's T-shirt and shook it from side to side.

"Were you that into her? Huh?"

Takumi shut his eyes, frowned a little, then nodded his head.

"Why? Why did you do it? Getting all dressed up in cosplay like that to have sex, then having it spread all around the internet! Only a complete idiot would let something like that happen!"

I shook the neck of his T-shirt again, and his head lolled limply from side to side with it.

He covered his face with his hands. *Go ahead and cry if you want to*, I found myself saying inside, just like a bully would do.

"Because I was in love with her," Takumi said from the other side of his palms in a muffled voice. Just then, the door opened. Mrs. Saito, seeing me sitting there on top of Takumi, quickly shut it again without saying anything.

"Sorry, sorry!" I heard her voice loud from the other side of the door, then the sound of her powering down the stairs, so I jumped off the bed, opened the door, and called out to where she was standing at the bottom of the stairs.

"Sorry for barging in without telling you I was here." I bowed my head in apology.

"So, um . . ." she said as she climbed the stairs slowly and came in to Takumi's room again. She looked between the two of us. I felt myself blushing to my ears and had no clue how I should behave. For some reason totally unclear to me, I decided it would be a good idea to sit down on the tatami with my back straight and my knees tucked under me, as if I was attending some formal gathering.

"So, now . . . What was I here for again?" Mrs. Saito rubbed her temples with her two middle fingers.

"Oh, yes! I remember. I got such a surprise it went clean out of my head."

She smiled broadly, in a way that made her look even more like Takumi. From outside the window I heard a whoosh of running water. Had the rain got even worse?

"So they're saying it's possible we'll be flooded tonight, what with all this rain. There's been a torrential downpour in the mountains, and they're saying that if the dam overflows we might be in trouble here. I've got two women in at the moment. One of them has already given birth, and her family's coming to pick her up, but the other one might just give birth tonight, so I've arranged for her to stay with a friend of mine who's also a midwife, somewhere higher up. When this area starts flooding, it fills up in no time. After I've cleared up downstairs, I'm going over there in the car. But you guys um . . . Sorry, your name was . . . ?"

"It's Nana. Nana Matsunaga."

"And where do you live, Nana?"

"Right next to Dairoku elementary school."

"Oh, that's the place where several houses got washed away before, right? There's a good chance that bridge might become unusable, so you'd better get home. Soon as you can. Your parents will be worried, I'm sure. Takumi, you go and take Nana home now, while you still can. If the rain gets really bad, you don't have to come back. Go over to Ryota's. I can't imagine the water will get all the way up there."

As Mrs. Saito rattled all that off in a fast voice, she grabbed a towel from the basket in the hall and handed it to me.

"Come on, Takumi, get a move on! Nana, you'll get soaked with just an umbrella, so I'll lend you a raincoat and boots."

Saying that, she went clattering down the stairs.

I put on the magenta Gore-Tex coat Mrs. Saito had loaned me, and Takumi and I set out across the bridge. The coat was too big, and my hands got lost in the sleeves. The boots were huge on me, too, so the rain had no problem finding its way inside. By the time we set foot on the bridge, my toes were already icy cold.

Takumi walked slightly ahead of me, still in the same T-shirt and shorts he'd had on in his room. There was a strong wind blowing from the east, so the left half of his body got quickly soaked, and that part of his T-shirt stuck to his skin. The rain would come falling down with insane power, and then stop just as suddenly. Sensing something dark flash through the sky, I looked up to see a group of big black birds that looked like ravens being blown about and thrown off balance as they tried to make their way toward the mountain. The river was usually so piddling and short on water that I'd often wondered why they'd bothered making the bridge so long, but today the cloudy water took up the entire width of the river, and was rushing past at a crazy speed. Now and then, I saw a plank of wood or a chunk of white polystyrene go whistling by. The wide grassy riverbeds on either side of the river were totally soaked. I watched as a homeless man carrying a blue vinyl sheet walked unsteadily across the middle of the flooded sports field there.

When we reached the middle of the bridge, Takumi stopped walking and peered down at the surging water. All of a sudden, a siren sounded very close by. On impulse, I rammed my fingers into my ears, and of course the rain took that opportunity to come flooding into my sleeves, dribbling all the way down my arms. Opposite the bridge was the old apartment building I'd once followed Takumi inside—the place where the housewife lived. On the days Takumi hadn't come to work, I'd sometimes spied him standing on that bridge, staring moronically into the distance.

"Are you going to see her again?" I looked up at him, feeling the raindrops slapping down on the skin of my face, running into my eyes. I could see it hitting Takumi's face, too, totally without mercy.

"She's not there anymore."

A car driving too close to the curb sent dirty water flying up, spotting Takumi's white T-shirt with brown. The spray hit me in the face, too.

"Things might be easier if I just jumped off," Takumi said.

I began to shout at him. "If you want to die, then go ahead and jump, right now! I'm not gonna stop you. You've had your fair share of fun times, after all, so I guess you might as well. Goodbye!"

I set off, using the umbrella to shield myself from the rain. As soon as I stepped off the bridge, the dark sky was lit up with a flash as if a giant camera had gone off, and immediately after, there was a clap of thunder so huge it rattled my insides. The shock of it made me stumble in those enormous rain boots, and I fell flat on my face like a toddler. I felt so pathetic, and my knees hurt so much, I burst into tears, lying right there facedown on the ground. My face and my clothes were wet with some mixture of tears and rain. A passing car sent dirty water flying into my mouth.

Enough of the ribs of the umbrella Takumi's mom had lent me had bent that it was now basically ruined. I got up slowly and looked behind me to see Takumi standing there, watching me expressionlessly. After a while, he came over, took my arm, and helped me up. I held onto his arm while I took off each of my boots in turn and emptied them out. I was surprised by how much water came gushing out.

"I wanted to have sex with you, you know."

"I can't do it anymore." Takumi looked away from me as he spoke, and with the huge noise of the rain, it was hard to make out what he was saying clearly, but I caught it. "It's no good. Nothing happens, whatever I look at. Ever since I split up with her."

It was only evening, but the sky was as black as if it were the middle of the night. The headlights of a passing car picked out Takumi's face so it glowed white against the surrounding dark. I thought suddenly of Hinata's thingy pointing straight up at the ceiling in the hotel. That had been just earlier today.

"My grandma always used to say that the gods punish the wrongdoers. It must be your punishment from the gods, for being so mean to me!" But even as I was saying the words, I wondered if there was any god that would punish Takumi just for having sex with the person he was in love with.

Even now, when I was totally wet through and chilled to the core, the tears running down my face felt warm. It struck me for the first time that all the liquid inside the body must stay pretty warm. Takumi went off striding ahead down the bridge toward my house without looking back at me. I broke into a run and followed after him. At the foot of the bridge, men in yellow raincoats were piling up sandbags.

"They've issued an evacuation order for this area!" one of them shouted. "Go and take shelter in Daiyon middle school, quickly!"

When I turned back to look, the grassy riverbeds were now totally submerged, and the water level was nearly up to the top of the banks. A flash of silvery blue lightning lit up the sky above the mountain. It looked just like fireworks. I'd never seen the river like that before, a thick black current that appeared to get more powerful by the second. It seemed like it could swallow up a whole town at any moment, just like my brother had said it would. When I imagined my house submerged by that water, a shiver ran down my spine. Without thinking, I grabbed Takumi's arm and was surprised to feel it trembling.

We turned onto the road by the river, where my house was. The water that had made it over the riverbank was seeping its way onto the street, little by little. It only reached to Takumi's calves, but it came all the way up to my knees. I held onto his arm as we waded slowly through the water. I was sharing his umbrella by now, although we were both so soaked it was basically pointless. Apart from the sirens, the only sound was that of the rain beating down. It was kind of eerie.

My cell phone had no reception, so I couldn't even send texts. Finally, my house came in sight. I could see a figure on the balcony. My brother was standing there with his binoculars, his white shirt soaked through.

"My God, what an idiot," I said. I only realized I'd actually spoken the words out loud when Takumi turned and looked at me.

"My house is just there," I said, while inside I carried on cursing my brother. *Idiot, idiot, idiot.*

Wading through water used up a surprising amount of energy, and my teeth were chattering with cold and exhaustion.

When we turned the corner that led to my house, I saw that the lights of all the other houses around were out, and there was no sign of anybody anywhere. Only the light in my familiar old hall was on. The whole garden was deluged, and a garden sandal and a few of the plastic dishes we put under plant pots were bobbing around on the surface of the water. It took a joint effort between Takumi and me to pry the front door open.

"Mom!" I called, and she came running out of the back room.

"Nana! My God! I've been calling and calling, but I couldn't get through!"

Mom's eyes turned to Takumi.

"This is Takumi, who lives in the maternity clinic. He brought me home."

Takumi bowed his head at Mom, then said, "Goodnight." He made to open the door, but Mom reached out and took hold of his arm.

"No! You can't go out there now, it's too dangerous. They say it'll stop by tomorrow morning, so you stay the night here."

Mom's voice was so urgent and fierce it took both Takumi and me by surprise.

"Everyone else has already taken shelter in the school, but you hadn't come home, and Yusuke . . ." Mom trailed off and looked up the stairs. "Anyway, for now, take your shoes off and come in. You'll catch a cold if you don't change out of those clothes."

Mom insisted, so Takumi and I took turns going into the bathroom to dry ourselves off. When I put the towel up to my face, the smell of the fabric softener Mom always used felt like the most comforting thing in the world. I took off my crumpled dress, and there was my polka- dotted bra. I unhooked it, and just as I tossed it into the clothes hamper, there was a huge peal of thunder and the lights went out. It was pitch dark, and I couldn't see a thing, but I somehow managed to put my clothes on and then, feeling my way with my hand along the hallway, made it into the living room where Mom and Takumi, now wearing my brother's shirt, were standing, looking out the window, at the rain pouring down the windowpanes. It was like the whole house was being given a good clean in a car wash. Mom squealed as she lifted a foot in the air. I looked down to see a stream of water flowing slowly into the room from under the door to the hall. Now it was my turn to squeal.

"Mom, we saw Yusuke standing on the balcony when we came in."

Before I'd even finished speaking, Mom was away up the stairs, so fast it was hard to believe it was the same mother of mine who usually struggled so much for energy. Takumi and I followed. The door to my brother's room was locked, so we went out onto the balcony from my room. My brother was sitting there with his legs crossed, the rain tipping down on him like a waterfall.

"Get inside, right now!" Mom's voice was practically drowned out by the sound of the rain and the roaring of the wind. I grabbed my brother's arm and pulled, but his body didn't move an inch. It seemed like he had no intention of going inside.

"Those glasses are really dangerous with all this lightning." Saying this, Takumi plucked Yusuke's glasses off his face and threw them onto the bed in my room. My brother stood shakily to his feet. His white shirt stuck to his skin. He pointed toward the river and shouted with a smile.

"You see! I told you! In no time at all, the river will breach its banks and come for us. It will sweep this house away. We shall all be engulfed!"

At that moment there was a noise like a match being struck, and the pitch-black sky grew as light as if it was full of burning magnesium, like I'd seen in science class. Then there was this noise, like a bunch of enormous drums were being beaten all at once, and a thick, blue-white band of light dropped straight down into the center of the riverbank. We saw it touch the top of the big tree in the baseball field, and then, for just a moment, the outline of the whole tree was picked out of the darkness. The strip of light that ran straight down the tree divided itself into thin threads, spreading out in all directions across the ground.

Takumi threw himself on top of me, covering my body with his. I looked to my brother to see Mom had wrapped her arms around him and was clinging to him tight. He was staring dazedly at the flames rising up from the top of the tree. Takumi and I grabbed my brother's arms and pulled, while Mom shoved him from behind. She made it inside the room last, and fastened the balcony door behind her. All four of us were soaked through and panting. Mom stood up shakily from where she was squatting on the floor, went up to my brother, and whacked him over the top of the head.

"I won't let you die in this house, you hear? Your father built this place. He worked himself to the bone and built this house to protect you and Nana."

Mom was standing with her hands on her hips in front of my brother, in a super-imposing way. I remembered how, before she came down with menopausal disorder, she'd often used this pose when she was telling me off for something or other. My brother had covered his head with his hands and was staring at the floor.

"I won't have it, you hear? I won't let you die before me!"

Mom's shoulders heaved as she shouted, and she looked as though her whole body was going through the wringer. With each new bolt of lightning, the dark room would light up just for a moment. Between the noisy gusts of rain, I thought I heard a sniffling noise. At first I figured it was my brother, and looked at him. Then I realized. It wasn't my brother that was crying, but Takumi, next to me. Soon enough, Mom and my brother noticed, too, and looked at him in surprise. It seemed like he was trying desperately to hold it in, but his shaking shoulders gave him away.

"I'm really sorry, I just, I cry at everything," he said in a hiccupy voice. Mom looked at him, then at me, and a faint smile came across her face. Someone's stomach let out a big rumble.

"That wasn't me!" I said.

Mom smiled. "I know it wasn't," she said. She went down the stairs, and I followed. The water was lapping against the bottom step, and all our slippers and sandals were floating their way down the hall. With water washing round my ankles, I moved down the pitch-black hallway, pulled a bunch of towels from the rack by the bathroom sink, and carried them back upstairs, where I handed them to my brother and Takumi. My brother was leaning up against the wall and Takumi against my bed, both of them hanging their heads. Mom came upstairs cradling bottles of water, tea, and juice, and a bunch of tins of food to her chest.

"I didn't make any dinner today. I couldn't get to the shops. I know a canned meal is hardly ideal right now, but please help yourself, Takumi."

Mom peeled back the lids from a selection of cans—mackerel broiled in miso, grilled chicken, sweet corn, peaches—and placed them open on the floor. I took the plastic plates and forks out of the rucksack Dad had prepared for earthquakes and other emergencies and handed them out. I lit a scented candle and placed it down in the middle of where we were all sitting. Takumi started in on the miso-marinated mackerel that Mom had dished out onto plates. My brother picked up the can of grilled chicken and began shoveling its contents into his mouth at extreme speed.

"I think it was Yusuke whose stomach was rumbling," I said meanly, but Mom darted me a look that meant *stop it*.

"This isn't going to be enough, is it?" she said and went back downstairs, and I went with her, into the kitchen.

"I think this rice should still be okay." As Mom opened the lid of the rice cooker, steam rose up, and beneath it I could see the white rice sparkling in the dark of the kitchen. The nori in the drawers under where the plates were kept had gone soft with all the moisture in the air, so we left it, and made just plain rice balls with salty dried plums in the middle.

Most of the rice balls were gobbled down by Takumi and my brother in record time. Watching the two of them silently making their way through the rice and the tins, Mom looked very pleased. The candle flame flickered, casting shadows of the four of us on the wall. The whole thing reminded me a lot of camping. After a bit, Mom went out onto the landing and shone the Maglite from the emergency rucksack down the stairs to get a better look at the first floor. It was too dark to see well, but it seemed as though the water level was rising even higher. The wind and the rain were showing no intention of easing up, and I had the sense that this house was going to be submerged, along with the entire town, just like my brother had warned. Because my stupid brother had left the balcony door wide open, his room was totally drenched, and so it was decided that we'd all sleep in my room.

"I'll stay awake and keep watch, so you all go ahead and get some rest," Mom said.

"We'll take turns," I said. "You can sleep first."

I persuaded her to lie down on my bed, and Takumi, my brother, and I settled down on sheets and blankets laid out on the floor, with me at the foot of the bed and my brother and Takumi close to the door. I lay sucking on the rainbow-colored hard candies that I'd found in the emergency rucksack, turning the handle of the wind-up radio.

Interspersed with a scraping noise like someone running their nails down a wall, I could hear snippets of meaning: *rainfall exceeding four inches per hour . . . The M—— River has exceeded the critical water level . . . 874 households in T—— City have been inundated above floor level . . .*

Hearing the male presenter's voice coolly announcing these facts, I suddenly started to feel scared, and turned the tuner knob until I found a music station. They were playing slow music, the kind we used to listen to in the car when we were with Dad. Every summer, Dad had taken us on vacation to a seaside town. I remembered how, after all the traffic jams, the car sickness, and the fights with my brother in the cramped back seat, I would catch a glimpse of the blue line of sea in the distance. Ignoring Mom's warnings not to, I'd open the car window just a crack and race with my brother to see which of us could smell the sea first.

"Oh, this sounds familiar," my brother said from where he was lying staring up at the ceiling.

"'Summer Day Love,' it's called," Mom said from the bed. I turned the handle of the wind-up radio again, as if I was reeling in a fish I'd just caught, and then set the radio down beside my head.

The station kept on playing the kinds of songs we had listened to in Dad's car. At that time, I'd found the music boring, old-fashioned, and impossibly uncool, but now I could have happily listened to it forever. After a while, I heard Mom and Yusuke snoring lightly. The rain was still falling heavily, and the whole house seemed to be swaying in the wind. I heard a moaning sound, then saw Takumi turn in his sleep. His body was lying right alongside mine. I lifted myself up and looked at his face, which was down by my feet. In the light of the candle now placed on my desk, I could see it pretty clearly. He was sleeping like a baby.

I looked up at the ceiling, stretched my arms and legs, and let out a huge sigh. It had been a long day. And this, I thought, this was my summer vacation—the summer vacation of my fifteenth year. I was still a virgin in an A cup, and now I was trapped inside my own room by the rain. Sleeping next to me was Takumi, who was depressed because someone had spread photos and videos of him having cosplay sex with a housewife all over the internet and he couldn't get hard any more, and who also happened to be the person I liked the most in the whole world. I turned to the left, so my face was right beside the sole of one of his bare feet. Then I stuck out my tongue and licked it. It tasted kind of salty. Once the rain stopped, I thought, I'd have to go and return the towel and the raincoat and stuff to Takumi's mom. Then, I'd march up to Takumi's room, sit on top of him, and punch him. I'd sit smack bang in front of him with Ryota, and down a whole can of tangerine juice in one go. I didn't care if he started to hate me. I'd keep going to his room until I felt satisfied, I decided. I kissed the sole of his foot. Then I shut my eyes and felt myself falling straight into a deep sleep.

"How on earth did this wind up here?" Dad smiled in amazement as he picked up a plastic potty from where it was lying in our garden and flung it into a garbage bag. Our garden was in a total state, full of all kinds of crap the river had carried here. Around Dad went, picking each thing up with his rubber-gloved hands. The night of the crazy rain, he had driven all the way back here from Tohoku. He was so worried that he couldn't get in touch with us, so when he'd opened the door to my bedroom and found me, Mom, Yusuke, and Takumi all lying there snoring, he felt kind of angry in spite of himself. He smiled as he told me that.

It's been decided that, starting in September, my brother will go live with Dad. He's going to take a break from college and work for a while in the factory. Since the day of the storm, my brother has started coming out of his room and spending more and more time in the living room. He's started eating Mom's cooking like before, or rather in even greater quantities than before, so that his body, which was all skin and bones, has rapidly filled out again.

Now, he was watching a program on the TV called *Total Eclipses Around the World*. He looked so serious and into it, and I could see Mom and Dad throwing worried looks in his direction, so I called out, "Hey, this isn't giving you funny ideas again, is it?"

"No, no, no! It's nothing like that, I assure you," my brother said, blushing like crazy.

I'd sat down Mom on a stool and was dyeing her hair, which was going pretty gray. I daubed the dye around her temples and her part, taking care not to get any on her scalp.

"Hey, Yusuke, you're the only one who's not doing anything," I said. "Why don't you make us some lunch? Anything's fine, curry or whatever you can do. There's rice already cooked."

Hearing this, my brother stood slowly to his feet and looked at me. "How does one make curry?"

"There's some roux in the cupboard. It's all written in the instructions on the packet. A person who can't make curry from a packet isn't going to make it to the 2035 eclipse, you know!"

Mom slapped my backside.

For the next few minutes, we heard a whole variety of noises from the kitchen: crashes, and thuds, and *ow*s, and *ah*s. Then silence. After a while, I smelled something burning. I ran into the kitchen and saw the largest pan we owned filled to the brim with curry, bubbling over furiously. My brother was sitting on the chair in the kitchen, absorbed in some book. I turned the hob off, and thrust a ladle right down to the bottom of the pan. Just the texture of it told me that the curry was burnt beyond any possible salvation.

"You're *such* an *idiot!*"

Hearing this my brother finally took his eyes off his book and looked up at me.

"I think the same thing about myself sometimes," he said, dead serious.

Although the curry tasted of little except burned matter, and although the carrots and potatoes that were supposed to be lumps had now dissolved into mush, we ate it for lunch anyway.

"Hey, this is perfectly edible!"

"It's actually pretty good!"

As I watched Mom and Dad piling compliments on the first meal my brother had ever made, I thought there really was something kind of weird about them. Still, despite all their praise, they didn't eat very much of it. I, on the other hand, was so hungry that I had a second helping of what had to be the most disgusting curry I'd ever eaten. From the TV, which had been left on, we heard a voice say, "The next total solar eclipse visible in Japan will take place in 2035."

How old would I be in 2035? I wasn't smart, and I couldn't do the calculation quickly. But even if the world was going to end then, I was going to stick around until that point. I'd have lots of mind-blowingly amazing sex (hopefully with Takumi), and lots of babies (hopefully Takumi's). They could just try to stop me. As I thought that, I took my third helping of curry. My brother shot me a look like I was some kind of bizarre, exotic species of animal he'd never seen before. A dragonfly came flying in from somewhere, perched on the index finger of my hand that was holding the spoon, and then flew off again. It wouldn't be long before summer was officially over.

4

A Goldenrod Sky

BACK WHEN I WAS in elementary school, I went on a school trip to the local transportation museum.

I remember how all the boys in our class stood with their noses pressed up against a glass case, totally enraptured by the model railroad inside. The case was about the size of the tatami-floored room I slept in. Inside it was a diorama of a miniature town with a river gently snaking through it and a set of mountains behind it. Encircling the town was a golden train track. The town had a station, a shopping arcade, a hospital, a factory, a bridge, a bus stop, and lots and lots of houses with little pointed roofs.

Around me, my friends were pointing excitedly at the trains racing by, globs of spit speckling the glass as they shouted out, "It's an 100-Model Shinkansen!" and, "Look, look, a Super Azusa!" and "An eight-carriage Naha!"

What I was staring at wasn't the trains, though, but the tiny people dotted about the town. A man in a suit carrying a briefcase, a station worker cleaning the platform, a mother pushing a stroller, construction workers mending the roads, a farmer tending his field, and schoolkids with big leather backpacks on their backs—the town contained all kinds of people.

Then I glanced toward the river and noticed the figure of a man in a gray shirt and black trousers lying facedown right in the middle of the road. A bright yellow train, the kind used for cleaning the tracks, raced along the sharply curved railway track right next to the man and off into the distance. I stared at that man for a long time. I felt like I'd seen that outfit, the gray shirt and the black trousers, somewhere before. Then I realized. I was pretty sure it was the same thing my dad was wearing in the photo of him holding me as a baby. He'd died not long after that.

The lights in the miniature town gradually dimmed, marking the shift from evening to night. The utility poles, the stations, and the windows of the pointy-roofed houses all lit up in orange.

As if from afar, I heard our teacher calling out for us to gather round, that it was time to go. Even after my friends dashed to the exit, I stayed on, staring at that facedown figure. It seemed as though, among all the people in the town with their specially allotted roles—station worker, businessman, mother, schoolchild—only the man spread-eagled on the road was without a proper part to play.

The teacher came up again and said in a low voice, "Come on, Goldie, let's move it."

His fist came flying at my head.

Goldie is what everyone calls me. It's a bit of a long story, but basically it comes from goldenrod, which is the name of a kind of weed that grows down by the riverbank. The goldenrod plants are really tall, and I was the tallest in the class, and it has these yellow flowers that are exactly the same color as the sweatshirt I was always wearing. I can't remember precisely when it happened, but at some point the name stuck, and even the teachers started using it. As I rubbed the part of my head that had been thwacked, I took one more look at the man lying down before I walked away. He looked like he might be having a tantrum slap-bang in the middle of the street, lying there sobbing and refusing to get up. *You're a grown-up*, I thought as I walked away. *You're supposed to be a grown-up, so just pull yourself together.*

In front of the station is a strip of shops—a supermarket, a couple of convenience stores, fast-food restaurants, and a secondhand bookstore. Walk a little farther, and you find an arcade with shops of the same kind you'd find if you got off at any station on this train line, and some relatively new residential areas with apartment buildings and houses. In the gaps between these, you find the odd pear orchard. Encircling this plain old town, with nothing much to distinguish it from any other, is a band of low mountains.

Take the road that goes straight from the station, in the opposite direction from the main hospital, and it leads you up a mountain and to a crematorium. Keep going, and you'll come to a section of road paved in parts seemingly at random, like an asphalt quilt. Follow the road up to the top of the mountain and pass through a short dark dank tunnel, and you come to an estate complex, a group of buildings so old and shabby that their name, New Town, seems pretty ironic. Alongside the complex is a dirty old swamp about the size of a school swimming pool. Some people living in the complex call it a "pond," while others prefer the term "swamp." I don't really have a preference either way. It's just a big puddle of fetid water, so I figure people can call it whatever they like.

Some of the rainwater that falls on the mountain flows down into the center of the town via the river, and the rest makes its way into the swamp. The water that ends up in the river will someday make it to the sea, but the water that finds its way into the swamp mixes together with the liquid already in that stagnant puddle, whose oily surface gleams in metallic rainbow colors, and probably doesn't go any farther. Down there with all that water is a whole load of goldfish and turtles that the people living around here couldn't be bothered to keep, not to mention dead cats and dogs and who knows what else. When the westerly wind blows, it gives off a smell of rotting protein like from a garbage bag, meaning it's more or less impossible for the people living around here to open their windows during the summer. Growing around the swamp are a few Manchurian ash trees.

A long, long time ago, on a very hot day, someone hanged themselves from the branch of one of the ashes, but, after a while, the branch broke under the weight and the body slipped down into the swamp below without anyone noticing. Three days later, the body suddenly floated to the surface, all bloated and covered with the grunge from the depths, so that it looked as if the body was coated in chocolate. That person was my dad, who had killed himself to escape from his endless battle with debt. People in the complex say that if you walk by the swamp before dawn in midsummer, when Sirius appears in the east, you're likely to see a mud-drenched figure appear before you, but I come back to my complex from my paper route at dawn every day and I've never once seen my dad's ghost.

When school was over for the day, I went back to my apartment and carried my bike up to the fifth floor. Leave it in the bike rack, and either the saddle or else the whole thing was sure to get stolen. Of course, the building, which dates from sometime around the fifties, way before I was born, doesn't have any elevators. I made my way around and around the spiral staircase, and when I reached the fifth floor, used a long chain to attach my bike to a water pipe in the hallway. I opened our door, so badly rusted that all the paint was peeling off, and heard the sound of running water in the kitchen. The water gushing out of the tap was splashing off the bowls, cups, and plates in the sink, steadily soaking the clothes of my grandmother, who was standing motionless in front of the tap. Seeing me, she opened her mouth slowly and said, "Welcome home, Yoshio!"

For the record, Yoshio is not my name. Yoshio was the name of my dad, who hanged himself. Yoshi-o, meaning *good man*. They took one of the two characters, the one meaning *good*, to create my name: Ryota. Ryo-ta, meaning *good* and *big*.

"Hi, Gran."

My gran was getting very deaf of late, so I had to raise my voice when I spoke to her. I turned off the tap, then guided her by the arm and sat her down by the table in front of the TV, flicking through until I found a kids' program. My gran looked at me and grinned. I wiped off her wet hands and clothes quickly with a towel, then returned to the kitchen and opened the lid of the rice cooker. All the rice I'd cooked this morning was gone. Even taking into account the rice we'd eaten for breakfast, the rice balls I took to school, and the rice my gran would have eaten for her lunch, there should have been some more left. Still, a fat lot of good it was doing those kinds of calculations now. I'd had the feeling for a long time that there was a rice thief living in this house. I sighed and started rinsing more rice. There was only a little left in the plastic container we kept under the sink. That meant I'd soon have to go to the shopping center across the mountain where they sold it cheap and buy a new bag.

Eyes fixed on the screen, my gran was moving in time to the dance of the big animal characters. As my eyes passed over the kitchen table, they fell on a crumpled envelope with a bank logo on the front and "Takako" scrawled on the back in pencil. I looked inside to see three ten-thousand-yen notes. Takako was my mom's name, and the thirty thousand yen was, I guess, a message from her, meaning *you'll have to make do with this until the end of the month.* It would be at least half an hour before the rice would be ready, so I made some instant ramen and ate it straight from the pan, standing there in the kitchen. Noticing this, my gran stood up and stared at me fixedly.

"Do you want some?" I asked, and she nodded firmly.

At these times, and these times only, my gran seemed to be able to hear the faintest of sounds. I transferred a few noodles and some soup into a small bowl and passed it to her along with some chopsticks. She lowered herself back down in front of the TV, holding the bowl with immense care as if it were an extremely precious object. She picked up the noodles one by one with her chopsticks and ate them slowly and silently.

"Okay, Gran, I'm off to work now," I said.

She stayed studiously gazing at the period drama that was now on, not even gracing me with a reply.

In the morning I had my paper route and in the evenings my job at the convenience store. In between, I went to school. Throughout the summer I'd worked as a lifeguard at the pool, which had paid a decent hourly wage, but now that vacation was over I was back to early-morning paper deliveries and a night shift at the convenience store every day until 10 p.m. Along with my gran's pension and the odd few notes my mother occasionally brought over, what I made had to support both my gran and me.

I unlocked my bike and carried it down with me. Chiaki, a little girl from one of the first-floor apartments, was standing barefoot in front of her door. Her left cheek was red and swollen. Like many of the men in these projects, Chiaki's dad drank heavily from the time he woke and, come evening, started beating his children. In between the kicks and the punches, he'd yell her name at top volume. That was how I knew it.

"Did he hit you?" I asked her, but she didn't reply. I reached out to pat her head, but before I could get there she shouted, "Don't touch me, you perv!" From my pocket I took out a piece of the mint-flavored gum I chewed when I needed to stay awake and put it down on the ground by Chiaki's feet. Her feet were grubby, and she had almost no toenails to speak of. I guessed that she ate them when she was hungry. I'd done the same thing back in the day. I said bye to Chiaki, who was staring fixedly at the gum by her feet, got on my bike, and rode past the swamp and along the road that led down the mountain.

A pickup truck loaded with a jumble of discarded furniture and other garbage came lurching up the narrow mountain road toward me, so I stopped my bike in the parking area outside the crematorium to get out of the way. From there, I looked down at the town spreading out from the station like a scale model—a lot like the model railway town I'd seen on that school trip. Turning my head, I could see the gray housing projects looming up behind the narrow chimney of the crematorium. *Project kids*—that was what the people from town called us. Poverty, benefits, alcoholism, child abuse, personal bankruptcy, suicide, murders—the sort of events people in the town spoke about with deep frowns on their faces were a fact of life for me. The kids in the projects grew up surrounded by adults with eyes like those of the giant salamanders that lived in the swamp—tiny, dull, barely visible.

"What the hell are your parents doing?"

I stepped into the stockroom of the convenience store to see the manager holding a phone to his ear and looking pissed off. He was sitting on the fake-leather coated swivel chair and glaring in turn at each of the three kids standing in front of him: two boys and one girl of about eight or nine. I felt like I'd seen them somewhere before. In all likelihood, they were project kids.

"It's dinnertime and no one's at home in any of your houses! What's going on here?"

They're likely off playing pachinko, I thought as I put on my clownishly bright uniform that never got any less embarrassing to wear. The manager flung the phone onto the sofa. Scattered across the table was the assortment of small candies the kids had stolen. As if reading from a script that left him totally cold, the manager intoned:

"This convenience store is not your refrigerator. If there are things you want, things you feel like eating, you have to pay for them. If you take things out of the store without paying for them, that makes you thieves. Didn't your mothers ever teach you that?"

He reached out to grab the arm of one of the boys, who flinched reflexively. The girl next to him was glaring at the manager with big, moony eyes. The manager stared up at the ceiling and let out an ostentatiously loud sigh.

"Okay. I'll just have to call your school tomorrow. You go straight on home now, you hear!"

The children walked out without a word, swinging their backpacks, and the manager spun around in his chair to look at me.

"Those project kids are a dead loss," he said.

"Sorry," I said quietly.

"It's no good you apologizing! Truth is, I'm no good at this telling-kids-off business. Or with kids in general."

Saying this, the manager, who was now slumped back in his chair, glugged thirstily from a plastic bottle of Coke. I watched his big belly wobble as he drank. The buttons on his uniform looked ready to come flying off at any moment. He'd inherited this convenience store from his parents, who'd converted it from an old liquor shop. Although he was still only in his twenties, the hair on the top of his head was already thinning, and his forehead was bathed in sweat, though it wasn't even that hot. The door opened, and Taoka, the guy in charge of the part-time workers, came in.

"Yo!"

"Oh, Taokaaaa!" the manager groaned in a gross, wheedling sort of voice. "I'm begging you! Will you deal with the shoplifters next time? You were a teacher at a cram school, right? You must be good at that kind of stuff."

"Oh, no, I'm no good at telling off little kids."

Taoka hung his biker jacket on a coat hanger in his locker.

"Right, right, it was a university cram school you were at, wasn't it?"

Just then we heard a voice calling out, "Excuse me! Excuse me! I think the copier's got stuck!"

"Not again!" the manager said. "When is that damn maintenance man going to come?"

Tsk-tsking, he made his way into the shop.

"You done your homework yet?" Taoka said as he tied up his shoulder-length hair.

"Yep."

"I'll take a look during my break if you want. Your midterm tests are coming up, right? We should start preparing."

With that, he picked up the cleaning stuff and headed out into the shop.

I was fifteen when I first started working at the convenience store, and Taoka was the one who showed me the ropes. He was in his late twenties, and he basically ran the store in place of the manager, who didn't really have a clue about how to do the job his parents had entrusted him with.

"You almost feel sorry for him when he's standing next to Taoka," one of the other part-timers had commented, and it was true. Unlike the manager, who was short, fat, and balding, Taoka was tall and long-legged, and though his way of speaking was hardly what you'd call refined, he was pretty popular among the girls and middle-aged women we worked with.

"It's those eyes of his that do it," said one of the college students who worked there part-time. "Kind of icy and sadistic-looking."

I didn't really get what she meant.

I discovered soon enough that the job at the store involved way more things to pick up and intricate tasks to master than I'd initially thought and, pathetically enough, I got in a panic over each one. As I was flapping about in front of the cash register, Taoka would come up beside me and say quietly, "Deep breaths, deep breaths," then help me to bag the stuff. My instinct whenever I ran up against some kind of problem was to keep silent and try to sort it out by myself, but he told me over and over again, "If something goes wrong or you're not sure about anything, ask for help right away."

I didn't really know anything about his life, but I did find it very odd that someone who could clearly do this kind of job with his eyes shut and who, according to the manager, used to work in a cram school that sent lots of kids to top universities, would be working in a dump like this.

Several times, while I'd been sweeping outside, I'd see Taoka running after kids who'd been caught shoplifting and given a telling-off by the manager and were now heading home with their tails between their legs. I watched him hand them bags containing ice cream or candies, crouching down and patting their heads, smiling as he spoke to them. Then he would wave them off and come back. Once he spied me watching him and said, "When they've been told off by Daddy, it's Mommy's job to make them feel better." Then he went inside.

I had no idea what he was talking about.

After the first few months, during which I made a ton of mistakes and generally was a big nuisance, I'd gotten to the stage where I could operate the cash register and bag up people's stuff without keeping them waiting. Once you'd mastered the basics, there wasn't anything desperately demanding to the job, but the amount of shoplifting that went on did get me down. I recognized most of the kids who got caught—they were project kids.

When I first started working there, a college student named Nakamura took joy in pointing out every little thing I did wrong. And whenever there was an incident of shoplifting, he'd say, "Kids from your part of town, again!"

One time, when I ran to catch a little kid who was trying to make off with something, I slammed hard into a container of steaming *oden*, and its entire contents, including all its hot broth, spilled onto the floor. The strong fishy smell stuck in the back of my throat so I felt like I might choke, but Nakamura and I set about picking up all the components of the stew and cleaning the sopping-wet floor. As I was kneeling down, tossing lumps of stewed radish, fish sausages, and little knots of seaweed into the garbage can, Nakamura tramped back and forth across the place where most of the hot liquid had collected so that it flew up into my face.

"Just look! My new sneakers are all covered in stew!" he said as he stepped in the patch of liquid time and time again, sending the hot broth flying up into my eyes.

"There were never this many shopliftings before you came. Bet you go around giving tip-offs to all the project kids, don't you?"

In a second I was up on my feet and flying at him, but before I could land a single punch, I felt a dull pain running down from my left temple. For a moment, the world in front of me swam. As I went in for a second attempt, Taoka came up from behind and grabbed both my arms, saying, "What the hell is going on here?"

"I've seen you!" I yelled. "I've seen you stealing cigarettes from the stockroom!" My voice was shaking and got stuck in my throat, making me squeak like a little kid. I felt like a total loser.

"What?! That's enough of your bullshit, poor boy." Saying this, Nakamura made to high-kick me in the stomach, but from his position behind me, Taoka somehow managed to catch hold of his foot. Standing there on one leg, Nakamura lost his balance, and fell back awkwardly, right into the puddle of oden broth. His head struck the floor with a thump, sending a tofu fritter skittering. "I can't take this shitty store a minute longer!" he said, tearing off his broth-soaked uniform shirt and throwing it on the floor before storming out.

In the back room, Taoka handed me a wet towel for my face.

"It wasn't just cigarettes that little shit was nicking," he said, smiling, then handed me a bottle of a new kind of juice that had just been delivered, a toxic-looking shade of fuchsia.

"I'm really sorry that the project kids cause so much trouble."

"You're always apologizing on their behalf, but it's not like you've any responsibility for them. Last I heard, you weren't the fricking project ambassador. Or are you?"

Taoka smiled and took a swig of his canned coffee. The side of my head where I'd been punched stung badly.

"Is this yours?"

Holding a piece of paper soaked through with oden broth between his thumb and forefinger, Taoka dangled it in front of my face. It was my English midterm test that we'd been handed back that day. During the scuffle, it must have fallen out of the pocket I'd stuffed it in. Through the folded paper, you could see my mark written in red pen: 17/100. Taoka was holding it out beyond my reach. When I extended my arm to try and take it, my temple throbbed with pain.

"Hold on a sec," Taoka said. He unfolded the paper with his thumb and index finger, and pinged it into a plastic clipboard lying on the table. He started studying it, his face suddenly turning serious in a way I'd never seen it do before.

"Even leaving aside the longer passage, there are a lot of simple slipups here where you could easily have picked up points. These words and idioms here, you could have got another ten marks just by learning them by heart. You're making mistakes on words you learned in the second grade. See—here, and here, and here."

Taoka looked at me with an incredibly sad expression.

"Bring your textbook along on your next shift. I'll help you during your break."

"Nah, I hate schoolwork. It's fine, don't worry."

"You can't say that when you've only just entered high school! You've still got lots of time until your exams for college."

"I'm not going to college anyway. I can't afford it."

"No. No, no, no. Hold it. Do you know how hard it will be for you to find a job if you don't go to college? Besides, even if you've already decided you're not going, lessons are bound to be boring with an attitude like that. Where's the fun in sitting in class not understanding a thing? It's a total fucking waste of time."

"Lessons are meant to be boring, that's the point of them. Everyone sleeps through half of them."

"That's only because the teachers are incompetent."

"Yeah, well. I'm at a bad school. The whole thing's a farce, students and teachers alike."

I thought I saw Taoka's eyes flash as I spoke.

"Right . . . Well, at this rate, you'll get married as soon as you're out of your bad fucking school, have a slew of kids, be worked to the bone by assholes like Nakamura, and live out the rest of your life in the projects. But hey, that ain't such a bad life, eh?"

He smiled and patted me on the back, and I wanted to kill him. At the same time, I remembered the guy lying facedown on the road in the model-train town.

That was when it hit me.

All my life, I'd never once thought about my future, or how my life would end. But now, it struck me that if I just traveled along the track that stretched out in front of me, the chances of me slipping up and ending up facedown on the road were extremely high. Debt, pachinko, habitual violence, heavy consumption of alcohol and cigarettes, sitting in a musty room with the TV blaring all day every day—these were the ingredients that made up the lives of the adults living in the projects. It seemed weird to me now that I'd never thought about them in conjunction with my own future—never tried them on for size.

"There's no way I'm going to let that happen." My voice was so loud it took even me by surprise.

Taoka burst out laughing.

"Right, then. Well, you better get studying!"

The following day, Taoka handed me a big sheaf of papers.

"We'll start by reviewing the middle-school stuff. Each of these is designed to take you about ten minutes, so you can do one per break."

On the top sheet, Taoka had written in big letters MASTERPLAN TO INCREASE RYOTA'S TEST SCORES BY 35 POINTS. I turned over the cover to the English section, and the exercises began with revision of the alphabet.

"Write out the uppercase and lowercase letters," read the first question. I got the feeling I was being taken for a total blockhead, but I worked through the sheets nonetheless during my breaks. I'd put the ones I completed in Taoka's locker, and he'd return them to my locker, marked, the following day.

For about a month, I reviewed the math and English that made up the curriculum for the final year of middle school. When I got everything right, Taoka would write, "You're a genius!" and draw me a *hanamaru*, the big flowery circle that signified full marks. I knew it was ridiculous, not least since these were middle-school questions and I was a high-schooler, but the truth was I'd never been praised by a teacher before and I couldn't help feeling just a little bit pleased. I didn't want to admit it, of course, even to myself. I still found it weird that I'd suddenly turned into this much of a try-hard at this late stage.

I'd always thought of myself as naturally pretty dumb and had loathed any kind of schoolwork. I was convinced that my bad grades were all a result of my lack of effort. But once Taoka started tutoring me, I began to think that maybe it wasn't entirely my own fault that I'd done so badly. However many times I made the same mistakes or asked stupid questions, Taoka never once pulled a face. Instead of giving up on me, he kept explaining the same things until I understood. When I made a mistake, he'd write out explanations in red ballpoint pen—often so long they were practically spilling off the page.

Taoka understood what it was I didn't get, why I didn't get it, and why I tripped up on particular questions. It was as if he could see straight inside my head. Until he started tutoring me, the stuff I'd learned in middle school was scattered at random throughout my brain, but Taoka went sifting through all that stuff, throwing away the parts I didn't need and organizing the rest by sorting it into levels of importance. As I worked through the printouts he made for me, the middle-school stuff gradually started to gather itself into solid lumps inside my head. I could feel myself making definite progress. It felt a little like stacking up a lot of solid, weighty bricks, one on top of another.

There was a girl named Akutsu working in the store who also happened to live in the same complex and go to the same school as I did. At break times, she would watch in silence as I worked through Taoka's printouts. She'd sit there glancing up from her phone, which had a whole bunch of novelty toys and stuff hanging from it, and pulling a face as if she found the whole thing totally repulsive.

Taoka helped me prepare for my first end-of-term test in high school. This time it wasn't just English and math he was coaching me with, but also Japanese, and world history, and health and physical education, and just about everything else. For English and math, he produced special end-of-term-test printouts, and for stuff like history and biology he looked over what the test was covering and printed out summaries for me that he told me to memorize. All I had to do was remember the information that was on there, and I'd be okay.

Our homeroom teacher at school was a young woman straight out of college. Everyone called her Notchy. When the time came to hand out the results slips, she looked at me with a face sparkling with excitement and said, "You came fourth in the year!"

Takumi tore my results slip out of my hand, then looked at me and mumbled, "What the hell's with you?"

During vacation, having no family trips planned or summer school to go to, I did my paper route in the morning, worked as a lifeguard at the pool during the day, and went to the convenience store in the evening. On breaks, I continued to work through the sheets. The whole studying like crazy thing had started as just a way to fill time, but at some point I'd really gotten into it.

At the end of vacation, Taoka handed me a few sheets of paper, saying, "This is a review of what we've done up till now. Have a go at it at home. You shouldn't be spending longer than an hour on it."

The following day, after passing an eye over my efforts, Taoka pinned me with a particularly serious look, and said, "You really ought to think about going to college, you know."

"I don't have the money."

"Shit, man, I'm telling you. Don't be so defeatist. There's lots of ways around it—scholarships, recommendation programs, super-cheap colleges, all that kind of stuff. I can take you through everything you need to know. With these kinds of grades, it'd be a waste for you not to go just because you can't afford it."

"But aren't there lots of people who can't get jobs even after going to college?"

"Listen to me, okay? As you are right now, you're totally unprotected. You don't have rich parents, or special talents, or anything else to fall back on. Don't you think it makes sense to equip yourself with at least one item to up your game? Okay, sure, a degree isn't totally bulletproof, but even idiots like Nakamura are still considered useful in the eyes of the world so long as they've managed to make it into a decent college. . . . In the absence of pressing evidence to the contrary."

Taoka was raising his voice slightly.

"But you went to a good college, didn't you? So why are you here, working in a convenience store?" I shot him my best know-it-all face.

Taoka looked at me, unflinching. "Yeah. In my case, they've got pressing evidence."

Akutsu, who was sitting on the sofa, lifted her head from her phone screen and looked from me to Taoka in turn.

"I'll tell you about colleges another day, okay?" He looked at his watch. "Hey, you guys are done for the day already. Take care getting home, you hear?"

Both Akutsu and I clocked off at ten. With hardly a street-light to call its own, the road back to the projects was very dark, so Taoka had made me promise to always go home with Akutsu. I pedaled along, my eyes on Akutsu's back as she rode her bike up ahead of me. All that talk of colleges had left me feeling a little wired.

Inside the grounds, the noise from all the TVs was loud enough to drown out the chirping of the crickets. The block Akutsu lived in was a ways away from mine, and because it wasn't at all unusual for men to pop up beside the unlit bike racks and grope young girls, I always took the long way around so I could see Akutsu back to the block she lived in. Since we'd entered the projects, Akutsu had been pushing her bike in silence, but now she turned back to look at me and said, "Why are you grinning like that, Goldie?"

Now that I was in high school, Akutsu was the only one who still called me Goldie.

"I'm not."

"Don't bullshit me. You're all pumped up because Taoka said you should go to college, right?"

"No!"

"You should watch out for him."

I got a whiff of the sickly smell of the lollipop Akutsu was sucking on.

"Why?"

"Why? Because he's a faggot, that's why."

I'd heard the same thing said about Taoka by a few different members of the shop staff. Taoka didn't really talk much about his private life, so the people at the store took it upon themselves to dream up exotic scenarios and exchange nasty rumors about him. Several times I'd heard people saying he and the manager were secretly a couple. Despite all the part-timers bombarding him with questions, the only things that had emerged as definite were the fact that Taoka didn't have a girlfriend or wife and that he lived alone in an apartment building close by.

One time, a college student working at the store developed a crush on Taoka and followed him home on the sly. After seeing where his building was, she ran back to the store in a state of extreme excitement to share her findings with her colleagues.

"It's those luxury ones by the station! You know, the ones they always have flyers for in the newspapers! My mom was saying they're not renting them out, they're for sale only! Which means that all the people living there own their apartments. They're all, like, huge, like, a hundred square meters!

And there's a reception desk with a concierge! What do you think the story is with him?"

A hundred square meters meant nothing to me, and nor did the word "concierge," which I couldn't even pronounce. In fact most of what she said went right over my head, but I understood enough to grasp that Taoka lived in a fancy apartment complex very unlike the projects I called home.

"You shouldn't go saying that kind of stuff about him. You've no evidence, right?"

"I've seen you making that kind of face before, back in elementary school and stuff."

Akutsu shot me a look that seemed to say words weren't enough to express how much of a loser I was, then stuck her lollipop back in her mouth. Crunching away with her front teeth, she looked up at me mockingly. "You're just excited cause you think you've found yourself a new dad."

From an apartment somewhere, we heard a man shouting and a kid wailing.

"But you're never gonna get a new dad. Do you remember, Goldie, after it all went to crap? How you used to slap me around the head on like a daily basis?"

"I'm sorry."

In fact, I'd wiped all of that stuff out of my mind entirely, and this sudden reminder from Akutsu knocked me for a loop. What a little shit I'd been.

"So I'm just saying, don't get your hopes up too far, 'kay? I'm not having you taking it out on me when it all goes wrong."

With that, Akutsu fastened her bike to the utility pole and went sprinting up the narrow staircase, the hood of her parka swinging from side to side.

For a while there'd been talk of my mom remarrying, and when it all fell through I'd been really cut up about it. That was when I'd started hitting Akutsu. It wasn't long after that her family had vanished from the projects without warning, only to return just before the entrance exams for high school.

Right before she'd moved, Akutsu had gone around telling people: "My dad's taking over the company! He's gonna be the CEO!"

I didn't have it in me to laugh at her. Back in elementary school, both Akutsu and I were still the kind of stupid, naïve children who believed everything their parents told them.

Back home, I found my mom sitting at the kitchen table, looking wiped out and eating rice steeped in green tea. She looked like she'd lost more weight in the two weeks since I'd last seen her.

"Where's Gran?"

"Asleep already. Oh, I finished off the rice from the cooker."

My mom pushed her bowl away and lit a cigarette.

"Hey, you know that money I left on the table? I need it back, just for a while. I'll bring it back soon."

I said nothing. I just went to my room, took the envelope out of the cookie tin on the top of my bookshelf and handed it to my mom. She checked the money inside then stuck it into her wallet, which was covered in tiny beads. Since I'd started high school, my mom had been living with her boyfriend in his apartment by the river. She rarely came back to the projects. Occasionally, like today, she'd pop in without any notice to check on how I was doing.

"You know, you can come and live in his apartment with me if you want," my mom had offered back when she'd moved out.

"And what will we do about Gran?"

"Oh, we'll just have to let her handle with things. It's not my duty to look after her, you know. We'll leave her to it, and then hopefully . . ."

My gran was my dad's mother, so my mom didn't feel the obligation of any blood ties. For me, though, she wasn't only a blood relation but also the person who'd taken care of me and brought me up in place of my mom. There was no denying that she was pretty senile these days, but living with her still seemed way better than the prospect of living with my mom and her boyfriend, who I'd never even seen, let alone had a conversation with. My mom had left back in May, just before the national holidays. To be totally honest, it was kind of a relief to have her gone.

On a whim, I asked, "Mom, you know my bank account with my present money and stuff? Where's the bankbook for it?"

The account contained the very small sum left to me when my dad died, and the money my gran would give me every New Year. Before I'd entered high school and started working part-time jobs, it had been the entirety of my savings. My mom rubbed her eyelids sleepily. The room was silent. The smoke from the cigarette she was holding motionless between her fingers stung my eyes.

"I'll give it to you when you're twenty. I haven't touched it since you were a kid, so it's exactly as it was." Saying that, she yawned. "It's late, so I'm gonna stay over, okay? I'm on the early shift at the factory tomorrow. It's quicker to get there from here."

Leaving her bowl and chopsticks on the table, my mom went into the room where I usually slept. Inside the bowl was a bunch of twisted cigarette butts.

Now and again, I found myself checking with my mom about that account. I knew deep down that my savings didn't exist anymore, but seeing her look all nervous like that somehow made me feel a little better. My stomach let out a long, low rumble. Bearing the hunger as best I could, I set about rinsing the rice so it would be ready for tomorrow morning.

When school started again after summer, I'd heard rumors about what Takumi had been getting up to. At the start of the fall term, girls hanging around in the corridors or in the corners of the classroom would sometimes shoot me these looks as if they wanted to say something to me, but, when our eyes met, they'd quickly look away. I heard them whispering words like *cosplay* and *online* and *amateur porn*, but it never crossed my mind that any of this was in relation to Takumi. He'd suddenly stopped turning up to work at the pool midway through summer vacation, and when school began he was often absent. Takumi was weirdly popular with the girls, and a few of them came up to ask me if it were true that Takumi was going to quit school.

Shortly after the midterm tests, I arrived at school early after my paper route to find the PE teacher standing in the corridor in his tracksuit, frantically ripping down pieces of paper stuck to the walls.

"Good morning, sir," I said.

The PE teacher looked at me and said quietly, "Morning."

He scrunched the papers in his hand into a tight ball and went off in the direction of the staffroom.

It was still before eight, and I was the first one to get into the classroom. It was stuffy, so I opened the windows to let some fresh air in. My plan was to get the math worksheet Taoka had given me out of the way before the first lesson began. Lifting the lid of my desk to put in my textbooks, I noticed a folded square of paper and, when I opened it, I saw a number of pictures of some guy dressed in some kind of funky costume. He was wearing a purple button-down jacket like a lab coat, pulling various poses, and staring straight-faced right into the camera. It took me a good few seconds to realize that the guy was Takumi. In the biggest photos, you could see the white thighs of a girl in a sailor uniform in the frame, standing right in front of him. In a flash, I understood what all those mentions of *cosplay* and *amateur porn* had been about.

"You fucking idiot . . ." I found myself saying out loud. For some reason I was grinning. "You absolute fucking idiot!"

The same photocopied sheet of photos had been put into all the desks in our homeroom, and that day the entire school was in uproar. It seemed like absolutely everyone was walking around clutching a copy and talking about Takumi. Some kids took pictures of the photos with their phones and started sending them to heaven knows who.

At break time, people from other classes and higher grades came to our classroom, wanting to see the photos, and then chaos really broke loose. One girl got hysterical, shouting, "It's disgusting!" and tearing up the printout into little shreds. Nana was going around with a garbage bag in her hand, collecting the copies in the corridor or in the trash and saying to people, "In here! Put them in here please! The teacher said so!"

When I caught her eye in the corridor, she raised her eyebrows into a troubled expression, as if she was close to tears.

"I'm sorry to ask you this, Ryota, but would you give this to Takumi?" our homeroom teacher Notchy asked me once lessons were over. Sitting on her chair in the break room, twirling her dyed brown hair around her index finger, she handed me an envelope.

"Tell him it's about the payments for the third-year trip, will you? And also . . ."

Notchy was on the chubby side, and when she shifted her weight the chair let out a nasty squeak.

"I'm really sorry to have to ask this of you, but . . . Will you see how he's doing? I mean, he's barely come into school at all this term, and then there's all this stuff today. I've been thinking I should go myself, soon. But, I mean, I know you two are pals. I was thinking I'd get you to scope out the situation first."

She looked up at me with an almost guilty expression.

"Okay, I'll go before work this evening."

Notchy looked a little relieved and grasped my arm with both hands.

"That would be great, I'm really sorry." Then she started lavishing me with praise for my grades shooting up so dramatically. Finally, she reached into the pocket of the white lab coat she was wearing. "Here, a little reward," she said, handing me a throat lozenge.

I was sucking on that overly mentholated lozenge as I pushed my bike toward the school gates when a couple of shifty-looking middle-aged men who clearly had nothing to do with the school called out to me.

"Hey! What year are you in? Do you know Takumi Saito in freshman year?" A narrow black voice recorder was thrust toward my mouth. One of the men, a tall guy in a striped shirt, showed me a copy of the piece of paper with Takumi's cosplay photos that had been in everyone's desks. I snatched it away, scrunched it into a ball, and threw it down on the path.

"Hey, what are you doing?" The man grabbed my arm angrily. I turned back toward the staffroom and called out as loud as I could, "Hey, teachers!"

Notchy stuck her head out of the window, and not long later she was running toward the gate along with a few other teachers.

"Shit!" the men said as they jumped into their car.

I was getting on my bike when two girls in the kind of maid uniforms I'd seen people wearing on TV came up to me.

"Hey, Lord Muramasa goes to this school, right?" The girls spoke in high-pitched, lispy voices like they came straight out of an anime. One of them was also clutching a piece of paper, this time with a single picture of Takumi in cosplay blown up very large. I tore the paper out of her hands, ripped it in half, and threw it on the path. "Hey! What are you doing to Lord Muramasa?"

I got on my bike and pedaled away, the sound of the girl screaming hysterically following after me.

What the hell was going on? And who was Lord Muramasa? The only thing that seemed beyond doubt was that whatever was going on, Takumi was slap-bang in the center of it.

"I'm coming in," I said as I opened the door to Takumi's room, which was even messier than it had been when I'd come with Nana during summer vacation. What with the manga, CDs, computer games, and convenience store bags full of what looked like trash strewn across the floor, there was now no room to step at all. As I stood there, a random pile of manga I must have caught with the door cascaded to the floor. The duvet on the bed had a lump in it, which I knew had to contain Takumi, but I couldn't get to it for all the stuff.

"Notchy told me to give this to you. And here are your handouts."

I put the envelope and a bunch of papers on his desk. It was piled with books that looked as if they'd never been opened. On the corner were a few bowls and plates wrapped in plastic. Most likely today's lunch. There was a heaped bowl of rice, one of miso soup, and a main dish of potato croquettes with a garnish of shredded cabbage and tomato. My stomach rumbled.

"Have you given up coming to school or what?"

No reply.

"It was crazy today. Someone handed out all these photos of you."

Still no reply.

"There were these weird journalist people and girls in maid costumes and stuff."

The lump in the duvet moved a little, and I got a glimpse of Takumi's face. His already pale skin seemed to have got even whiter, so it was practically see-through. Was that what happened to you when you didn't leave the house? His hair had grown down to his shoulders, and there was stubble around his jaw. He was fast asleep. I could hear him snoring softly. Looking down at my feet, I saw the opened case of a brand-new game that had just come out. The controller lying under his bed was connected to the TV at the corner of the desk, whose screen said GAME OVER. November sunlight was streaming through the window, shining on Takumi as he slept there like a baby and all the dust-covered objects filling the room around him.

"Lord Muramasaaaaa!" I whispered.

No reply. I picked up a manga and threw it at the lump in the futon. The lump in the bed stretched and let out a long, sleepy groan, then curled up again. Suddenly, it struck me how ridiculous all this was, and I walked out. On the way downstairs, I heard voices from the big tatami room that joined with the kitchen. Peering through the glass door, I saw Mrs. Saito explaining something to a group of women with huge pregnant bellies. From time to time, as she was speaking, Mrs. Saito would pound her back with her right fist, as if she was in pain.

I was making my way toward the front door when I heard a scuttling sound from the direction of the kitchen sink, as if there was a crayfish or something moving inside there, and then a jet of water came spurting out and landed with a splash on the floor. Alarmed, I went to peer into the sink, and saw that the some of the clams left to soak there in a silver bowl had opened their shells and extended their siphons, waving them around in the water as if they were looking for something. I reached out a finger to touch one of the clam's siphons, and it let out another spurt of water as if in protest. I gently flicked the edge of the bowl with my finger, and the clams hurriedly drew their siphons back inside their shells. There was just one whose siphon was still dangling out. I picked up the solitary clam and squeezed its shell tight shut between my fingers. There was a little sucking noise, and after a while, the siphon stopped moving, as if all its power had drained away. I stared down at the clam now resting on my palm then put it back into the water. Feeling strangely satisfied, I put on my sneakers and left Takumi's house.

That evening, the temperature dropped suddenly, and it was freezing cold. Akutsu and I had finished work and were bicycling back home. The road leading up to the tunnel that we had to pass through to get to the project snaked this way and that, and sometimes taxis and trucks looking for a shortcut back into town would come racing down those bends. That night, a truck appeared out of nowhere, hurtling at breakneck speed right toward where Akutsu was pedaling in the middle of the road, standing up in order to make it up the steep hill. The driver slammed his fist on the horn. I was convinced he was going to ram right into her, but Akutsu immediately cut her handlebar hard and swerved to the left, losing balance and toppling to the ground along with her bike. The truck went thundering past without even so much as slowing down, passing right beside her head. I stopped my bike by the side of the road and ran up to her.

"Are you okay?"

"Stupid fucking truck!" Akutsu said, getting to her feet and brushing herself off. She'd scraped her elbows but seemed to have avoided any serious injuries. The nylon tote bag that had been stuffed inside her front basket now lay in the middle of the road, and its contents—her cell phone, a handkerchief, a bag of candies, a small fabric pouch, and a clear plastic folder with a bunch of paper inside—were strewn across the road. Thinking to help her collect her things, I leaned over to pick up one of the pieces of paper, but Akutsu dashed over and snatched it right out of my hand.

What the hell? I thought. Looking down in the light of the dim streetlamp at the papers scattered across the road, I realized what they were. It was the photos, the cosplay photos of Takumi that had been in our homeroom desks.

Crouched down on the road, Akutsu gathered up the papers one by one. Her shoulder-length hair, which had come undone, was hanging over her face. The cold breeze came in through the thin fabric of my coat and seemed to chill me to the very core. Rubbing my hands together to warm them, I leaned against the guardrail and looked down at the town. I could make out traffic lights, streetlights, houselights, and the headlights of moving cars. It looked like a different world from the place I was in right now. I thought of Takumi curled up in his house by the river and Taoka living in his fancy apartment by the station. When I thought about how far away they were from me, standing here with the cold night wind blowing around me, I felt a weird prickling feeling in my chest. I wanted to be in a warm room that didn't let the draft in or else have someone prepare me three meals a day or something. I wasn't really bothered about the details of the situation—I just wanted to feel protected by something. Anything.

I turned around to see the mouth of the tunnel hanging wide open. The sight of it with its orange lights inside made the hurting in my chest even worse. Akutsu put the stack of papers she'd collected back inside the transparent folder. Under the glow of the streetlight, I could see she'd scraped her face just above her lip, and it was bleeding a bit.

"Give me half of those," I said, reaching out a hand.

She looked me and smiled, then reached up her tongue and licked at the blood on her lip.

"I don't have a bike."

It was the next morning. I'd finished with my paper route and was waiting for Akutsu by the swamp when she came up from behind me and spoke quietly. Though it was really the last thing I wanted to be doing, I let her get on the back of my bike and headed for school, praying silently that no one would see us riding together.

175

There was still almost an hour before lessons started, and though the school gates were open already, there was hardly anyone around. Thinking we'd be too easily noticed going in through the main gates, we went around to the back and entered by the door near the gym, taking care not to be seen by the brass band club who were in the middle of their early-morning practice.

I hurried in the direction of the freshman-year classrooms with the bunch of papers Akutsu handed me, while she ran up the stairs to the third floor where the sophomore-year classrooms were. Diving inside the neighboring homeroom, I went around putting the sheets with Takumi's photos on inside each of the forty or so desks. It was pretty similar to my paper route. I could hear the muffled sounds of the brass band in the distance. The ticking of the clock above the blackboard seemed excessively loud. My face was hot, and my mouth got so dry I could feel my tongue sticking to the roof. When I was about halfway through, I thought I heard someone coming down the hall. As the sound of shoes squeaking on the linoleum got louder, the beating in my chest grew faster and faster. Hugging the papers to my chest, I crouched down and hid underneath one of the desks. I heard the door slide open and the footsteps draw closer. I screwed my body up as small as I possibly could and shut my eyes tight.

"I'm gonna do the ground-floor lockers next," said Akutsu's voice from above. I opened my eyes and saw her knee-high socks just inches away. When I peered up, I saw she was smiling and rolling her eyes.

"Once a wimp, always a wimp! Isn't that right, Goldie?"

I finished distributing the sheets Akutsu had given me and was making my way back to my homeroom when I heard someone saying, "You're in early!"

I looked around to see Notchy standing there in her lab coat.

"Uh, yeah! I thought I'd come in and get some work done," I said hesitantly.

"Listen, if you find any more of those things of Takumi's, do me a favor and bring them to me, will you? Seems like there's someone intent on leaving them all over the place. Heaven knows why."

I nodded and promised to do that, feeling the sweat run down my back. Glancing ahead, I saw Akutsu heading toward us down the hallway carrying a stack of papers.

"I'm, I'm feeling really hungry! I might go and buy something from the shop," I said in an excessively loud voice, so as to be sure Akutsu would hear. I was so pained by my appalling attempt at acting I felt ready to cry. Akutsu looked at me and nodded, then turned and disappeared into the girls' bathrooms.

Notchy held out a plastic bag from the convenience store containing a bun filled with sweet red bean paste and a carton of coffee-flavored milk.

"Here, have this. Please. I know you have a part-time job and everything. You shouldn't push yourself too hard." Saying that, she went down the stairs toward the staffroom. I felt the energy suddenly drain from me, and I sank down to the floor, watching her disappear from sight.

Later, on the way home from work that night, it was Akutsu's back I was staring at as she walked along in front of me, engrossed in something on her phone. As I watched her, I thought about when we were back in elementary school. As kids from the worst projects in town, Akutsu and I didn't have even an inkling that shoplifting was a bad thing to do. We learned how to do it from older kids, and we passed the knowledge down to the younger ones.

In the shop by the school that sold cheap candy, Akutsu and I had stood and waited until the shop lady was distracted, then started dropping little paper-wrapped chocolates into our pockets, one by one. It wasn't long before our pockets were full to bursting. The very moment the chocolates came spilling out onto the floor, I felt the lady's hand grip my arm. She escorted Akutsu and me into the back room, where she made us sit up straight on our heels while she lectured us.

When I saw the huge Buddhist altar behind her, crammed full of memorial tablets, I suddenly felt scared. I didn't think I'd done anything wrong, but big round tears came pouring from my eyes and I apologized immediately. Akutsu said nothing.

What bad little children needed to set them right, the shop lady informed us as she opened a drawer in her wooden tea cabinet, was moxibustion. She brought out a moxa set and deftly formed the dried mugwort into a cone, which she placed on the back of Akutsu's hand. Then she took out a match and lit the tip of the cone. Something about the combination of its smell, which caught at the back of my throat, the plume of smoke rising up toward the ceiling, and the sight of the red flame gradually creeping closer toward Akutsu's skin sent me into a total panic.

"We're sorry, we're sorry!" I shouted, but the lady didn't say a thing. It looked to me like the dark, wrinkled hand gripping Akutsu's tiny arm could break it with a single flick of the wrist. Akutsu kept her eyes open, staring at the red bead of flame. Even when it was almost touching her skin, she didn't shut her eyes. There was a smell like burning meat, and Akutsu twisted her arm and the rest of her body. Her eyes filled with tears but, unlike me, she didn't wail or cry out. Just then, we heard a customer calling from the shop. The moment the shop lady got up, I grabbed Akutsu's hand, and we ran for it, dashing past the shop lady and running outside.

I remember we walked back to the projects in total silence. When we got to the swamp, Akutsu looked at me and said, "Hold out your hand."

She pulled out three small chocolates from her pocket and placed them on top of my palm. I looked down at them, three chocolates in different flavors sitting there.

"Let me have the strawberry one," she said, and then unwrapped it and popped it into her mouth. "See ya."

Akutsu walked off toward her apartment block. When I looked at her hand clutching the strap of her backpack, I saw not only the red burn mark left by the moxa from before but other round brown scars like stains on her hand that I'd never noticed.

I wondered, now, if the marks were still there. Still pushing my bike, I charged forward until I was walking alongside her and tried to look at her hand as she fiddled with her phone, but it was too dark to say for sure if there were any scars.

"I'm done with it," I told her as we walked along.

Akutsu looked up from her phone at me.

"Fucking wimp," she spat.

"You're like best friends with Nana, and she's going out with him. Why would you want to do something like that? I don't get it."

Akutsu returned her eyes to her phone, typing something at breakneck speed.

"Do you have a thing for him or what?"

"You did it, too, remember!" she said, glaring up at me once more. "And you're supposed to be Takumi's friend! You're just as bad as I am. I don't see what right you have to go lecturing me! I think you're jealous of Takumi, and that's why you did it. I know Takumi's mom is a single mom and shit, but his situation is still a lot more cushy than yours."

I didn't know how to reply. Just then Akutsu broke into a run down the road toward the station, the opposite direction from the projects.

"Hey! Where are you going?" I called after her, but she ignored me and crossed the street. I turned and went after her.

"Leave me alone!" she yelled, without turning to look at me.

"You haven't even got your bike. You know it's dangerous to walk back home alone."

"You sound like Taoka," Akutsu said, turning off into an apartment building by the road. From her bag, she took out a bunch of the same papers she'd had at school today and with a grim look, began wedging them into the thin slots of the mailboxes. I left my bike standing in the road and went up beside her.

"Give me half."

Akutsu glared at me.

"Look, I'm used to doing this from my paper route. Give me some. With a technique like that, it'll take you all night."

I wrested some papers from Akutsu and began to put them inside the mailboxes at twice the speed she had been doing it. We did a few blocks of apartments near the station, until almost all of the pictures of Takumi in cosplay were gone. Outside the entrance of our last block, we sank down onto the sidewalk, utterly exhausted. There was a sudden honk very close to us, and we both looked up startled.

A black minivan making its way down the road stopped beside us, and the window rolled down slowly.

"What the hell are you doing?" Taoka said, sticking his head out the window. We stood up and went over to his car.

"Oh, we were working. Giving out flyers." My breath came out white. It struck me that I was telling a lot of lies today.

Taoka stared at us, then said, "Jump in. I'll give you a ride home."

As I was wondering how to reply, Taoka said, "C'mon, don't be shy," and jumped out to open the back door. His car had the sickly sweet smell of air freshener, and the back seats were littered with the kind of small soft toys you got in those claw crane machines in arcades.

"Gross! No way!" Akutsu said and ran off.

"Sorry. I've got my bike over there, so don't worry about it."

I bowed my head repeatedly at Taoka, then followed Akutsu, secretly feeling grateful for how she'd managed the situation.

From somewhere behind us, I heard Taoka yelling, "Just don't catch a cold, okay?"

That Sunday, both Akutsu and I worked in the convenience store from morning till evening, and when we came out, we heard the sound of a car horn. The window was wound down, and Taoka stuck his head out.

"Get in. I'll buy you dinner."

Akutsu and I looked at each other.

"There's something I want to talk to you about. It won't take that long, and I'll drive you home after."

Before she had the chance to run away, I took hold of Akutsu's arm. She tried with all her strength to wrench it back.

"I promise it won't be for long. Come on."

Taoka was smiling, but there was a hint of anger in his voice. With his eyes fixed on us like that, every passing second felt more and more unbearable. Unable to stand it any longer, I said, "My gran's waiting for me, so it'll have to be just an hour."

Still holding Akutsu's arm, I practically shoved her into the back seat and hopped in next to her. No sooner had I put my butt on the seat than Akutsu stamped down on my foot as hard as she could. Taoka drove out of the parking lot, whistling.

"What do you want to eat? What do you guys like?"

Akutsu said nothing so I replied, "Oh, anything. Anything's fine with me."

"That's the kind of line girls hate, y'know," Taoka laughed.

Akutsu glared at the back of Taoka's head in the seat in front of her. I looked at his face in profile from where I was sitting, behind him and to the side. He had a bunch of piercings in his left ear. I knew that piercings on one side or another meant you were gay, but I couldn't remember which side it was. Unlike the last time, I couldn't see a single stuffed toy. My heel brushed against something under the seat, and when I looked down I saw a slightly grubby stuffed Pikachu lying there. I picked it up and placed it on the seat next to me.

There was a fair amount of traffic on the road. I looked across at the car that had stopped next to us and saw two little boys horsing around in the back. Both of them were holding big paper cups of popcorn. When their mother in the front seat turned around and scolded them, they sat still for a while, but soon enough they were back to playing around like a pair of kittens. The older-looking boy poked and shoved the younger one so much that he spilled his popcorn all over the seat, at which the mother reached around and slapped the older boy's knee. I couldn't hear what they were saying, but I felt as though I could practically hear the mom shouting and the child crying.

Each time I saw a motel sign, I'd start to get a little jittery. I noticed that Akutsu's hands were gripped into tight fists where she'd rested them on top of her thighs. Finally, though, the car came to a stop in front of a steak restaurant.

Taoka told us we could order anything we liked, but Akutsu and I found it impossible to decide, so in the end he ordered three of the same thing. Soon enough, three steaming, sizzling steaks landed on the table in front of us. My mouth welled up with saliva. I sawed off a big piece, wondering how long it had been since I'd eaten a hunk of meat like this one. And man, did it taste good. The onion sauce and the rice alone would have made a fine dinner. I ate with ferocious speed, taking alternating mouthfuls of rice and meat.

"You don't have to eat that fast, you know. It's not going anywhere. If it's not enough, you can order more. Eat as much as you can." Taoka was smiling.

Akutsu gave me a disdainful look. She hadn't even picked up her knife and fork yet.

"What are you playing at?" Akutsu, who'd been silent all this time, finally said to Taoka. "I know you're planning something funny. You're a perv, everyone knows that. I've heard all kinds of rumors."

His knife and fork in hand, Taoka looked Akutsu in the eye.

"You really go straight for the jugular, don't you?" He took a sip of water from his cup. A kid of about three ran past our table screeching. "I have absolutely no plans to do anything to you or Ryota, today or any other day. You don't need to worry about that. I mean it. So look. Why don't we eat first, and then let's talk."

Akutsu carried on glaring, but then seeming to realize that Taoka wasn't going to discuss anything until he'd finished his dinner, she took her knife and fork in her hand and tucked into the steak. None of us said another thing until the meal was over. When we were done, Taoka ordered coffee for him and ice cream for me and Akutsu.

"I'm thinking about starting up a cram school near the station next year." Taoka looked at Akutsu and me in turn as he poured a generous amount of milk into his coffee.

"You mean, give up working at the store?" I asked.

Taoka nodded and took a sip of his coffee.

"Look. There isn't really a good way of saying this, but at the cram school I was working at, the kids were mostly from families whose parents were prepared to spend any amount of money to get them into a good university. And I started to get really grossed out by the whole thing. Like I was helping the ones who came into the world with a natural advantage anyway. I started to feel I wanted to help improve the grades of kids not from those kinds of homes. You know, charging as little as possible."

"For poor kids like us, you mean?" Akutsu said, sticking her spoon into her mouth.

"Well, I prefer the expression 'children who have extremely limited time and opportunities to study,' but yes, without bells on, I guess that's what I mean."

"I want another ice cream," Akutsu said.

"Of course. Ryota?"

I stayed silent and shook my head.

"And a cream soda."

"Sure thing." Taoka was smiling as he called the waitress over.

"Seeing Ryota studying so hard, and his grades going up like that . . . Well, I guess it gave me some confidence. You found my materials easy to understand, right?"

"Yes."

"I know this sounds bad, but the truth is I really want to know more about guys like you, who go on to high school without ever really getting your heads around middle-school stuff. The kinds of mistakes you make, the kinds of things you trip up on."

The waitress refilled Taoka's coffee.

"So the reason I brought you here today is to make you an offer. I'd like for you guys to read through the printouts and materials I put together, answer the questions, and then tell me what parts you found hard, or where you wanted more of an explanation and so on. I'd start giving Akutsu printouts like I did to Ryota, and checking where she slips up, seeing what kinds of explanations work best, and so on. If we say for every sheet . . . No, wait. I'll give you the equivalent of one hour's wage at the store for every two printouts you complete. How's that?"

Both Akutsu and I had trouble grasping what Taoka was saying. We both just stared at him, our mouths hanging open slightly.

"One hour's wage for every two sheets?" Akutsu said, without removing her straw from her mouth.

"Yes. I'm not just talking about reading through and answering the questions, though. You've got to give me lots of suggestions about things I could change, things that could be better."

"In other words, you're gonna pay us for doing schoolwork?"

"I don't think it's a bad deal. When I open the cram school in spring next year, I'd like for you guys to help out there, too. I figure it'll be better than working long hours in a convenience store, at least. Also, and I know this is a big if, but if you guys decide you want to go to college, then I'll help you out until you get in." Having reached the end of his piece, Taoka took a big gulp of water from his glass.

"College . . ." Akutsu whispered.

"Yup. If I start tutoring you and you begin preparing now, you've still got enough time. You can keep on earning money while you study, too."

The same waitress from before came up to the table and refilled everyone's glasses with water.

"So what you're saying is, you can't get your head around the way dumbasses like us think, so you're paying us to tell you. That's it, right?" Akutsu continued. "You know, maybe I really am dumb, 'cause I don't even know if it's a good deal or not. Or if I can do all the stuff you want me to do."

"Of course, that makes sense. I think it's best if you start off gradually and see how it goes. At first, I just want you to reduce your working time at the store by an hour or so, and do two sheets at home instead, so that it's not too much of a burden."

I was convinced there was no way Akutsu, who loathed schoolwork with a passion, would take Taoka up on an offer like that, so I was genuinely surprised when she said, "Okay, fine. So long as it's only a little, then sure."

It hadn't been long ago that she'd been warning me not to get my hopes up.

"What about you, Ryota?"

"Is it okay to think about it?"

As Akutsu let her guard down, I was becoming more cautious. Taoka was obviously making an attempt to get closer to us, and I didn't know if it was okay to trust him.

"Sure," Taoka said, and looked at his watch. "Do you mind if we stop into one more place after this?"

We left the restaurant, and Taoka pulled up into the parking lot of the new shopping mall. He strolled ahead of us whistling "Jingle Bells" and walked in through the door of a toy store. Inside, he passed me and Akutsu an enormous cart that looked like it could have fit ten toddlers inside.

"My brother's baby's due around Christmas, so I want you guys to choose a present. And if there's anything you want for yourselves, just put it in the cart. Think of it as a way of saying thanks for you giving up your time today."

Akutsu squealed in delight and ran off to the back of the store. I walked along behind her, pushing the cart. The glaring neon lights of the store made me blink. After no time, Akutsu came up and threw two baby toys in boxes into the cart, then ran off back down the aisle toward the back of the store.

"Jeez, did she even look at them?" Taoka said as he examined the boxes with a smile.

The shelves were heaving with the kinds of toys I would have died for when I was in elementary school—transformer belts, super-alloy robots, huge jigsaw puzzles. I'd wanted all that stuff so badly when I was a kid, and I still wanted it now, even though I was fifteen.

"Whoa, an N-Gauge. I remember these!" Taoka stopped in front of the model railway section. "My dad was really into model railways. He was always so uptight about them, though. We'd get into trouble if we laid so much as a finger on his trains. Wouldn't you like one of these, Ryota?"

"Is this a kind of charity service or something?"

"What?" The N-Gauge box still in his hands, Taoka darted a look at me.

"Are you like a volunteer or something? Sasaki at the convenience store said your parents run the huge hospital across the mountain. And you live by yourself in that great big apartment. I mean, you don't really need to work in the convenience store, right? You just do it because you feel like it. Like today.

You take me and Akutsu out and are all nice to us, feeding us and buying us stuff, just because the urge takes you. I was really grateful when you tutored me and stuff, but I don't feel very comfortable about this. I feel like whatever you do for us I'm going to have to pay back in some way."

Taoka had seemed in such a good mood, but now the smile vanished clean from his face. He put the model train inside the cart, then said, "My parents do run the hospital, that's true. But I've had to break into my savings to start the cram school and cover the down payment on the apartment. The rest is a mortgage that'll take me decades to pay off. Not that that really matters anyway."

Suddenly, Akutsu was standing beside me. She was holding a small stuffed rabbit and a few sheets of shiny stickers.

"Is that it? You don't have to hold back, you know."

As we moved toward the cash register, Taoka reached out to grab bags of gummies and cookies off the shelves and flung them into the shopping cart. Seeing how Akutsu's face was slightly flushed with excitement, I found myself at a loss for words and walked all the way back to Taoka's car without saying a thing.

On the way home, the roads were more congested than before. Akutsu opened up a bag of Haribo, and the smell of the artificial flavors filled the car.

"Do you want some?" Akutsu held out the bag, but Taoka and I both shook our heads. After a while, Akutsu nodded off.

"Is she asleep?" Taoka asked.

"Yes."

"Eating till you're full, then falling asleep. That's the way it should be, eh?" he said with a laugh. Then he turned around and looked at me. "Do you mind if I talk to you for a bit?"

I shook my head.

"The thing is this. I really love teaching. When there's a kid who doesn't understand a subject, and I help them get their thoughts in order, and then they finally pull a face that means, *Shit, I get it*, that's the best feeling in the world for me."

The car edged forward the tiniest bit.

"I knew I wasn't suited to be a schoolteacher, so I became a cram teacher. But the schools around here won't employ me. There are rumors going around about me, like Akutsu said."

Each time the car moved then stopped again, Akutsu's body would lunge forward then sink back.

"I know you're not supposed to say this stuff about yourself, but when I was working at the cram school, the kids there really liked me. I got lots of them into good colleges, and the schools and the parents trusted me, too. But then out of the blue, I got fired. The official reason was that I lost a USB stick with lots of the kids' personal information on it."

A classical piano piece started playing on the radio.

"But the truth was, that stick was stolen. Someone took it from my bag. Cram school teachers are surprisingly competitive. I don't know the real reason, but I guess the person who took it wanted to see the handouts and textbooks I'd prepared for the new term. But then there was other stuff on there, including a bunch of photos that really made their day."

"Photos?"

"Of kids." Taoka sunk into silence for what felt like a long time. Then he said, "Naked photos of young boys."

I had absolutely no idea what to say, so I kept my mouth shut. The car had stopped just in front of the turning for the bridge and wasn't moving an inch.

"I never asked to be into that stuff, you know. The gods just kinda gave me those preferences."

Suddenly, out of the blue, I heard the sound of sleigh bells. It took me a moment to figure out it was a Christmas song coming from the radio.

"The rumors flew around the cram school like wildfire, and soon everyone knew. We're talking not just the teachers, but also the students. Then they started being embellished. People were saying how I'd been caught messing around with some kid years ago in such-and-such a place, and so on. And of course, because I'd been found with those pictures, I couldn't defend myself against the other stuff. It was a free-for-all. So I guess when I open up my new own school, the rumors will come back to haunt me. The people spreading them won't pass up that opportunity, you can be sure of that."

I suddenly remembered the pictures of Takumi that Akutsu and I had given out, and my heart started racing.

"My parents run a big hospital, and I'm not stupid or bad-looking, even though I say so myself, and I'm a good teacher. To people who are bored out of their minds with their lives in this poky town, the idea that someone like that would get off on looking at naked pictures of kids is about the juiciest morsel of gossip in the world."

Without warning, the line of cars began to move forward and Taoka stopped speaking. Some kind of hymn came on the radio.

"But they don't know how much I . . ."

I waited for Taoka to finish, but he shut his mouth and didn't say anything more. I listened in silence to the words that kept repeating over and over: *the Savior comes.* Halfway across the bridge, the car came to a halt again.

Taoka turned around and said, "Look, I know I'm hardly one to go around lecturing you, but you and Akutsu should call it quits with handing those things out."

The traffic around us began to move, and Taoka turned to face front, pumping the accelerator. I started to feel like I couldn't breathe and opened the window a crack. Without turning around, Taoka continued, "Akutsu left the original in the copier at work. Then two weird reporter types turned up at the store with the same sheet of paper. Not to mention the one you put in my mailbox. Trust me, if you've got spare time on your hands, you'd be better off spending it figuring out how to get away from those projects as quickly as you can."

"Okay," I said, and looked down.

Since my earliest childhood, however badly teachers or other adults told me off, I'd never once felt like I'd done anything wrong. But now, somehow, with Taoka, I felt ashamed of myself.

The car stopped. I looked up and saw with surprise we were outside the projects already. Akutsu still showed no signs of opening her eyes, so I shook her awake and dragged her out of the car.

Taoka said, "It's a little early, but happy Christmas," and handed me a big box beautifully wrapped in Christmas paper.

It was the model train from before.

"Remember to brush your teeth and get to bed early," he shouted, sticking his head out of the car window, and drove off, back in the direction of town.

I kind of knew that if it had been just some regular rich kid who had taken a serious interest in my future without having any obligation to do so, then I wouldn't have trusted him as much as I did Taoka. It was the darkness Taoka carried around with him that meant that someone like me who'd grown up in the projects could feel as close to him as I did.

After thinking on it for a while, I decided I'd try working for him for a month and see how it went. Akutsu and I both arranged to cut our shifts short by two hours and spent that time studying instead. Akutsu said she found the temptation of the TV too much when she was at home, so she asked me to study with her in a nearby cafe. As a thank-you, she paid for me to use the unlimited-drink bar.

"How do you read this?" Akutsu showed me a kanji on the printout she was working on.

"We learned that in the first year of middle school."

"Okay. I'll write that I can't read it." The printout was already bathed in little red writing, but she somehow found a space and printed *can't read this* in even tinier letters.

"Shit, I didn't realize it was this late! I've got to go and make dinner."

"Oh, yeah, I forgot. Here." Avoiding my eyes, Akutsu passed a plastic Tupperware box from her bag across the table. "This is for your gran, from my mom. It's simmered pumpkin."

She started erasing something furiously, and, although she was holding the paper flat, it quickly grew crumpled.

"Thanks," I said. When I picked up the box, I felt it was still warm.

Now that my shift at the store was shorter, I could be at home for dinner, which was a great help. It seemed like my gran was getting more senile every day, and she'd started disappearing out of the house in the evenings, sneaking out when I was in the kitchen chopping leeks or whatever, without even bothering to put her shoes on. When I went to look for her, I'd inevitably find her sitting on a bench by the swamp, or crouching down in the parking lot, muttering something to herself over and over. I'd take hold of one of her arms, spindly as a dried twig, and say, "Let's go home," and then she'd allow herself to be escorted back, but it wasn't long before she'd make a break for it again. It had gotten to the point where she was escaping multiple times in the few hours between dusk and the time she got into bed, so I started to lock the door to keep her in. But sometimes in the middle of the night she'd wake up and start pounding on the rusty door with a strength I found frightening. When I told her to stop, that she'd wake the neighbors, she'd look at me with a tragic face, and say, "Yoshio isn't here."

Now, in addition to the letters asking us to pay the rent, health insurance, and utility bills and the reminders from school that my fees were late, envelopes addressed to my mother from a private loan company had started showing up. Then phone calls started coming in the evening, warning us that the repayments were overdue. My mom was supposed to be taking care of the rent, utilities, and my school fees. I tried calling her cell phone. It didn't go through.

Until now, the money I made from my jobs had just about covered the cost of food for me and my gran, but her superhuman appetite meant we got through everything so quickly, and we were starting to feel the strain. Then the debt collectors called us a bunch of times late at night. I disconnected the phone and continued studying.

It turned out that while I was at school my gran was unlocking the door and wandering around the grounds. I only found this out because one particular day, she found her way into one of the apartments on the floor below whose door had been left unlocked, opened the fridge, and helped herself to its contents.

The moment I got back, the man whose apartment it was started hurling abuse at me. When I went down to collect her, I found her sitting in front of someone else's TV, munching on rice crackers.

"If it happens again, I'll throw the old hag in the swamp!" he snarled, but when he saw me standing there looking so wiped out and my gran cackling away at the TV, he lowered his voice and asked, "What's your mom up to these days?"

Not long after, I got home from school to find the bankbook and personal seal, which I kept inside the plastic tub where we stored our rice for safekeeping, had disappeared. As if that wasn't bad enough, there was visibly less rice than there had been that morning. I jumped on my bike and pedaled as fast as I could to an ATM, where I used the bank card I kept in my wallet to check the balance of my account.

Nothing. All the money I'd saved up little by little from my various jobs had been withdrawn. I got on my bike and rode to the apartment by the river where my mom lived. I climbed the metal staircase, my feet making an unpleasant clanging sound, and saw that the surname that had been there the last time had been taken down from the nameplate. I peered inside through the crack in the kitchen window and saw there was not a single piece of furniture left. All that remained were the dirty cream curtains on the windows.

Back at home, an hour after I'd served her a sizeable dinner, my gran started shouting that she was hungry. I tried to explain that she'd just eaten, but in her current state that information meant nothing. I cooked more rice, made rice balls, and gave them to her. There was only a little rice left. I knew I had to prioritize my gran's hunger over my own.

In a bid to forget about my growling stomach, I would try solving equations and drumming English vocab into my head, though I knew it wasn't really a good substitute. One day, I stupidly forgot to lock the door, and my gran, seeing I was wrapped up in my schoolwork, took the opportunity to slip outside. I was weak from a lack of food, and tearing after her was beyond me. Instead I lay stretched out on the fraying tatami. Suddenly, I remembered the model train set Taoka had given me, still sitting in the top of the closet where I'd left it. I ripped off the paper, opened up the box, and linked the pieces of track together. I plugged it in and pushed down the lever, and the little Nozomi train shot forward. Noisily, it raced around and around the short track. That was it—that was all it did. Here was a toy I would have given my back teeth for as a kid, and I couldn't take even a scrap of joy from it. I turned off the power supply and lay back on the tatami. The wind came whistling into the room through the cracks in the badly fitted window frame. Maybe, I thought, maybe Gran will come home of her own accord, but the thought only lasted a second. I got to my feet and went unsteadily out the door to look for her.

When I got to school after my morning paper route, Takumi was sitting at his desk. I watched how, each time anyone came into the classroom and saw him, their eyes grew round with shock. Then they'd either ignore him entirely or watch him from afar. It seemed like it wasn't just me who had no idea how to deal with him.

At break, Nana went up to Takumi's desk and began talking at him. Takumi didn't look at her but nodded, making an inscrutable face. Then Nana went away, and Takumi came over to me.

"Thanks for the handouts," he said.

"How nice it must be to have so many people looking out for you." I injected my words with as much bitterness as I could, but Takumi just stared at me hard and said nothing.

* * *

"You are all here on this earth because your parents *loved* one another."

That afternoon we went to the gym to listen to a lecture by an ob-gyn doctor I'd seen a bunch of times on TV. She was a fat, middle-aged woman with a very wide jaw, who went on and on about contraception, abortion, AIDS, and how precious life was. Needless to say, everyone was dozing or sneakily reading manga or playing with their phones. It felt like not a single person in the gym was listening to what she had to say.

"God only gives us challenges that He believes we are capable of overcoming."

The doctor had informed us at the beginning that she was a Christian. As her speech went on, she got more and more into what she was saying, and her voice grew really loud. Occasionally, her microphone made horrible squeaking and thumping noises.

I sensed some kind of commotion behind me, so I looked around to see the boys on either side of Takumi nudging and poking him.

"What about you, Saito? Did you use 'adequate protection'?"

"With all that lovin' there must be a few of your kids knocking around, no?"

Takumi was staring straight ahead with a tense expression I'd never seen him pull before. I watched as a graying gym shoe came flying out of nowhere and struck him right on the back of his head. Taking their cue, the other kids began pelting him with shoes or balls of scrunched-up paper. Still Takumi said nothing, just sat there staring straight ahead. I stood up and went over to him, forcing my way through the metal folding chairs. I took one glance at the boy next to him, grinning as he dug his finger into Takumi's cheek, and swung at him with all the strength I had, my fist catching him under his jaw. Still in a seated position on top of his chair, he went sailing back onto the floor in slow motion.

"Every child chooses the parents he or she is to be born to, and the life he or she is going to lead," the woman on stage said in an excited tone. Her words took away any hope I might have had of checking the violent impulses bubbling up inside me. My ears began ringing like tuning forks, drowning out the voice of the speaker and the shouts and shrieks of the other kids around me. Again and again I punched and kicked at the kids trying to hold me back, and those pointing at Takumi and laughing. Eventually, Notchy, looking like she was on the verge of tears, came up with the PE teacher. The PE teacher grabbed my arms from behind and the two of them dragged me out of the gym. I heard people whistling and cheering. There was just one thought going around my head: *Everyone, everyone in this whole fucking place is a fucking idiot.*

"With your grades, you could get a school recommendation for college, you know! You shouldn't go doing that sort of thing, or you'll blow all your chances!" Notchy was in tears as she told me off in the teachers' room. "And just when Takumi's finally come back to school and everything!"

Her mascara was running, forming black patches under her eyes.

At last, she let me go, saying, "If you're ever in any kind of trouble, you have to just tell me, okay?"

I hurried back home to discover my gran was gone. I turned on the rice cooker, dissolved miso paste in hot water to make soup, without any of the usual wakame seaweed or tofu or anything, then dashed out. Notchy's lecture had gone on so long I didn't have the time to be looking for my gran. That day, I was supposed to be at the shop for three hours to cover for Mrs. Aoki, a part-timer whose kid was ill, but I was over half an hour late, which earned me a dressing-down from the manager. When I opened my wallet during my break to buy a rice ball, I saw there was no money left. I put the rice ball with its salty plum filling back on the rack where it had come from.

I had no idea what to do about the fact that my mom had disappeared, or what my gran and I were going to eat tomorrow. I didn't know who I was supposed to talk to when I ran out of money. I didn't have the courage to look a person in the eye and tell them I was in deep, deep trouble. Each time I opened the cash register, my eyes would be drawn to the row of notes.

I somehow managed to get through my hours of work, dizzy with hunger, and went to the back of the shop. The clutch bag the manager always carried around under his arm was lying on the sofa. It was unzipped, and I could see his cell phone, his keys, and his bulging wallet poking out. Before I knew what I was doing, my hand was reaching toward the wallet. I opened the clasp slowly, so it wouldn't make a sound. It was like the shoplifting I'd done when I was a kid—I didn't feel guilty in the least. And then the manager had come in through the back entrance of the store without me seeing him and was standing there staring at me as I held his wallet. I watched as his sweat-beaded face turned puce before my eyes, then threw the wallet down onto the sofa, dashed out the back door, and jumped onto my bike. I pedaled so fast that the wind rushed through my ears with a metallic ring.

I made it back to the projects, and I was starting to climb the stairs to my block when I heard what sounded like lots of voices coming from above. It hadn't been raining before, at least not that I'd noticed, but with every step I took now, drops of water came flying down from above, soaking into my sneakers. When I reached the fifth floor, I saw a crowd of people standing in front of the door to my apartment. Catching sight of me, the man from the apartment below started yelling.

"It's all come leaking into my room! It's gonna ruin all my stuff!"

A middle-aged woman stood next to him cast me a pitying look. There was a guy with a can of beer in hand, laughing as he peered into my apartment.

"Your damn gran left the kitchen tap and the bath tap running and then started throwing water around the room with a bucket! She was throwing it off the balcony, too!"

I rushed in through the door to find Akutsu mopping the kitchen floor with a towel. My gran was sitting in front of the blaring TV, laughing to herself. I apologized endlessly to the man from the apartment below, bowing so many times I lost count.

"It's compensation I want! Compensation!" he kept yelling, until another man dragged him away, saying, "Let's deal with it tomorrow. Give the kid a break today."

"Don't worry about the rest," I said to Akutsu when they'd gone. "I'll do it."

"Let me do the floor at least. You can't deal with this all by yourself."

Akutsu kept on mopping the floor.

I draped a blanket over my gran, who'd dropped off to sleep on the sofa, and lowered the volume of the TV. Looking at the coffee table, I saw a paper bag I hadn't noticed earlier.

"It was hanging on the door," Akutsu said. From the bag, I drew out a slip of paper in Takumi's handwriting. "This is for you, from my mom." Nesting inside the big plastic lunchbox were heaps of rice balls, fried chicken, and omelet rolls.

I gorged myself like I never had before. Akutsu said she'd had dinner already, but she still managed two of the rice balls before she got back to wiping the floor. When my stomach was full, I felt suddenly overcome by drowsiness. I asked Akutsu to wake me in five minutes and, slumped forward on the table, I fell into a deep sleep.

"Hey! Your gran's gone!" I woke to Akutsu's voice in my ear. "I was just cleaning the bathroom, and then when I came back in here, she . . . she . . ."

Akutsu looked ready to burst into tears.

On the sofa where my gran had been lying was now only a rumpled blanket. I looked around the apartment, but she wasn't anywhere to be seen. Stepping into my sneakers, I headed outside, and Akutsu followed me. We ran around the projects looking for her, checking the parking lot, the staircases and landings of the other blocks, the communal gardens, but no luck. I even peered down at the surface of the swamp—right now, it seemed like anything was possible—but the only thing there was a narrow sliver of moon flickering on the surface of the water.

I got on my bike, and Akutsu got on behind like it was the most normal thing in the world, wrapping her arms around me. We passed through the dark tunnel and started down the road leading down to town, passing the crematorium and coming out in front of the hospital. Just to be sure, I asked at the emergency room reception to see if they'd heard anything, but an exhausted-looking security guard waved me away. We came onto the big road that led to the station. Standing outside the doughnut shop was a group of boys from our class. Seeing me and Akutsu on the same bike they called out, "Ooh, look at you two! Lovebirds!"

I stopped the bike and walked over to them. They took me in nervously.

"You haven't seen an old woman in a beige dress, about this tall, have you?"

"Your gran?" one guy asked. My question seemed to have shocked him into taking me seriously.

The guy next to him looked at me with equal earnestness and said, "Have you lost her?"

I nodded limply, and the guy who'd spoken said, "I'll ask around. At this hour, there's a ton of people coming back from cram school and part-time jobs, so they might know something." He took out his cell phone. Realizing I didn't have a phone, he said, "If I hear anything, I'll call Akutsu. I'll keep an eye out on my way home!"

We put the doughnut shop behind us, along with our classmates who were now typing into their phones with grave expressions, and began searching the town. When we passed the convenience store I glanced inside to see the manager standing alone at the cash register, and a long line of customers waiting.

We came out beside the river and moved slowly along the bike path, looking at the wide stretch of land leading to the river. I was exhausted and parked my bike beside a vending machine. Akutsu bought a couple of cans of sweet red bean soup and handed one to me. We knelt down and drank the soup, feeling its sticky sugariness spread throughout our bodies.

"Look, it's late. You should get on my bike and go on home. Your family'll be worried."

Ignoring what I'd said, Akutsu said, "Do you remember those mugwort sweets your grandma used to make? They were amazing."

In the spring my gran had always gone out picking mugwort, which she used in making sticky green rice-dumplings full of sweet red bean paste. Once, when I was a kid, she'd taken me up a mountain at the edge of town, saying the shrine at the top was full of the stuff. I'd helped her pick those green leaves for hours on end and had been so tired afterward that she'd given me a piggyback home. Once the sweets were done, my gran would take them around to Akutsu's apartment and to other families in the projects. She also set a whole pile of them down in front of my dad's memorial tablet, the only one in the family altar.

"When you think about it though, that mugwort had probably been peed on by dogs for all we know. And absorbed loads of exhaust fumes and stuff. I'll bet it was really dirty." Even as

I said this, all I could think was how I'd have died for one of those sticky green sweets right this moment.

I remembered being a little boy and standing next to my gran beside the steamer, staring down at the plumes of billowing smoke, just waiting for the sweets to be ready.

"You're just like Yoshio!" my gran said. "He loved these mugwort sweets, too."

Then she put a spoon of freshly made bean paste, still warm, inside my mouth.

Just then, Akutsu's cell phone beeped. I saw her pass her eyes over the new message, and then jump to her feet.

"It says someone saw a woman by your gran's description over by the foot of the bridge."

We got back onto the bike and headed to the bridge we'd passed before. When we got there, we jumped down onto the flat expanse of riverbed, and started calling out at the top of our voices. We ran the width of the riverbed, passed over the patch of big rocks, and stood right by the river's edge. Along with the sound of running water, I thought I could hear a voice. It sounded like my gran.

"Over here!" Akutsu said, parting the leaves that stretched far above her head and making her way through them. I sprinted to catch up, but I'd already lost track of her, so I made my own way through the thicket, coming out right in front of the patch where all the goldenrod grew. It was covered in fluff like the artificial snow people hang on Christmas trees. I felt, all of a sudden, like my path had been blocked. Unable to go on, I looked up at the sky instead. I could see a sliver of moon up there. No stars, though.

In truth, there had been another reason why I'd been nick-named Goldie. As a kid I'd always been dirty, covered in dust, and kind of unkempt, and someone had spread it around that being near me made people sneeze. Just like that goldenrod by the river, someone else had said. Our homeroom teacher had said that you couldn't get hay fever from goldenrod, but nobody had paid him any attention, and the name had stuck. Had I really chosen this life for myself, like that obstetrician woman had said?

I looked up at the sky. If there really was a god up there, I thought, then it had to be a pretty cruel one. I clicked my tongue, and then spat in its direction.

Then I heard Akutsu's voice coming from somewhere ahead. Without pausing to think, I plunged into the colony of goldenrod and charged ahead.

Finally, I parted the grass ahead to see the baseball park stretched out in front. On the field, my gran was marching around and around in circles. Where she found that kind of stamina in that wizened old body of hers, I honestly had no clue.

Akutsu and I did our best to take hold of her arms, telling her it was time to go home, but she brushed us off and continued walking. Then she began to sing at the top of her voice. The song was pretty nonsensical, but now and then we'd catch a word or two: *birdcage* and *canary*. At first Akutsu and I followed my gran faithfully around and around the field. After a while Akutsu crouched down, breathing heavily.

"Let's just wait until she tires herself out," I said.

We sat down on a half-rotten wooden bench overlooking the ballpark. The wind was freezing, and both of us were shivering. For a long time, I sat hugging my knees to my chest, but after a while my hands got tired. When I let my hands sink down on the bench, one of them brushed up against Akutsu's. It was the same hand she'd once put the stolen chocolates on top of, the hand that had once been covered in brown marks. Her palm felt dry and rough.

Akutsu's cell phone rang. She held it to her ear and then, looking at my face, said into the receiver, "Ryota." There was a pause. "Yeah, his gran escaped."

Akutsu talked to Taoka for a while, then hung up.

"He was worried, apparently. He said you went running out the store today in the middle of your shift. Did something happen?"

I ignored her question and kept silent. Not long after, we heard a car parking by the top of the riverbank and saw Taoka come walking toward us.

"Where is she?" he asked, and we pointed. Taoka went off at a jog toward the moving figure. We watched as he accompanied her around the baseball field a bunch of times, before bending over to whisper something in her ear. Then he hoisted her up on his back and made his way toward us.

Taoka loaded my gran, who was by now dozing off, and Akutsu, who was just about lifeless with cold and exhaustion, into the back of his car, lay a blanket over them, and shut the door.

"As soon I've smoked this, we'll go," Taoka said, taking a pack of cigarettes out of the pocket of his biker jacket and lighting one. It was the first time I'd ever seen him smoke.

"I'll take you to the hospital."

I shook my head, panicked. "I haven't got the money."

"It's okay. I know someone there. I'll speak to them and make sure you don't have to do anything. I told you, when you're in trouble, you should always come to me first."

"Yeah, but . . . I know I've asked you this before, but why are you so willing to help me out like this?"

Taoka stayed silent for a long time, not answering my question. He smoked his cigarette right down to the butt, breathing out halos of white smoke. Then he crushed the end beneath his shoe and moved his foot back and forth over it for what seemed like way longer than was necessary.

The shrill cry of a bird marked the start of a new day. In the eastern sky, gradually morphing from indigo to purple, I could make out the morning star. Taoka took out another cigarette and put it to his mouth. In the orange flash of his lighter flame, his face looked utterly exhausted.

"There's parts of me that are unbelievably awful. So unless I make the other parts unbelievably good, I'm done for."

He spoke so quietly I could barely catch what he was saying. If the wind had been blowing any harder, I probably wouldn't have.

"I had fun the other day. When we had dinner together and went to the toy shop," he said.

I nodded, and Taoka brushed off the goldenrod fluff that was sticking to my hair.

"We should do it again," he said, and grinned. He looked just like a little kid when he smiled like that. I thought back to that weird Sunday drive: the sickly sweet smell inside his car, the dirty old Pikachu on the floor. For some reason I had the feeling that Taoka was going to disappear on me, just like my mom and my dad.

Sure enough, a week after my gran was hospitalized with pneumonia, Taoka was arrested on suspicion of indecent assault.

Ms. Shimizu, the social worker Taoka had introduced me to, had helped me out a lot with the fees and about what to do once my gran came out of the hospital.

"He was going to therapy, taking it very seriously. There's no way he'd do something like that," Ms. Shimizu had said angrily, with a frown, when she heard about Taoka. But when we came out of the room at the hospital, she said to me very quietly, "He didn't try anything with you, did he?"

"No," I said.

"Okay. Sorry for asking," she said, a slightly guilty expression on her face.

When I went into my gran's room, she was sitting up in bed and rubbing cream into Akutsu's hands.

"She's been doing it for ages! She won't let go. My hands are so sticky!" Akutsu said, beaming. My gran kept on and on, stroking Akutsu's hands as if she were handling something extremely precious.

With Taoka no longer around, utter chaos had descended on the convenience store. I'd been planning to apologize for trying to steal money and submit my resignation, but when I went in to do just that, the manager gave me a tearful look and refused to let me go.

"My wallet fell on the floor, and you were just picking it up. I know, I know! The shifts for next month are up over there, so take a look before you go, okay?" He mopped sweat from his brow with a handkerchief, then ran to the registers where there was a line of customers waiting to collect the Christmas cakes they'd ordered. I opened my locker to see a brown envelope in there. Inside was the book of questions Taoka had created based on Akutsu's and my feedback.

"Apparently he'd go around offering to help kids with their schoolwork, then drag them into his car, strip them naked and take photos of them!" I heard one of the part-time women saying, sounding almost rabid with excitement. Then everyone else out the back of the shop started talking about him, saying they'd always known there was something suspect about him or how they'd never trusted that glint in his eyes.

On the way back home, I stopped my bike midway up the slope leading to the projects and looked down on the little town below. Watching those lights, I decided to myself that I was going to study like crazy, take everyone by surprise by getting into a prestigious university, and leave this place for good. Then I thought about Taoka, and I directed a single prayer to the cruel old god up above: *Wherever he is tonight, please don't let him be feeling too lonely.*

5

Pollen Nation

WHEN THEY MAKE IT this far, it means they're almost there.

With my surgically gloved right hand I could feel the crown of the baby's head, all warm and slimy. For a couple of minutes now, it had been popping out of Mrs. Oshima's vagina, then disappearing back inside again.

"Not long to go," I said to her. With her arms still wrapped around her husband's neck, she dropped her eyes to the floor and nodded limply. She was wearing just a pale-pink tank top, kneeling on the tatami with her legs spread wide. I went around to sit behind her, reaching my hand between her legs to support the baby's head.

At first, it had seemed like the sight of his wife howling like a wild beast had totally knocked Mr. Oshima sideways, but now he'd apparently managed to locate some balls somewhere and was being much more helpful, wiping the sweat from her brow and offering her sips of water.

No sooner had the New Year arrived than the weather had suddenly taken a cold turn. A big freeze had made its way over from mainland Asia, the forecaster had announced on the evening news. From time to time, a strong gust of wind would rattle the badly fitted windows of the old wooden house. I glanced up at the window, whose curtains I'd left open, to see the bare branches of the cherry trees lining the bicycle path rocking and shaking in the wind.

Mrs. Oshima had asked a little while back that I turn off the heating unit as the noise was bothering her, and yet she, her husband, and I were all still dripping with sweat. For some reason, as soon as I'd switched off the heating, the labor had started to go far more smoothly. I don't know why, but those kinds of semi-miraculous turns of events often seem to happen in childbirth. The patches of sweat staining the husband's green T-shirt were gradually expanding, and beads of sweat from his hair were dripping onto Mrs. Oshima's pale, delicate skin.

"AAAAAAAAAAAAAAAAAH!"

Staring right into her husband's eyes, Mrs. Oshima let out a long, loud yell. The atmosphere in the small room suddenly turned soupy and intense. I felt as if I'd crept in unannounced to their bedroom, and I made myself as inconspicuous as I could. I concentrated all my energies on ensuring there was as little burden on Mrs. Oshima's body as possible, so that the baby would be more likely to come out in one uninterrupted gush.

"Relax your body. Breathe in short, shallow bursts. Say *ha, ha, ha*."

I'd barely finished speaking when there was a sound like a balloon bursting, and warm water spilled out onto my palms. Mrs. Oshima breathed for a while like I'd told her to, then I saw her take a long breath through her mouth, and out popped the baby's head. I used my fingers to clamp her anus shut, while also supporting the baby's body that was twisting around as it emerged. The shoulders and the back followed quickly.

There was a moment of silence, and then the baby let out a mewl. I slipped my hand gently under the back of its head and hoisted it up onto Mrs. Oshima's chest, still attached to her by its umbilical cord. Her cheeks flushed a vivid red, Mrs. Oshima kissed the back of her newborn baby's head, still wet with amniotic fluid. Her husband wrapped his arms around her from behind: man hugging woman hugging baby. Cradled at his mother's chest, the baby soon stopped crying and began with closed eyes to seek out her breast.

"Here, it's here," Mrs. Oshima said, guiding her nipple into its mouth. Watching how the baby, without having ever been shown how, began slurping away with a noise like a little suction pump, a tear ran down the husband's cheek. I looked dazedly at the three of them, this freshly created holy family in front of me, and let out a long deep breath from the very bottom of my lungs. Then it began to hit me how hungry I was.

A delicious smell greeted me as I stepped into the kitchen. I lifted the lid of a pan on the stove to find golden dashi stock, glistening in the dim. I dunked a ladle in and raised it to my mouth. There was the patter of slippers making their way down the hall, and then Mitchan came into the kitchen, carrying a great pile of folded towels. She looked at me and frowned.

"Again with the bad manners, Doctor! How many times have I told you about drinking straight from the pan?"

"Your stock is just too tempting, Mitchan. I feel like it's restoring me to life."

"If you can just hang on a few minutes more, I'll make you some soup with it. Go on, have a seat."

Mitchan transferred some of the stock into a small pan. She took some steamed fish and greens out of the fridge and began chopping them at a furious pace, then tossing them into the pot. I looked up at the clock. It was past midnight.

"As soon as you've made that you should go home," I said. "You've barely slept these two days."

"I really think you're in more need of it than I am, Doctor. You'll die at this rate." With a smile, Mitchan set a bowl of soup and a pair of chopsticks down in front of me.

Mrs. Oshima had come in the morning the day before yesterday, her contractions ten minutes apart. But just when it seemed like things were heating up and starting to look promising, the contractions would slack off again, and in the end the labor had gone on for two full days. There'd been other deliveries taking place simultaneously, too, and as a result, neither Mitchan nor I had slept properly. Mitchan hadn't even been home but had stayed here the whole time, grabbing the odd moment of shut-eye when she could. This kind of thing was hardly a rarity. I took a sip of the soup and felt it warming my esophagus, all the exhaustion and tension starting to ebb away.

"My God, this is good."

Mitchan let out a strange cackle. Her hair was cut so short I could see her earlobes turning red.

Mitchan had been working here since the year before last. Not only was she a midwife, but she was also in charge of preparing meals for the women staying at the clinic. She still wasn't at the stage where I could leave her alone to deliver babies by herself, but when it came to cooking she rivaled most professional chefs. As soon as she'd joined, there'd been a sudden rise in comments on the feedback sheets that the mothers submitted after their stays that the food had been incredible. We served traditional Japanese meals at the clinic, more or less exclusively. Mitchan insisted on extracting her own dashi stock from bonito flakes and kombu seaweed, rather than using the instant stuff. She also eschewed the electric rice cookers everyone else used, cooking her rice in an earthenware pot. Along with rice and soup, there'd be a main dish of either meat or fish as well as two small vegetable dishes and a little helping of some kind of seaweed. All of this she managed to rustle up quickly and efficiently and at minimal cost. To top it all off, at the end of each day, she'd enter a detailed record of the meals she'd cooked into the computer.

Whenever another midwife or I complimented her on her cooking, though, she'd get all embarrassed.

"When I was a kid my mom was always off playing pachinko, right? She didn't do a thing around the house. Well, I had seven brothers and sisters, and I was the oldest girl, so I just learned. I didn't think anything of it," she'd say. Then she'd go on to tell us what a bad seed she'd been. "Basically, you name it, I tried it—except murder."

We'd had a lot of people who started working here, especially younger women, who couldn't cope with the strain of the round-the-clock job. Mitchan had been here the longest of anyone.

"It went quite smooth in the end for Mrs. Oshima, then?"

"Yeah, the end was surprisingly quick. She was totally exhausted! I think if it had lasted much longer the baby would have got tired, too. We'd probably have ended up taking her to the hospital."

As I spoke, I pressed my fingers to my throbbing temples. Seeing this, Mitchan said poutily, "Honestly, Doctor! I'll clear this up. Will you *please* just go up to bed?"

I went upstairs as I'd been told and knocked on the door to Takumi's room. No reply. I waited a little before turning the doorknob. Seeping in through the crack in the curtains, the light of the streetlamp shone upon a lump in the duvet. I stepped over the manga, books, and convenience store bags full of trash strewn across the floor and went up to his bed. Quietly, I peeled back the edge of the duvet so his face came into view. His eyelids were firmly shut, not moving at all. I moved the duvet back farther and held my finger beneath his nose until I felt the faint, warm touch of his breath. He was alive. Having ascertained that much, I stood up and walked out of the room.

Without turning on the light, without even taking off my clothes, I dove into the futon left out on the floor of my bedroom. The throbbing in my temples was really bad. The right side of my lower back felt heavy, as if I'd strained it. If this went on, I'd have to watch it not to put my back out like I had before. I felt a shooting pain from the inside of my right shoulder blade, like someone was sticking a needle in. When I closed my eyes, the ceiling began spinning, and I felt gravity pulling my body down, deeper into the futon. Well, at the very least, I thought, as my consciousness began to fade, today had ended disaster-free. There were still plenty of pending problems to be dealt with, of course. I had no idea how long I'd be able to sleep, but I prayed that even just a few hours would be enough to take this exhaustion away.

With my scarf wrapped several times around my neck, I got on my bike and set off down the bicycle path in the opposite direction from the station. I didn't know why he never asked me to meet him at the station and instead specified some out-of-the-way spot, but I guessed he must have had his reasons. Besides, I knew that calling him out on it would only end in a fight, so I tried not to think too much about it and concentrated instead on getting to the specified meeting point as quickly as I could. The big bridge of the next town came into sight. I parked my bike by the path and walked across the wide expanse of riverbed.

He was sitting on a battered wooden bench by the baseball field, slumped over in the same shabby plum-colored down coat he'd been wearing when I last saw him at the end of the year, his hands hanging down between his legs so they brushed his feet. Seeing me, he lifted his left hand and waved it. I stood in front of him and pulled out a little envelope. It was the kind of envelope that people put money in to give to kids at New Year, with a Hello Kitty picture on it—I'd been in a hurry when leaving the house and hadn't had time to find anything more suitable. When I reached out to give it to him, he smiled a little, taking it into his outstretched hands. Then he put his hands together in a prayer of gratitude.

"Bye," I said and made to leave, but he grabbed my left arm. With sudden force, I shook his hand off me.

"Look, I want this to be the last time, okay?"

I lifted my face as I spoke. The piercing light of the winter sun, now nearing its zenith, made me wince, and I shut my eyes.

"Okay," he said. I tried to pretend I hadn't noticed how gray he looked all of a sudden or that the laces of his sneakers were so frayed they seemed as though they might fall to pieces at any minute. I turned my back to him and began to walk away.

"Say hi to Takumi from me," he shouted after me.

I strode across the baseball field, pretending not to have heard.

When we'd met, in the very beginning, he'd been working as a photographer's assistant. He'd showed up at the maternity clinic where I was employed, asking for permission to shoot one of the births. Back then, he would work hard for a while to save up some money, then use it all to go off to India or Thailand or whatever. Even after we'd got together, there were several occasions when he disappeared off the radar. If he didn't want to do something, he wouldn't do it—that was the kind of person he was. At first I mistook that aspect of him for a kind of integrity. After he was kicked out of his apartment for failing to make his rent, we fell into living together, and then I got pregnant and had Takumi. To get by, I had to put Takumi into day care and start working almost immediately. His cameras and equipment gathered dust in the corner of the room. When I dragged myself home from work, exhausted, collecting Takumi from day care and returning to our apartment, I'd find him stretched out asleep, the fan and the TV left on.

It wasn't him that changed—it was me.

I started to lecture him. "You're a father now!" I would practically shout. "Isn't it time you got a proper job?" Claiming the moral high ground like that always left me with a sticky lump inside. I'd married him out of admiration for his unfettered way of life, but the moment a child came on the scene, I'd tried to foist the responsibilities of a husband and father onto him. Until that point, I'd always claimed to have such an enlightened view of life, saying that the housework should be done by whoever found it easier and the living costs should come from whoever could afford them. But now, without ever stopping to properly consider how I wanted me, him, and newborn Takumi to get along in this world, in fact without even really exploring the available options, I flew at him, brandishing all the tenets of common sense that I'd had drummed into me throughout my life.

We went through a phase of furious shouting matches, then a phase of picking holes in everything the other did, before finally settling on ignoring one another entirely, despite still living in the same house. At one point he got into producing organic vegetables. On another occasion he decided he was going to be a translator and started studying for that. His approach to life, which involved doing exactly what he wanted at that particular time, hadn't changed at all. But nothing he did ever yielded results. Meanwhile, I was gaining experience as a midwife, improving little by little. The year I set up my maternity clinic at home, he announced that he'd found a younger woman and left. My abiding memory of that period of my life is the sound of Takumi's sobs from a distant room mingling with the wailing of the babies I'd just delivered.

"Is he doing okay?" he called out at my back now, as I strode across the field. I turned around and shouted back.

"Why don't you go and see for yourself?"

He hadn't been to see Takumi once since leaving. I hadn't banned him from coming or anything. He just stubbornly refused. If I asked him about it, he'd come out with the kind of things I'd never expected to hear him say, like "I'm too bad a father to face him at the moment."

I had robbed my son of his father, and robbed his father of his innocence. The guilt at having destroyed my family was forever there at the back of my mind, like a pile of smoldering embers. Every now and then, a gust of wind would come along and rouse the embers into flames. Cursing myself for always giving in to him, for always handing over money so readily whenever he said he needed it, I ran up the steep lip of the riverbank and onto the bicycle path.

"We're fully booked all the way through till April, Doctor! I'm not seeing much evidence of the declining birthrate around these parts, I've got to say." Eyes glued to the computer screen, Mitchan let out a big sigh.

I knew to what it was we owed this popularity. Maternity wards were closing their doors one after another, from the hospital in the next town to the big one in the neighboring prefecture, and there had been a sharp rise in expectant mothers looking for a place to give birth. Not that we could accept everyone—because we had no medical equipment, we weren't allowed to take on women with any kind of medical complaints or those whose births had been deemed high-risk, so whenever anyone like that made inquiries we had to politely turn them away, however guilty we felt. Of course, when I'd first started the clinic, the flow of customers had been sparse at best, and I'd spend each day worrying about how on earth I was going to make ends meet, so the fact that now so many women were expressing a desire to give birth here should have felt like a dream come true.

I had just given the babies their morning bath, going through the motions as quickly as I could, when a young expecting mother named Mrs. Nishimura turned up for an appointment. She was wearing a knitted dress of soft white wool with stripy legwarmers. I had it written in my notes that she was thirty-four, but she didn't look a day over thirty. She'd only just been told for sure by the gynecologist that she was pregnant, but she was so determined that she wanted to have her baby in this clinic that she'd already made an appointment for the birth. Mitchan and I asked her a bunch of in-depth questions about her physical condition, and then explained the options for the different types of deliveries we offered here. Mrs. Nishimura took out a notepad from her bag and wrote down everything we said in small neat handwriting.

"I'd like the birth to be as natural as possible," Mrs. Nishimura said, sitting perfectly upright and pinning her eyes on me. Most of the women we saw here had the exact same reason for selecting this clinic. I said nothing. After a bit, Mitchan raised her head from the woman's notes and looked at me expectantly.

"I understand that," I said. "The thing is, and of course I'm not saying this to scare you, but we do have to prioritize both your life and that of the baby. You need to be aware that if something happens that we're unable to deal with here, we will have to take you to the hospital. We have an arrangement in place with a particular hospital nearby."

"I don't want to give birth in a hospital."

The sun streaming in from the window made her light-brown eyes glisten. The sheer directness of her words and the force with which she spoke them set me back a little.

"Since before I got pregnant I've been taking great care with the food I've been eating, for the baby's sake. I've been on a strict vegetarian diet. I heard you cater here to the culinary requirements of your clients, and that's the reason I decided to give birth here. I'd like to have my meals while I'm here made with only organic vegetables, as they have been throughout the pregnancy."

Saying this, Mrs. Nishimura removed a leaflet about an organic vegetable delivery service from a transparent folder she'd brought with her, and placed it on the table. I felt Mitchan's toe nudge my calf under the table.

Just as she had said, it was our policy at the clinic to try, wherever possible, to cater to our patients' wishes. That included not just food, but other aspects as well. People who didn't eat meat or fish would be served meals without meat or fish, and people pursuing a macrobiotic diet would be served macrobiotic meals. If our patients told us they wanted us to hang blackout curtains on the windows so they could give birth in a pitch-black room, and if they wanted CDs of dolphin calls playing during their delivery, then we arranged that it would be so. Even requests that at first blush seemed somewhat demanding or greedy, we still did our best to oblige. The more the women had the sense of being accepted when they were giving birth, the more their bodies would naturally relax, and the smoother the delivery would go. In fact, not only did we go out of our way to comply with women's wishes, but we also encouraged our patients to make use of the range of various treatments we had on offer to help relax the body and mind, such as aromatherapy, moxibustion, and acupressure.

Time and time again, I would repeat the same things to expectant mothers: *Keep your body warm at all times. Don't put on too much weight. Try and walk as much as you can each day.* At times I felt as if I were on a constant loop—much like the moon, which every month would wax full, causing so many women to go "naturally" into labor. Even in cases where people followed my advice to the letter, and there were no physical problems with either mother or baby, some births simply didn't go well. Something they'd told us over and over again at midwifery school was that however much experience you had, no two births were ever identical, and that was certainly true.

That said, over time, I'd developed the ability to be able to predict, based on factors like the woman's personality and way of life, how the delivery would go. I knew that when assisting the births of a highly strung, finicky type like Mrs. Nishimura, I would have to treat her with kid gloves, making her understand the things I needed to get across without being seen in any way to criticize her or negate what she was saying. I also needed to work on trying to soften her rigid way of thinking as far in advance as possible before the birth. That was another important task of the midwife.

"You're fine to go on eating as you are now, and we'll certainly do all that we can to meet your wishes while you're staying with us. But will you promise me one thing?"

"What's that?" Mrs. Nishimura cocked her head like a sparrow and looked straight at me.

"From today, I want you to try to keep away from the internet."

I saw Mrs. Nishimura neatly print the words *no internet* on her pad.

"Your eyes soon get tired when you're pregnant, and the net only makes them worse," I said, not mentioning the real reason for my prescription. The information on the net was a real mixed bag, and perhaps because they were both mentally and physically more delicate, expectant mothers somehow had a knack for stumbling on the worst stuff. In the past, I'd seen women beside themselves with worry about diseases that affected one in every 300,000 children or those who became convinced, right before they were due to give birth, that a massive earthquake was about to strike and they mustn't by any means go into labor. Women like Mrs. Nishimura, who were very particular about what they ate, what they wore, and all those other kinds of lifestyle choices, were particularly susceptible.

"If I follow the instructions you've given me, I'll be able to have a natural birth, yes?"

Mrs. Nishimura shut her notepad and smiled up at me. I shot her a smile back that I hoped was open to multiple interpretations.

Natural, natural, natural. Every time I heard that word come out of the mouths of one of the host of expectant mothers who passed through these doors I would find myself swallowing a whole bunch of other words. I felt hugely uncomfortable about how it sounded coming from their lips—how casual it seemed, how flimsy it was—yet I was unable to express that feeling of mine linguistically. I knew that, to put it bluntly, embracing "totally natural" births meant embracing all those lives that would be "naturally" eliminated by such a thing. I knew the feeling that the phrase conjured up for them—something soft, fluffy, and dreamy, like organic cotton. I suppose in a sense that wasn't exactly wrong, but the truth was that even natural labor conducted in the presence of all kinds of sophisticated medical devices sometimes involved the ripping of warm flesh, the spurting of hot blood. From time to time both mother and baby lost their lives. Regardless of the advances made in medical technology, giving birth was still life-threatening.

Mitchan and I stood at the door to wave off Mrs. Nishimura in her chocolate-colored down coat. Once she'd rounded the corner and disappeared from sight, Mitchan turned to me and said, with an indignant sort of look, "Don't you ever just want to tell them the truth, straight up?"

Stooping to pick up a scrap of paper by the doorstep that had blown in, I feigned innocence.

"What do you mean?"

"C'mon, Doctor!" she said, giving me a gentle poke with her elbow. "I think if it was up to me, I'd explain everything to them, in painstaking, gory detail."

"She just has to listen to what we'll teach her in the prenatal classes. If I spent that kind of time on every single person, we wouldn't be able to keep this business going. Save the laborious stuff for the birth itself! That's more than enough, I say."

Mitchan widened her eyes at me and blinked. "You're really surprisingly cynical, aren't you?"

"What do you mean? We've got to make a living, haven't we? Doing this job."

The fact was, when I'd been Mitchan's age I'd gone through a phase of trying my best to bring my patients around to my way of thinking. But the more I tried to explain in a theoretical, heavy-handed way what labor involved, the more the women's faces would freeze up. This then manifested itself in hitches in the deliveries.

In fact, it had dawned on me only very recently that the things I truly wanted to get across to others were actually few and far between, and they didn't have to be conveyed in a loud voice or even in words at all. I only wished I'd realized that sooner. The knowledge may well have come in handy with my marriage, too.

I was standing in the kitchen eating the ham sandwich Mitchan had rustled up for me as a late-night snack, washing it down with coffee. Midway through, I bit into a glob of mustard that made my nose tingle and my eyes water—and which sent my sleepiness packing.

Whenever the full moon was drawing near, the clinic would start to get busy. There's no real medical explanation why people tend to go into labor at this time. Of course, over half of the human body is made up of water, and that proportion increases in pregnancy with all the blood and amniotic fluid, so there are some who say that, being so similar to seawater in its constitution, that water also falls under the sway of the moon's gravitational pull. Who knows? I suspect most doctors would ask me to first prove my assertions with solid statistical evidence before they'd even discuss it with me, but my thinking is that it's a midwife's job to come face to face with the mysteries of the body that can't be fathomed through numbers and figures alone.

In the absence of major mishaps, there would be two babies born before dawn. Mitchan had also been working through the night, assisting the deliveries without a dinner break.

Just past midnight, the birth I was overseeing finally reached its conclusion. I stepped into the kitchen, and in a single gulp drained the cold coffee left in my mug from earlier. As I was doing so, Mitchan came running into the room looking very concerned.

"Doctor, can you come and look at Mrs. Wakabayashi's baby?"

I followed her back into the room at the end of the hall. Mrs. Wakabayashi was sitting up, leaning forward, her upper body draped over a big red cushion. Seeing us come into the room, her face softened in relief. Her husband was standing behind her with a grim look on his face.

"I'll just check how the baby's doing, okay?"

I had Mrs. Wakabayashi lie down on her back, then rolled up her T-shirt and wiped the sweat from her stomach with a towel, using the monitor to check the baby's heartbeat. The contractions were coming at five-minute intervals, and each time they arrived the baby's heartbeat would drop. Mrs. Wakabayashi, who had been battling with the agony of contractions since she'd arrived yesterday morning, was nearing the limits of her physical endurance. Dusky rings had appeared under her eyes from the lack of food and sleep. I put on a pair of surgical gloves and checked her cervix. It was still clamped shut. By this stage, it should have been more dilated.

"Mrs. Wakayabashi, you've done a magnificent job. But the thing is, the baby's getting tired. I think it's best to go to the hospital, just in case. I'll call an ambulance right away, okay?"

Mrs. Wakayabashi looked at me for a while, then nodded silently. She looked utterly wiped out. Unlike Mrs. Wakayabashi, there were some women who wouldn't have assented so readily, despite the state they were in. They knew that if they were taken to the hospital it was likely they'd be given a cesarean, despite specifically choosing this clinic because they wanted a "natural" birth. But if there was ever any kind of trouble, we took the women to a hospital we partnered with so they could be operated on as and if necessary.

"You see!"

Until now, Mr. Wakabayashi had kept deathly quiet but suddenly, as we were waiting for the ambulance, he broke his silence.

"I told you we should have gone to a hospital! But you insisted on coming here! What if something happens to the baby now?"

Mrs. Wakabayashi stayed staring up at the ceiling as if dazed, not even looking in her husband's direction.

"I can totally understand why you're feeling upset, Mr. Wakabayashi," I said, placing my hands on his arms as I spoke. "But for now, let's just concentrate on prioritizing the safety of your wife and child. Okay?" As I finished speaking, I heard a siren in the distance.

We piled into the ambulance and went racing down the wide main road. It was the middle of the night, and there was barely anyone else around. It must have rained at some point, because the asphalt was glistening, its dark, glossy surface mirroring the green of the traffic lights. We were headed for the general hospital, where I used to work.

Mrs. Wakabayashi was lying on her side on a stretcher, her eyes closed. Occasionally, her face would distort with a spasm of pain. I rubbed her lower back, saying, "When the pain comes, make sure you don't stop breathing. Open your eyes and exhale slowly." I demonstrated like I was blowing out a candle.

Sitting next to me, Mr. Wakabayashi wasn't even looking at his wife. He stayed silent, a deep frown etched into his face.

"Not long to go now," I said, turning to him. "We're nearly at the hospital."

At this, Mr. Wakabayashi looked down and began rummaging around in his backpack with an air of panic, then held a plastic bag up to his mouth and vomited violently. In the cramped interior of the vehicle, the smell was unbearable, and I felt as if I might be sick, too. Mrs. Wakabayashi had her eyes firmly closed, clearly trying to bear the situation as best she could.

"A lot of people get carsick in ambulances, you know," the middle-aged paramedic sitting across from me said, and smiled.

We reached the hospital in fifteen minutes and wheeled Mrs. Wakabayashi into one of the consultation rooms. I told a young male doctor and a female nurse with dark bags under their eyes about the course the delivery had taken. I was pretty relieved that neither of them were people I knew; however, midway through my explanation, the head nurse, whom I had worked for, entered the room. I bowed my head at her, but she ignored me. She took the clipboard with the medical notes from the young nurse, put on her glasses, and passed her eyes across them.

"All this garbage about the benefits of natural birth! What's the point, when they all end up in the hospital like everyone else?"

"Yes!"

Apparently stirred by the head nurse's words, Mr. Wakabayashi began brandishing a finger at me. Before the head nurse had even finished speaking, he was shouting with such ear-splitting force that it was impossible to believe this was the same person as the hunched, green-faced figure in the ambulance just minutes ago.

"If anything happens to my baby, it'll be all your fault! You hear?"

His words rang out around the room. As if to cut him off, the young doctor addressed him directly: "We'll take her in for surgery immediately."

I gave him a deep bow.

"Not long now until you can see your baby!" I said to Mrs. Wakabayashi, who was clutching at a pink towel, her eyes squeezed tight shut.

"I was useless, wasn't I?" she said as she clenched my hand tightly, her voice so weak it seemed it could cut out at any minute. "I couldn't manage it. I'm a bad mother. I can't believe that after all this, I have to have a C-section."

"What are you saying? You did a great job. Nobody knows if they've been a good mother or a bad one, not as long as they live."

I felt Mrs. Wakabayashi's hot tears splashing down one after another onto my hand that was holding hers.

"Thank you," I said to the head nurse, bowing my head. "I'm sorry it's come to this."

But she wouldn't so much as meet my gaze. Dragging the stretcher with Mrs. Wakabayashi on it, she exited into the long corridor.

In fact, neither what Mr. Wakabayashi nor what the head nurse had said was entirely mistaken. Because I'm a midwife, people often assume I have a strong preference for natural births. In fact, I don't believe it matters if it's a natural birth or a medicated one or a C-section or whatever, so long as the mom and baby both come out of it alive and well. I don't stake my pride or my reputation on the number of babies I manage to deliver "naturally," and I'm not interested in getting into a competition over the mistakes each respective side might make. Insofar as they forgo their sleep and rest to deal with births all day every day in a way that grinds down both body and soul, doctors and midwives are exactly the same. However hard you try, there are sometimes things that happen as a midwife that you have no control over, and at those times you ask for the doctors' help in order to save the lives of the mother and baby. Can someone tell me what's so messed up about that?

It was around the beginning of fall last year that those weird, grainy photographs began turning up in the Saito Maternity Clinic inbox. Our email address is up on our website, and so, being a maternity clinic, we'd received the occasional obscene emails and photographs. In the past Mitchan had always dealt with them, deleting any unwanted correspondence. But suddenly, they were arriving in such numbers and with such frequency that weeding them out was becoming quite a job. It wasn't just via email, either—the same photographs turned up in our mailbox, laid out in rows like commercially produced flyers. When they came, Mitchan and I would take one look at them then scrunch them up and toss them in the trash. I tried not to let it bother me at all, but when it had gone on for a while, I started to suspect we might have a real weirdo on our case and began worrying about what I'd do if something ever happened to one of our patients. It was just around that time that Mitchan approached me with a piece of paper in her hand, saying: "I think you should take a look at this."

The person in the photo was looking directly at the camera. I saw immediately that it was Takumi, dressed up in some strange costume. He was with a girl, her white thighs exposed. Instinctively I closed my eyes, then forced them to open again and looked at the photo properly. I felt the anger and disgust rear up from the pit of my stomach.

"You're too young for this shit," I spat out. The vehemence of my own reaction took me by surprise.

Mitchan was looking down at the photos I was holding.

"Takumi, of all people," she said, shooting me a *this means trouble* look, then averted her eyes.

Since Takumi had started high school, I'd been vaguely aware he'd gone and got himself a love life of some kind.

One day, totally out of the blue, he stopped going in to his summer job, and when term time began, he started skipping school. I figured he was just having girlfriend troubles, so in the beginning I would peel off his duvet, rouse him, and send him in. But as fall wore on, Takumi started refusing to leave his room at all. I found his cell phone in the wastebasket, the screen bashed in. Once again, just like when his dad had left us, the sound of his crying would travel down the stairs and blend with the babies' wailing.

"Is that your son?" asked a woman who was up breast-feeding in the middle of the night. "He sounds like he might be crying."

"Yes . . . He's just had his heart broken," I told her. "I'm sorry, I know it's not nice to listen to."

"I remember what that was like," the woman smiled fondly. "Oh, the trials of adolescence!"

If only it had been as simple and innocent a thing as she and I had imagined.

But no. Somehow, even people of my generation got wind of what Takumi had been up to. At meetings of the neighborhood council (many of whose members had disapproved of my opening the clinic to begin with), there was no longer a single person who would speak to me. I started to get emails from people I'd never met, sent to both the clinic's account and my private one.

Mostly they were variations on YOUR SON'S A FUCKING PERVERT—which I could just about handle. The one that got me the most was a single line that said, WHAT DO U EXPECT WHEN U BRING HIM UP IN A MATERNITY CLINIC? Someone else wrote, NO WONDER HE'S TURNED OUT THIS WAY IF YOU MAKE HIM HELP OUT WITH THE BIRTHS! Heaven only knew where they'd gotten their information.

From a very young age, whenever Takumi saw babies who wouldn't stop crying or women in great pain, he would start crying in sympathy. When the mothers went to the living room to eat and the babies left behind in the bedrooms burst into tears, Takumi would crawl onto the futon alongside them and start gently rubbing their backs to soothe them. When he got slightly older, he began to help the women who, for whatever reason, had to give birth on their own without a partner—wiping their sweat and giving them water.

As I went without sleep and the women in labor suffered for days on end, Takumi had been there, taking it all in. He saw it and he felt it, and he wound up knowing it like the back of his hand. That was why, when he reached out those little hands in a bid to help, I found it was beyond me to brush him away. But maybe that had been a misjudgment on my part. Maybe that was why he'd grown up to be the kind of kid to have an affair with an older married woman and get off on dressing up like that.

"Boy, do the blows just keep on coming," Mitchan said as she went through deleting the emails that arrived one by one, chin propped up on her fist. I sat beside her, folding the piles of laundry I'd brought in from outside. "They're all just so fucking pathetic!" When she was really angry, Mitchan often got all potty-mouthed. "Have none of these people ever fallen for the wrong person, or what?"

She lifted one of her knees so her foot was resting on the chair.

"Hey! No feet!"

"Sorry," she said meekly, restoring her foot to the floor and taking a gulp of the green tea in her cup.

As far as possible, I tried not to look at the flood of emails, but in among the nasty ones were inquiries from people thinking of giving birth here, so on Mitchan's days off I had no choice but to pass my eyes over them. Once, hidden away right at the end of an email masquerading as a booking inquiry, I found the line: LIKE MOTHER, LIKE SON! IT SEEMS LIKE INFIDELITY RUNS IN THE FAMILY. So it looked like I wasn't going to be let off for my sins even of twenty years ago. As the thought ran through my mind, I felt a great sigh leak from my body.

With a pile of folded laundry held to my chest, I stood in front of the mirror over the bathroom sink and stared at the haggard face reflected in it. There was a small scar underneath my right eye, a reminder of doing what Mitchan had called "falling for the wrong person." The first place I'd worked after nursing college was the general hospital where I now sent my patients in emergencies. When word got out that I was involved with the deputy director, who was a good few years older than I was, his wife never once insulted or badmouthed me. I don't think she had the guts for that. Probably, her good upbringing got in the way. Instead, she chose to punish us— her husband and me together—by having us stand in opposite corners of her living room for a whole day, holding a bucket full of water in each hand. It was the same punishment they'd given kids who forgot their homework back when I was at school.

Then she ignored us. She pretended that we quite literally didn't exist, drinking her tea leisurely at the table and turning the pages of her book. Very occasionally she would raise her head and contemplate us in turn, as though we were pictures hanging on a museum wall.

When it was time for lunch, the wife took an apple over to the table, peeled it very slowly with a silver knife, cut it into small pieces, and ate it. At the smell, my mouth filled with saliva. Little by little, the sunlight filtering in through the large window shifted angle. My arms tingled and throbbed with pain. At some point I realized my body was slumped over forward, the water sloshing around in the buckets.

Yet the deputy director and I endured the punishment without resistance.

Thinking of it now, I imagine the sense of solidarity born between us at being given the same punishment must have enraged the wife even more. I managed to withstand the hunger, but she also prevented us from using the bathroom. With each tiny movement of my body, I felt my bladder wobble and my field of vision grow dark. At some point I remember deciding to give up and just go, unclenching the lower half of my body, but no urine came out. My bloated stomach had grown hard as a stone.

The wife was sitting on the sofa with her back to us. I looked at her delicate back, clothed in a white cardigan. Her glossy, chestnut-colored hair curled up where it brushed her shoulders. It was winter, and dusk had come earlier than I'd expected. Suddenly the wife stood up and walked over to stand beside me. Her slippers made a ridiculous squeaking sound as she moved across the shag pile rug. She stopped right in front of me, a head shorter than I was, and looked me right in the eyes. I noticed a little frown line forming between her eyebrows, then she reached out an arm, pinched my right cheek between her thumb and forefinger, and twisted it. My face distorted with the pain, and tears rose to the corners of my eyes.

"Aren't you going to say sorry?"

"I'm shorry."

With my mouth wrenched out of shape, the words came out all funny. The wife pinched harder, driving her nails into my face. I heard the noise of my skin ripping apart. It wasn't pain I felt spreading across my body but a strange heat.

"Stop it!" The deputy director set his bucket down and made to run over, stumbling over my bucket on the way so its contents went flying across the floor. He stood behind his wife and grabbed the wrist of the hand that was twisting my cheek. As the wife let out a scream, I felt the liquid go gushing out from between my legs, making its way toward where she was crouching beside me. The deputy director didn't make so much as a sound, just stared vacantly down at the floor. Try as I might, I couldn't move my body an inch. I just stood there, stock still, until my bladder was completely empty. Then I set my buckets down, took out a towel from my bag in the corner of the room, and began wiping the floor.

"I'm so sorry."

It was the first apology I'd uttered that day that I actually meant. I put the towel, now stained a faint yellow, back into my bag, and rushed from the house. The wife's long, trailing sobs followed me out the door.

After the hospital let me go, only the director of the one private maternity clinic in town would agree to take me on.

"Show me your hands," said the director, who was already nearing seventy, at our first meeting. She put on her glasses, placed my hands on top of her palms, then proceeded to examine them with great care. I watched her silver-haired head bob up and down. Before I could start asking myself what palm reading had to do with midwifery, she spoke.

"You've got nice, round fingers. These are hands that can protect the most important parts of a woman in labor. Yes, these are a midwife's hands all right. I'll be expecting you tomorrow."

With those words, I found myself employed once again. On my way home, I scrutinized my hands for a long time. It was the first time I'd ever been told my hands or my fingers were suited for assisting births.

The director had a pretty unique take on things and in magazine articles and conferences would come out with statements like: "People who are good in bed are good at giving birth," or, "If childbirth goes well, it feels amazing. It's better than any sex," or, "You must make sure not to turn your back on eroticism after having kids." This line went down very well with a certain kind of person but was met with fervent opposition from others. When another midwife working at the clinic asked the director gently if she could tone down her remarks, she cackled and said, "What's wrong with telling the truth? It's not wartime anymore."

I heard other midwives at the clinic speak of the director's "magic touch," and it wasn't long before I observed it myself. I can't count the number of times she would turn around deliveries that seemed to be going nowhere fast, despite all our most fervent efforts. The moment we passed the baton over to her, cervices that had previously been clamped shut would dilate like flowers magically springing into bloom, and babies would come slithering out into her hands.

There were certainly times when the discrepancy between my abilities and those of the director made me feel tempted to pack it all in, but I also knew that, now that my marriage had bitten the dust, I needed to be able to get by on my own. I had neither the courage nor the financial legroom to take Takumi and leave town. Yet every time I witnessed the director performing one of her superhuman feats, a huge iron ball would form inside my stomach. It was no good carrying on like that—I had to learn to keep up with her. Once I'd made that decision, things became easier. I stopped scanning the small print making up the newspaper's Help Wanted section.

As I ran up the stairs of the old building in front of the station, I could hear the sound of merry laughter pealing down from above. I prized open the door of the clinic to see Dr. Liu in a white shirt, thin black necktie, and pristine doctor's gown, surrounded by a flock of elderly women. Noticing me, he clapped his hands together and said, in a loud, crystal-clear voice: "Okay, my next patient has arrived, ladies. Let us call it a day, shall we?"

As they put away their folding chairs with a great clatter, several of the women snuck a glance in my direction.

The Chinese pharmacy had been in the building for five years. I'd discovered it a while back, when I'd mentioned to a colleague of mine that I was interested in seeing whether the chills, constipation, and other mild ailments that often afflicted pregnant women could be cured with alternative treatments such as traditional Chinese medicine, acupuncture, and moxibustion, and she'd introduced me to Dr. Liu. Things had gone from there, and now Dr. Liu came into my clinic to speak to the pregnant mothers as part of the prenatal courses we offered. We provided four sessions, both in the first stage of pregnancy and before entering the final month, covering the things women should be doing during pregnancy and the course that births take. One of these sessions was run by Dr. Liu, who spoke about self-care as a means of preventing health problems.

Dr. Liu had such an immaculately handsome face that Mitchan was convinced he'd had plastic surgery in Korea and, unsurprisingly, his session was a great hit with expectant mothers. He must have been my senior, but with his blemish-free face and full head of jet-black hair, he looked considerably younger.

Once, Mitchan had asked Dr. Liu the secret to his youthfulness.

"Chinese herbal medicine developed because the ancient Chinese emperor wanted to be immortal," he had replied, looking her right in the eyes, his Japanese a little more faltering than usual. "If a person will keep on taking it for years as I have done, it only stands to reason he will hold on to his youth."

"No wonder the women all fall at his feet if he looks at them like that!" Mitchan had reported to me excitedly afterward—and this from a woman who would say openly that what she valued most in men was broad shoulders and muscles rather than a handsome face. "Honestly, he could sell them anything he wanted!"

Now, the same Dr. Liu was sitting in front of me, inspecting the tongue I'd stuck out for him. In Chinese medicine you can apparently understand a lot about a person's physical condition by looking at his or her tongue.

"You've been going without sleep again, haven't you? Listen, it doesn't matter if you don't actually sleep, but it's important to lie down. Even for a short time. Think of it as saving up a little strength. If you continue just using it all up, you've no hope of making it through to your twilight years." He lowered his thick crop of eyelashes and started writing something on the paper on his desk. "Your body's screaming out for a rest, but still you ignore it," and, saying this, he disappeared into the dispensary.

I had started coming to see Dr. Liu at his pharmacy six months ago. That was after he had leaned over to me one day at the clinic where he'd come to give his class and said: "Never mind the health of the mothers-to-be. It's yours I'm worried about."

He had a point. I felt tired all the time in a way I couldn't seem to shake, and for a while I'd been getting dizzy spells and bad headaches. So for the last six months I'd been taking the medicine he prescribed for me. There hadn't been any miraculous improvements in my condition, but it did seem as though the exhaustion and dread I felt upon waking were gradually easing.

After he had finished mixing up the herbal medicine, Dr. Liu came back into the room carrying a tray with a pot and teacups and a small dish of pine nuts resting on it.

"It's not just you, either. Why do Japanese women feel the need to work so much? That's the reason so many childbirths go wrong. It's like you're constantly revving the body's engine while it's out of gas. I guess you believe that so long as you can summon up the mental energy, your body will somehow find a way. But I warn you: do that at your age and you'll shave years off your life. I can tell you that with absolute confidence. Isn't there something you can do to reduce the burden placed on you? Take on more midwives or something?"

"That's not financially viable, unfortunately."

"Because you're trying to keep staffing costs down? Because you want to be rich? Richer than you are now?"

Smiling, Dr. Liu poured tea from the iron pot into small, jade-colored ceramic cups.

I remarked how nice it smelled and Dr. Liu grinned, revealing his perfectly aligned, white teeth. He took a sip of his tea, then said, "It's doesn't do to torment your body by working too much."

The winter afternoon sun caught the steam rising from the teacup, lighting its gentle upward motion. It felt like a very long time since I'd taken the time to sit down and really enjoy a cup of tea.

"The job of a midwife isn't just to help make sure that babies are born safely, you know," I began. Dr. Liu looked directly at me. "Both back when I was working in the hospital and now, there are a lot of babies that don't make it. Many more than you'd expect."

His teacup still held aloft, Dr. Liu listened fixedly to me.

"However hard you try, there are some that die almost immediately after they're born. I start thinking about them, remembering their cold, stiff little bodies, and then I can't sleep. I feel like I've got to do their share of living, too. Like I've got to live for the babies who never even had a chance at life."

"Hmm," Dr. Liu said, still looking at me. He reached out to the small dish on the tray and crunched a couple of pine nuts. Then he tilted the dish in my direction to indicate I should do the same. I put a pine nut into my mouth, just as I'd been instructed, and bit down on it with my back teeth.

"But it's not your fault," he said. "That's just their lot in—" A car with a loudspeaker blasting out some promotional message moved down the street, drowning out the rest of Dr. Liu's sentence.

"Their lot in life," I said, and fell silent.

I didn't have any confidence that I could explain this vague, confused feeling I had inside me to Dr. Liu in a way that he, as a Chinese person, could understand it. What he was trying to tell me—that the babies' untimely deaths could be put down to their lot in life, their fate, their given lifespan, and that there was therefore nothing to be done about it—I'd heard this from other people. For whatever reason, the argument went, those babies had lived out their allotted time on earth in just a few short days. But if that were true, I needed someone to tell me why on earth they would be born into this world at all. That was what I would find myself wondering whenever I saw young parents clutching at the edge of the tiny coffin placed in front of them, their bodies convulsing with tears. There was no religious doctrine, no theory of past lives or reincarnation or any other New Age philosophy that could satisfy me on that point. I wanted someone, it didn't matter who, to explain it to me in a way that would make me say, *Ahhh, I get it. I understand what the meaning was to those babies' short lives.*

"But it's okay," Dr. Liu said after a while. "You won't be rushed off your feet for that much longer. A doctor studying reproductive science at the same university as me used to tell me that only around 20 percent of the sperm stored in the Shanghai sperm bank was healthy. The same goes for Japanese sperm. I've seen data to suggest that the sperm count of men in their twenties today is half that of men in their forties."

He drank down the rest of the tea left in his cup in a long gulp. I noticed his Adam's apple bobbing up and down.

"Soon there won't be as many children born as there were. In Japan or in China. Then you'll be able to take it more easy."

"If that really happens, I'll be left high and dry! I've never had any other job!"

"Don't worry. If that happens, you can come and work here."

With a smile on his face, Dr. Liu looked me straight in the eye.

Taken aback at the way my heartbeat had quickened, I hurriedly reached for a pine nut and put it into my mouth, remembering something Mitchan had once said.

"So they say Dr. Liu came to Japan for a girl whom he'd met when she was studying in China," she'd told me. "He was top of his class in medical school in China but gave it all up to get his Japanese doctor's license. Can you imagine how hard that must have been! And then she jilted him and married a Japanese guy. Another doctor, no less! I guess he's the type who's got just about everything going for him but is enough of a romantic to throw it all away for love."

"Okay, well, if you could just fill out this form," I told the woman in front of me, who was visiting the clinic for the first time. She was short and chubby, with shoulder-length dyed-brown hair curled into ringlets.

She started to say something, but I interrupted.

"I'll be back when you're done." I hurried down the hall to the room where Mitchan was overseeing a delivery. Mrs. Hasegawa, who'd only just come in, was down on all fours, doing her best to weather the contractions. Both Mitchan and the woman's husband were kneeling down beside her, rubbing her lower back. From her face, I could see she was in considerable pain but not yet at her limit.

"Doctor, how long will it go on like this?" she asked, looking up at me.

"Well, you've still got a while to go. If all goes well, you may be holding your baby by midnight."

"I'm sick of these contractions already. It's someone else's turn." She looked about to cry, and, as she spoke, she grabbed at the neckband of her husband's T-shirt.

He had a white towel wrapped around his head like a bandanna, and said, "Trust me, I'd trade places with you if I could," then flashed a wry grin in my direction.

"If you've still got the energy for that kind of talk, it means you're still a ways away. I'll come back and check on you in a bit."

Just as I was leaving the room, Mrs. Hasegawa suddenly let out a loud shriek.

I turned around and smiled at her, "Okay, that's more like it. Now we're really getting started."

"What did I do to deserve such an evil doctor?" The woman glared at me with a frown.

I went down the hall to check on the new woman. As I slid open the screen door to the room I heard a wail, like a child crying. Startled, I went in to find the same woman with her head down on the table, sobbing.

"What! What's happened! Where does it hurt?"

"No, it's not me. It's that voice from the other room! She sounds like she's in so much pain," the woman said, hiccupping.

As I stood there too astonished to react, the woman reached for a tissue, still sobbing, blew her nose loudly, then took a pocket mirror from her purse and rearranged her bangs.

"Sorry, I'm really sorry. I'm Chie Nomura, Takumi's homeroom teacher." She stared at me, mascara smudging the corners of her eyes, then bowed her head. Each time we heard from the other room the sounds of Mrs. Hasegawa screaming, Miss Nomura's body would twitch. Mitchan brought us in some tea.

"I'm really sorry, Miss Nomura. I mistook you for the person booked in for this afternoon. I had no idea that you were expecting. When are you due?"

I watched as her exceptionally large eyes welled up with tears.

"But how did you know I was pregnant? I haven't told anybody!"

With this, she began sobbing again, tears stained black with mascara cascading down her cheeks. Mitchan had been on her way out of the room with the empty tray, but now she paused by the door, and we exchanged bewildered glances. From Miss Nomura's posture, the shape of her stomach, and indeed everything about the way she looked, there was no doubting that she was pregnant.

"I only came to talk about Takumi," she protested. She was so agitated, though, that she couldn't stop crying, so Mitchan and I began to inquire about her situation. She'd been to the gynecologist just once, when her periods had stopped, and had never received a Mother and Baby Record Book, which was standard issue for every pregnant woman. Mitchan shot me a musical-theater frown.

"I don't know if I'm going to marry my boyfriend, and I haven't even decided where I want to give birth—which hospital, you know?" She was still crying.

Barely audibly, Mitchan clicked her tongue in disapproval. I glared at her.

"First of all, you need to have a proper consultation with a gynecologist. So long as there aren't any complications with your pregnancy, you could think about giving birth here, if you like."

Snatches of Mrs. Hasegawa's screaming and wailing broke into the room from next door, and Miss Nomura's blubbering grew louder.

"I can't do it! I can't give birth if it hurts that much. I can't even stand injections."

At this, Mitchan pounded the table so hard with her fist that the tea came spilling out of the cups onto the saucers.

"You're already way too far gone to have an abortion. Are you crazy? You went and created it, so now you've just got to damned well have it! How are you're going to become a decent mother with that kind of attitude? Hmm?"

I stood up and took hold of Mitchan, who had jumped to her feet in her anger.

"Hey, hey! Mitchan, this is Takumi's homeroom teacher! Stop it. You're going too far."

But she pressed on: "I'm not having you causing Mrs. Saito any more problems, hear? If you want to give birth here, I'll take charge of your delivery!"

"I can't do it! I'm too scared! This woman's terrifying!"

Miss Nomura's whimpering mixed with the screams coming from next door and reverberated inside my skull, until my temples began to throb.

Miss Nomura, whom the students apparently all knew as Notchy, did as we asked, and went for an exam at the general hospital. There she was told that the maternity ward was all booked up, and so it was that, despite her terror of both labor and Mitchan, Notchy made an appointment to have her baby here. As Mitchan and I had predicted, she was already well into her sixth month, and was therefore due to give birth around the beginning of April, when the cherry blossoms would be out.

"She's as bad as those high-school girls who get pregnant and say they thought they were just bloated with constipation!" Mitchan ranted at me. "With those kinds of people becoming teachers, Japan is well and truly doomed."

Yet, in her own way, Mitchan did take care of Miss Nomura, who would pop in on her way home from school for regular checkups. To Miss Nomura's face, Mitchan would say in a severe tone of voice, "Remember, if you don't gain a single pound between now and your due date, you'll be doing just fine," but she would put some of the food she'd made for dinner in Tupperware containers and slip them to Miss Nomura to take home with her.

When I caught wind of the fact that Mitchan had summoned Miss Nomura's boyfriend to the clinic and given him a talking-to about his unwillingness to get married, I told her in no uncertain terms that, whatever the particulars of the situation, that was way, way out of line. Not long after, though, Miss Nomura was beaming as she told me that, "Thanks to Doctor Mitchan, we've set a date for the wedding!"

I found myself at a total loss for words.

Once her checkups were over, Miss Nomura would go up to Takumi's room, handing him homework printouts and filling him in on what had been happening at school. At first, she would often return hanging her head, telling me, "It seems like Takumi doesn't really want to speak to me," but after a few visits, she came bounding down the stairs with a big smile on her face, grabbed my arm, and said with great excitement, "I've got the feeling Takumi's going to be all right, you know!"

"Really?"

"Yes! He looked at my stomach and was like, 'Notchy, you've got to make sure to keep the baby warm.'"

Fat tears were spilling from her eyes as she spoke, and as I looked at her, I felt the tears forming in my own as well. For a little while, Miss Nomura and I stood there in the darkened hallway, crying together.

Ryota would also come by before he went to work in the evening. It seemed like he had nothing in particular to say to Takumi, and instead he just played games or read manga in Takumi's room, then left. Nana, whom I'd previously assumed was Takumi's girlfriend, came early in the morning, stood at the bottom of the stairs, and called out in a loud voice, "Takumiiiii!" She waited for ten minutes, and if there was no answer, she'd turn to me and say, "Is it okay if I look at the babies?"

She started giving me a hand with changing the newborns, lined up on the examination bed ready for their morning bath.

"You like babies, do you?"

"Yes. I want to do what you do. When I'm older, I mean."

"You want to be a midwife? There's no money in it, you know. You can't take vacations, either. There's really nothing to recommend it."

Nana burst into a peal of laughter. "Yeah, Takumi told me the exact same thing."

Suddenly, from the second floor, I heard Mitchan's booming voice and the sound of a vacuum cleaner. I quickly put the newborns, still all warm and toasty from their baths, back into their mothers' rooms and ran up the stairs with Nana.

"If we let the rooms get this dirty, the babies downstairs will end up breathing in the dust!" Mitchan had donned a surgical mask and gloves and was brandishing the hose of the vacuum cleaner like a weapon as she spoke. "Come on! Get up, get washed, then go eat breakfast!" Saying that, she thwacked Takumi on the backside with the vacuum hose. Still bleary-eyed with sleep, Takumi looked between me and Nana and then set off slowly down the stairs.

From that day on, Mitchan would wage a surprise attack on Takumi's room every morning.

"I had a younger brother, brother number four, who stopped going to school, too, but I set him straight," she said with tremendous pride. And in actual fact, from then on the amount of time Takumi spent up and about during the day began to increase. Nana came to the house every morning, and at some point he began going to school with her. Once a week became twice a week, then went back to once a week again. Little by little, taking baby steps forward and the odd baby step backward, Takumi began returning to life as a regular high-schooler.

Into February the days grew even chillier. As I wiped the condensation from the steamed-up windows, I saw someone jogging along the bicycle path, breathing clouds of white. As I was making breakfast for the patients, Takumi came into the kitchen in his school uniform and sat down at the table.

"You're up early!" I set down a bowl of steaming miso soup in front of him.

"Yeah, I've got a graduation ceremony committee meeting," he said, stirring raw egg into his rice. That Takumi was going to school every day, that he was eating breakfast—to other people these might have seemed like ridiculously normal things, but to me they were reason to rejoice.

The emails with attachments of photos of Takumi or saying libelous things about me and my clinic hadn't stopped coming, but, little by little, they were getting less frequent. I wished everyone would hurry up and get bored of whatever it was Takumi had done—that time would pass and people would move on and forget about it. Every day, I would pray for that to happen as soon as possible. I'd really had enough of the hatred directed at me by these faceless strangers, these unknown people in unknown places.

"Nana's sick in bed with the flu, so I'm going in by myself today." Takumi stood up.

"Okay, have a good day," I said as I washed up. Rinsing off the plates with hot water, I found I was humming to myself. Mitchan came in carrying a tray stacked with dirty breakfast dishes.

"Wow, your humming is majorly out of tune," she said, laughing.

It was then I heard the sound of something breaking outside the house.

Mitchan and I looked at each other, then rushed to the front door. Outside, Takumi was crouching down with his hands covering his face.

"What is it?" I reached down and shook his shoulder, but he brushed himself free of my hand and ran inside. I stared after him, watching him kick off his shoes and go hurtling up the stairs like a chased man. Mitchan came up beside me, holding a plastic convenience store bag that had been lying outside the door, and handed me a small lidded pot.

The pot was the size of a large teacup, and the lid was cracked—maybe as a result of Takumi dropping it, or maybe it had been like that already. I'd seen this kind of pot many times before, when I'd visited families' altars to light incense for the spirits of the babies that had died, both at the hospital I'd used to work in and here at the clinic. It was a small urn, designed to hold the cremated remains of babies and children. Realizing that, my hands began to tremble, and the cracked lid fell to the ground. Inside the urn was a small piece of folded paper with writing in smudgy black crayon. Written in a deliberately childish hand, the note said, The bones of yours and Anzu's child. The urn also contained a couple of gray-white bones. Standing next to me, Mitchan peered inside the urn.

"They've washed them clean and stuff, but I'm pretty sure they're just chicken drumsticks." She dropped the urn inside a vinyl bag and pulled it tight. "Honestly, people can be so fucking cruel. It's a good thing it's garbage day." And with that, she went running off in the direction of the garbage collection spot in her sandals. Standing there outside the house, I felt something cold and wet land on my face. I looked up to see snow, half mixed with rain, falling from the thick, overhanging layer of cloud. From that day on, Takumi stopped coming out of his room again.

In the supermarket, even when I was supposed to be shopping for stuff to make food for the patients, my eyes would always land on the ingredients for Takumi's favorites. There I'd be, thinking about making gyoza dumplings with plenty of garlic or burgers with slivers of burdock root inside, and then I'd come back to earth and remember I didn't have time to be rustling up such fancy things when the clinic had been chock-ablock for weeks. Instead, I'd take out the list Mitchan had given me and check it again.

Takumi hadn't just stopped leaving his room—he'd more or less stopped eating, too. Always wearing the same tracksuit, the only times he would stumble dizzily out of his room were to use the bathroom or to get a drink, and then he'd always disappear back inside immediately. When I glanced at him, I could see his eyes glinting sharply beneath his overgrown bangs. Now, when Mitchan barged in unannounced to vacuum his room, he stayed curled up on his futon, not moving an inch. Observing this, Mitchan had made the most of one of Takumi's bathroom trips to slip inside his room and root out all the scissors and cutters in there, which she concealed in her apron pocket.

"You just never know what might happen," she said to me gravely when she came downstairs. Her eyes weren't smiling.

Even when I was supposed to be concentrating on helping women give birth, that crayon-scrawled note and the little urn where it had been hidden would sometimes flash into my mind, and I'd find myself thinking about the person, whoever it was, who had made such elaborate efforts to show their malice. Couldn't they turn that energy toward doing something positive in their own life? I would think to myself. In the evening Mitchan would send me to the supermarket, saying it was important for me to get out of the house at least once a day.

As I was traipsing down the path, I heard a bicycle bell in front of me. I looked up to see Dr. Liu, wearing a heavy-looking black coat. He had stopped his bike in front of me.

"You look like a ghost," he announced loudly. "And you forgot to come and pick up your medicine. If you're heading to the station, come by on your way home."

He rode off without waiting for a reply, his gray scarf flapping in the wind.

Not long after, I was making my way up his flight of stairs. With my backpack full of groceries and a tote bag over my shoulder with a bunch of scallions poking out from the top, I found myself struggling to catch my breath. I opened the door to the pharmacy, and Dr. Liu stuck his head out from the back room.

"I'll get you some tea and something sweet. Just sit yourself down there for a moment."

It was pleasantly warm inside, and though I worried about what the temperature would do to the meat and fish I was carrying, I set the groceries down on the floor. A violin-and-piano piece was playing at low volume on the stereo. I removed my coat, sat down on the chair, and rested my head back against the wall.

I rarely watch television or turn on the radio. For years, I'd spent all my time listening to the moaning of mothers and the wailing of newborn babies. I stared at the speakers on the shelves in front of me, pretty fancy looking for a Chinese pharmacy, and thought suddenly of my dad. The year I'd started school, my dad had bought an enormous set of speakers about as tall as I was at the time, and he got into a huge fight with my mom about it. As it turned out, he'd spent nearly his entire bonus on those speakers.

My dad would play all kinds of things—Nat King Cole, Sergio Mendes, Andy Williams, Claude Debussy, folk music from far-flung countries—and ask me, "What about this one?"

Whenever I replied that I didn't really like it that much, he'd look really sad.

"It's nice music, no? It's a lullaby by Ma Sicong." Dr. Liu took a seat opposite me. "He was a wonderfully talented composer, but his scores and records were all burned during the Cultural Revolution." Saying this, Dr. Liu gestured to the tea and cookies arranged on a small glass plate he'd placed in front of me. "My father had a tough time back then."

"In the Cultural Revolution?"

"Yes. He was a doctor of Western medicine, you see, but he was suddenly ordered to study Eastern medicine, in Beijing."

"So the Cultural Revolution really did happen."

"That's right. It all really happened." Dr. Liu spoke quietly, his eyes cast down. "Then, while my father was away in Beijing, my mother got ill and died."

"Oh, dear . . ."

"But not everything that starts out bad stays that way forever. It was through watching my father that I decided also to study medicine. Although of course in my case, the loyal son eventually ended up as the prodigal one. So things that start out well don't stay that way forever, either." Dr. Liu grinned, flashing me his white teeth. Then he took a deep breath and began intoning in a low voice, as if he was reciting a magic spell, "If you can't shake yourself free of a bad thing, then stay holding onto it. One day you'll find it suddenly flipping, like a counter in that game Othello. Some day or other, that will happen. It will happen with what your son is dealing with, too. Try to think of it as something like this." As he spoke, Dr. Liu snapped his fingers. "No smaller, no bigger than that. Something like— like a pollen-carrying bee brushing up against a flower."

I averted my gaze from Dr. Liu, who was seeking out my eyes.

"Yes," I said, "If I could really feel like that, it would be great."

Just then my cell phone began to vibrate. It was Mitchan, calling to tell me that two of our women had gone into labor and were currently heading for the clinic.

"Okay," I said. "I'll come right away."

I hung up, zipped Dr. Liu's medicine into my backpack, and hoisted my backpack onto my shoulders. Somehow, as if automatically, I felt power flowing into my solar plexus.

"You look different, your eyes look different all of a sudden," Dr. Liu remarked. "It's good to have that, when you're working. But you have to let that go sometimes." Dr. Liu deftly wrapped up the cookies in a paper napkin, and tucked them into my coat pocket. "From time to time, you should drink good tea and listen to music," he said and, reaching out a slender finger, touched the scar on my right cheek. Then he added, "With me."

I ran back to the house to find Mitchan on the verge of tears.

"Doctor, they're both really close!"

I crammed the food I'd bought into the fridge and bolted up the stairs to get changed. The meal Mitchan had prepared for lunch lay untouched in the hall, so I opened the door to Takumi's room. The duvet had been thrown back to reveal the rumpled sheet underneath. I touched it with my hand and found it cold. The down jacket he always wore in winter was still hanging on the wall.

"Doctor!" I heard Mitchan calling from downstairs.

Both women would most likely give birth in two or three hours. There was no way I could leave them and go off in search of Takumi. I waited until there was a gap between contractions, then snuck off to where Mitchan wouldn't hear me and tried calling Ryota at home, but nobody picked up, and the phone just kept on ringing. Most likely he was at work. I thought of calling Miss Nomura, then thought better of it. It wouldn't do to give a heavily pregnant woman extra cause for concern. I even thought of calling Takumi's dad, but after deliberating for a while, abandoned that plan, too.

For the moment, I thought, I'd just concentrate on making sure these two women gave birth safely. I told myself that he wasn't the kind of kid to go and kill himself. I looked in on the two women in turn, the one whose birth Mitchan was supervising and the one I was overseeing. It seemed very probable they'd give birth around exactly the same time. I led Mitchan into the hall.

"You're okay to do this by yourself, right?"

Mitchan gave a little nod, but when her hand gripped my arm it was trembling.

I went back into the room where my patient, Mrs. Ohashi, was. In between contractions, I spoke with her to try and relax her. If you could get a woman giving birth to smile, things generally went better. We talked about the weather the previous day, the nice bakery near the station, and what her husband did for a living. In breaks between that intensely mundane conversation, the baby was making its way down the birth canal.

As she winced with pain, Mrs. Ohashi turned to me and asked, "Why did you decide to become a midwife?"

"When I was a kid, I visited the countryside where my dad had grown up and watched a cow giving birth."

I pictured the scene as I spoke. It was the house owned by one of our relatives, who kept cows. My mom was nagging at me, trying to get me to go home, but I refused to leave until the calf was born. I stayed there, crouched down and clutching at the iron railings, my eyes fixed on the scene. I remembered the calf's foreleg thrusting its way out of the mother's body, and the steam coming off the calf's body, glistening and moist with amniotic fluid.

Somehow, even at that age, I'd been spellbound. It seemed so different from anything I'd experienced in lessons or on TV.

It was something that was made of life itself. I remembered the first time I'd watched a woman giving birth, how fascinated I'd been by the warmth of the amniotic fluid that came gushing out of her body. Human lives that had begun in water so warm, so soft, finally coming out into the world. I wanted to be in the place where that was happening, always. Even if it meant not sleeping, missing meals, not making money, I wanted to be where the births were.

"You're amazing, though! Doing this job, and having a child of your own," Mrs. Ohashi said, her face scrunched up in agony. I had no way of telling her that my own child had run out of the house and was now missing as we spoke.

Mrs. Ohashi finally gave birth at around 11 p.m. When I looked into the next room, I saw that Mitchan's face looked even more rigid with fear than the face of the woman in labor.

I went up by her side and whispered in her ear, "I'll swap in for a bit, if you like. You go and take a rest."

When I spoke to Mrs. Yamada, her expression softened. Mitchan opened the screen door softly and went out the room, her eyes lingering on Mrs. Yamada. When I went into the kitchen to find her a little while later, I saw her eyes were red and puffy.

"What's wrong, Mitchan?"

"I can't do it the way you do," she sniveled. "Whatever I say just makes her more nervous."

"Everyone's been down that road, Mitchan. Me included."

"I just get so frightened."

"So is everyone. I still get frightened, would you believe. I still pray inside, for it to go okay."

Suddenly, a place popped into my mind. For some reason, I felt sure Takumi would be there.

"Mitchan, I'm here, okay. But today I want you to do this one by yourself. Call me only if you absolutely need me."

Mitchan stared at me for a few seconds with swollen eyes. She moved over to the kitchen sink, splashed her face with water, dried it off with a handkerchief, slapped her cheeks, then made off toward the back room.

I could tell from the noise of Mrs. Yamada's screams, which were getting louder and louder, that the awaited moment wasn't far off. I could hear Mitchan's words of encouragement, too. Around the time a new day began, I finally heard the sound of a baby crying. I opened the screen door to see Mitchan, drenched in sweat, getting ready to cut the umbilical cord. I put my hands on her shoulders from behind, and she turned around, startled.

"I totally missed you coming in!"

"You see, you can do it. All by yourself."

"Please don't make me cry." Mitchan looked at me desperately. "I'm feeling close enough as it is. I want to be able to see what I'm doing."

I made sure everything was okay with Mrs. Yamada and her newborn baby, then entrusted the two new mothers to Mitchan and made to leave the house.

By the door, I whispered to Mitchan, "Takumi's disappeared."

"Oh, my God, I'm so sorry." Mitchan looked as if she was going to cry again. I put on my backpack, into which I'd stuffed Takumi's down jacket, a flashlight, and a flask containing hot green tea, and set off down the pitch-black bicycle path.

When Takumi had been small, he'd often had a high temperature. There had been several times when, like today, I'd had to put off seeing to him because I was too busy with the births. Once I was done, I'd put Takumi, drowsy with fever, on my back and run down the road to the emergency pediatric ward. I may have delivered babies as a profession, but when it came to raising kids I was a total amateur. I pretended I knew what I was doing—that as long as Takumi grew up following my example, things would turn out okay, but underneath all that, I was a ball of worry. If I were being honest, I'd have to admit that when Takumi's dad left, and later when those photos of Takumi got out on the net, I'd felt at a complete loss and had taken refuge in the busyness of my work to get through. My skills and my career as a midwife weren't the slightest help in knowing how to deal with that kind of stuff. I'd been a mother for fifteen years, and I was just as uncertain about the choices I should make as ever before.

I pedaled through the center of our small town, now utterly deserted, then raced along the narrow road running by the side of the pear orchards. The closer I got to the mountains, the fewer streetlights there were and the chillier it felt. I parked my bike by the bottom of the flight of stone steps. The moon was bright, but no sooner had I stopped than it disappeared behind a cloud. I got out the flashlight from my backpack and shone it at my feet so I could see where I was going as I climbed the steps.

When I had dipped heavily into my savings so I could start up the maternity clinic, which I hoped would enable me and Takumi to get by, I had felt every single day as if the heaviness of the responsibility of birthing children was crushing me. The owner of the clinic I'd worked in previously, who'd been so good to me in so many ways and was as happy for me as if the clinic I was setting up were her own, passed away right before it opened. It felt as if I were being thrown into a raging sea in the middle of the night, with only Takumi for company.

Whenever I'd had any spare time back then, I would come to this shrine and pray. I prayed for all the children I'd delivered so far, for the ones I hadn't been able to deliver, for the ones who'd died right there in my hands, and for the ones I was going to deliver from now on. I used to go flying up this flight of steps in a single spurt, but now I came to a halt less than halfway up, gasping for breath. When at last I made it to the top, I passed under the shrine's red torii gate and slowly moved the flashlight around, lighting up the grounds. Gusts of wind stirred the beam of light shining on the leaves of the trees, distorting it into eerie shapes. One of the dried leaves at my feet flew up and hit me in the face. There was a tremulous sound coming from somewhere, like the call of a mountain bird or the groans of some huge creature. My earlobes and my fingertips were throbbing with cold. I walked slowly around the grounds until my flashlight hit upon a familiar pair of green sneakers, over by the hut where people purified their hands and mouths with water. I drew closer to find Takumi sitting on the ground, his head buried between his knees.

I went up to him silently, took his down jacket out of my backpack, and draped it over his shoulders. Squinting in the glare of the flashlight, Takumi slowly raised his head. Dirt and dust had stuck to his tear-stained face, making it look very dark. He stared at me for a while with glazed eyes, as he had done when he was feverish, then said, "Mom."

"You'll scare the babies if you cry that loud."

"It's okay. Only the gods are listening here."

Then Takumi's face began to crumple, and his mouth gaped open. For a second there was a gasp of air, and then his voice rang out across the mountain, like his throat was splitting open. I walked away from him, stood in front of the main building, and put my hands together in prayer. After a while, I began sensing eyes on me, and when I lifted my head to look I saw the moon poking its round silver face from between a gap in the clouds. I stayed there with my hands clasped in prayer until Takumi stopped crying.

Dear gods, please protect this child if you possibly can.

With her due date now very close, Miss Nomura's bump had grown very big.

I could hear her voice coming from the tatami room.

"Takumi, if you don't hand this in on time, you're going to *fail the year*. Do you understand that?"

"I can do it for him. I'm a genius, remember? I'll have it done in five minutes."

"Ryota, if you do it for him, it's totally meaningless. I'm supposed to be on maternity leave, but I'm so worried about whether or not Takumi's going to hand in his report I can barely get a moment's rest!"

I heard Takumi and Ryota laughing. When I went into the room with a tray of tea and snacks, Miss Nomura looked up at me and said, "Ah, it did it again. It keeps moving around." She ran her hand gently over the pale lavender tunic containing her hugely swollen stomach.

"It's reacting to everyone's voices," I said, placing my hand on her bump as I spoke. "Feel this hard part that's poking out? That's the ankle. Here, touch it and see." At my instigation, Ryota and Takuma both reached out their hands to touch Miss Nomura's stomach.

"Whoa, it's moving around like crazy. Like that thing in *Alien*. It's gonna eat through Notchy's stomach lining and come bursting out!" Ryota was grinning. "Wah! It just kicked me, like, really hard!"

"My God, you're so dumb! You're dumber than Notchy's unborn baby!" Ryota grabbed Takumi's head and mussed his hair.

"Stop fooling around like that in front of your teacher!" I shouted, and Miss Nomura, still with a smile on her face, looked up at me.

"My back has been very sore since I woke up this morning."

"Yes, well, when that pain starts happening at regular intervals, it means the contractions are starting." As I watched, the smile disappeared from Miss Nomura's face and was replaced by a look of anxiety.

"So this is finally it, eh? Good luck, Notchy!" said Ryota.

Miss Nomura thanked him, darting him a smile that looked like it could give way to tears any second.

"Come on! Hurry up and come out!" Takumi said in the direction of Miss Nomura's stomach.

Without warning, tears welled up in my eyes. To make sure nobody saw, I went flapping down the hall with deliberate haste, and began preparing the room for her to give birth in. I opened the windows to let in some air. The line of cherry trees spanning the bicycle path had taken on a delicate pink color—they were just about to blossom.

Staring at them, I tried snapping my fingers, as Dr. Liu had done in front of me. I couldn't make as satisfying a sound as Dr. Liu had, just a muffled kind of click, but as the sound faded into nothing, I had a thought. Even if I knew they'd be gone in just an instant, like this scene outside the window would be, I would still do all I could to help the babies that came into this world.

So come, I said to myself. *Come and be born.*

"Doctor!" I heard Mitchan calling.

"Yep!" I replied, slapping both my cheeks with my hands. Mitchan's habit for pepping herself up when the occasion called had caught on. From the open window I heard the wavering call of a bush warbler, very out of practice. It seemed like spring had come around again.